CH
REACTION

An absolutely addictive crime thriller with a huge twist

BILL KITSON

DI Mike Nash Book 12

JOFFE BOOKS

Joffe Books, London
www.joffebooks.com

First published in Great Britain in 2021

ISBN: 978-1-78931-679-7

For Val
My all-round superstar.

PROLOGUE

1989

The scream was involuntary, but it was sufficient to wake the boy, and send him running into his parents' room, fearing that this was yet another instance of the physical abuse both his mother and he had been subjected to in the past. What he saw made him stop on the threshold, his eyes wide with bewilderment. His father was clearly enjoying himself; his mother apparently less so. Despite the look of pain on her face, she was making no effort to stop her husband or even discourage him.

The interruption angered his father, and retribution came swiftly and brutally. He vented his frustration on the nine-year-old, courtesy of the wide leather belt from his trousers. It had come easily to hand, having been unbuckled before the boy entered the room. He supplemented the chastisement with a few blows delivered more directly, his fist being the weapon of choice.

For Elijah Nelson, the beating was merely one of a chain of such events that discoloured his childhood. The pain was intense and long-lasting, but even as he attempted to sleep while lying on his stomach, his curiosity as to what his father and mother had been doing was whetted. Over the weeks and months that followed, he resolved to try and discover more, but to go about it covertly, to avoid further recriminations.

His location, an old farmhouse, was set in woodland and formed part of the Harland estate, and made such voyeurism more readily available than for that of most children. The old coach house at the entrance to the manor house drive was now the Boar's Head Hotel, where his father was the chef, and his mother was employed as a chambermaid. The woodland gave Elijah ample opportunity to see the arrival and departure of guests, and, with his local knowledge, he was even able to witness some of their deeds — and misdeeds.

All the bedrooms to the rear of the hotel, away from the road, backed onto the woods where Elijah lived. Many of the occupants of those rooms, their priority being to consummate their desire for each other, were careless of their security. Their reasoning, that it was unlikely that anyone would be able to see what they were up to, was based on their ignorance of the surrounding area. With the aid of a pair of binoculars purloined from his father, Elijah watched human nature in action many times, and in a wide variety of ways.

By the time he was eleven years old, he had learned the meaning of what he had witnessed in his parents' room, and the activities he'd regularly viewed with growing interest from his place of concealment deep in the undergrowth at the edge of the woods. But it was several more years before he understood the emotional part of the procedure, and, with it, the pain that accompanied such pleasure.

His voyeuristic activities provided one huge surprise, in that he recognized one of the couples involved in a prolonged series of amatory encounters. Because he was aware of their identities, he kept this guilty knowledge secret, not knowing that when he reached a crisis point in his life, the information would prove extremely useful.

* * *

Five years later, after getting off the school bus, Elijah walked across the hamlet's main street to the hotel that stood at the northern end, where the road forked in two directions. The Boar's Head was renowned throughout the dale and much further afield, attracting visitors from the UK and abroad. Part of its appeal was its cuisine, comfortable rooms and excellent hospitality, which outweighed the outdated decor and fittings. The principal asset was the surrounding countryside, making the hotel an ideal venue for ramblers, cyclists and other tourists.

Elijah walked quickly past the inn and headed for home, anxious to get indoors, away from the biting northeasterly wind. He crossed the hotel courtyard and walked down the alley alongside the small stable block that had been converted to a row of mews cottages for the benefit of the hotel employees. Beyond there, the space widened into the hotel car park, and to the rear of the yard was a small footpath, the speediest route to Elijah's home. The only other buildings he passed were workers' cottages, now disused.

There was a knack to opening the front door. His father had promised to fix it, but, like so many other things, had failed to get round to it, except that today, the door swung open as he inserted his key. Did that mean Elijah would find his father passed out from drink? That was happening more and more often, ever since his mother had left some years ago. She'd gone suddenly, without a word. It was much later that his father told him what had happened. She had left them; left England to go and live with a man she'd met. Her lover had been a regular guest at the hotel. With his wife no longer available for Elijah's father to vent his anger and frustration on, his son had become his target of choice to deliver violent punishment for offences, be they real or imaginary. As Elijah grew taller and stronger, the beatings lessened and eventually ceased, and although they lived under the same roof, it was convenience, not affection, that kept them together.

The boy had been sickened on hearing that his mother had abandoned him. If he was angry and unhappy because she had deserted him, it seemed that his father was even more upset. Quite how distressed his father had become, Elijah didn't discover until he opened the kitchen door.

Having lived in the country all his life, Elijah was well used to nature in its raw brutality, but one look at the bloody mess the shotgun had made of his father's head was too much even for his stomach. He turned and bolted, reaching the garden before being violently sick.

After a long wait to recover, he ventured back inside. He didn't want to go in, but knew he had to, if only to use the phone. He went cautiously back into the kitchen and spotted a note on the dresser. Keeping his eyes averted from the table, from the bloodstained corpse and from the weapon with which his father had ended his life, he read the note. *I couldn't go on any longer.* Beneath that, another line read, *You'll understand when you read the diary.*

Elijah walked upstairs to his father's room. He saw the book on the dressing table, sat down and began reading. He gasped at the shock of what was written there. He took the diary and concealed it in his own bedroom before returning downstairs. He used a sharp kitchen knife to remove the second line of the suicide note, placed the scrap of paper on the fire and watched it burn. Only when the grey ash mingled with the rest in the grate did the boy replace the shortened version of the note, cross to the telephone, and lift the receiver. The time it took for the emergency services, headed by Detective Inspector Tom Pratt, to arrive, proved highly productive for the boy.

Now, as he stayed in the cottage, well away from the bloodbath in the kitchen, comforted by a female officer, Elijah tried to settle the jumble of thoughts and emotions that the terrible event had raised. Among them, the need to plan for his future surfaced. Conscious of what he'd learned from his father's diary, Elijah had to ensure that he had support to continue on the path he was beginning to realize was his only option. He needed to remain on the estate. It was then that the image entered his mind of the couple he'd seen disporting themselves in one of the hotel bedrooms some years earlier. Remembering this, and being aware of their particular circumstances, made him confident he would get the backing he needed. All he had to do was to let slip the extent of his knowledge. The fact that what he was considering could be construed as blackmail didn't occur to him. Nor would he have been worried if it had. At the time, it seemed straightforward.

Left alone, many sixteen-year-olds who had witnessed such a horrific act would have crumbled, but Elijah knew he would be able to count on support from his father's employer. The fact that this assistance would be provided not out of kindness, but from a more unworthy motive, that of self-preservation, didn't alter the end result. Elijah's continuing education and training were assured, as was his future as a member of the Harland estate workforce, and even more important, as the occupant of the tied cottage.

Elijah knew everyone would believe his father, obviously distressed by his wife's infidelity and desertion, had been unable to live with the pain. It was only later, when all attempts to trace her had failed, that questions might have been asked, but by then the authorities had other priorities, different, more urgent matters to contend with.

CHAPTER ONE

Present day

The Boar's Head Hotel had been subject to a takeover, and at last renovation work was underway. The new venture was the latest by a successful national company, who had acquired a ninety-nine-year lease on the property. The new proprietors had decided to expand the business. This would involve total refurbishment of the interior and a single-storey extension to the kitchen; replacing dated equipment with modern, state-of-the-art appliances. Even the layout would be drastically altered. "Gutting the place" was the term the contractors' foreman used when briefing his men before work on the project commenced.

The hotel had closed in June, courtesy of a defaulting tenant, and would remain shut until renovation work had been carried out, once the planning permissions had been granted — a process scheduled originally to be completed in six months. In the event, the closure remained in place far longer than anticipated. The expectation of being reopened by Christmas was dwindling daily.

It had been late autumn before the work could begin. The first order of business was the removal of all the units and appliances. Replacement of the antiquated heating system throughout the building also involved the dismantling of the boiler room and clearance of the adjacent storage area at the rear of the kitchen. It was during this procedure that one of the workmen, charged with sweeping up debris after his colleagues had swung their sledgehammers enthusiastically in the old storeroom, noticed something strange. Before inverting the shovel into the nearby wheelbarrow, his gaze fixed on two items that didn't belong there. He paused and bent over to get a closer look. Curiosity compelled him to pick up the two small objects. A split second later he dropped them, revulsion evident from his expression as he called the foreman over. 'Look what I've found. They were on my shovel. I swept them up.'

The foreman's reaction reflected his own. 'Oh Lord, that isn't good. I think we'd better get someone to look at this. If those are what we think, it's going to delay things even more, but we've no choice in the matter.'

* * *

DI Mike Nash had barely entered the CID suite when his phone rang. He listened to the message relayed by Sergeant Jack Binns before replacing the receiver. 'Clara,' he called through to the main office, 'we've work to do, out at Thornscarr. I'll get hold of Mexican Pete and the forensic' guys.'

Detective Sergeant Clara Mironova, his second-in-command, appeared at Nash's door, tucking her blonde hair into a clip as she entered. 'Mexican Pete and the forensic' guys sounds like a failed 1970s Glam Rock band. Any idea who the stiff is?'

Nash smiled slightly at her facetious remark. 'It isn't a stiff as such, not precisely. Workmen renovating the Boar's Head have found what they believe to be two dismembered fingers. It sounds as if they've been there a long time.'

'There's a lesson in that,' Clara refused to be daunted by this macabre revelation. 'Never sack the chef while he's holding a meat cleaver. Mexican Pete's reaction should be worth listening to.'

Nash winced at the suggestion and waved her out of his office while he rang the pathologist. Having listened to Professor Ramirez' blistering rhetoric about the too-frequent calls on his time, Nash managed to arrange for the backup team to attend. Once that was done, Nash turned to DC Viv Pearce. 'Viv, take care of things, will you? We shouldn't be too long on this one.'

The tall Antiguan detective looked up from his computer screen. 'OK, Mike,'

The detectives walked downstairs, where Jack Binns, an inveterate gossip, was eager to pass on all he knew about the area they were to visit.

'I don't know much about Thornscarr,' Clara admitted. 'I've been through it a few times, but that's all. It looks a pretty village, and there's that famous hotel, but that's about all there is.'

'I don't know much more than Clara,' Nash agreed, 'except that the village belongs to a big estate, doesn't it? Tell us more, Jack. Mexican Pete can't get there for another hour, and the body parts have been undisturbed for years by the sound of it, so we're in no hurry.'

'Hang on, Mike. You just told Viv we wouldn't be long,' Clara reminded him.

'Don't worry about him. He's too busy working out how to fit a cot and pram in their small flat. That'll keep him occupied.'

Jack Binns smiled and nodded agreement before telling them, 'For a start, you're both wrong. It isn't a village, it's a hamlet. There used to be a few people living there, estate workers or hotel employees, but that was back in the sixties and seventies, before mechanization changed the way farming works. The hotel has been on a downward trend; it's been sold to one of the big national groups. So the hamlet is a bit like one of those ghost towns from the Wild West.'

'You're becoming quite a social historian, Jack,' Clara teased him as they headed for the door to the car park.

* * *

On the outskirts of Helmsdale, they took the side road that would lead towards Wintersett village, where Nash lived, and beyond to Thornscarr. As he drove, Nash reflected on the grim discovery they were about to inspect. There might be an innocent explanation, but he couldn't think of one. The finding of two severed human fingers could hardly be explained as the result of an accident. The fact that the condition of the fingers suggested they had been there for a considerable time didn't make the cause any less sinister.

Nash had often admired the ivy-clad building that housed the Boar's Head. Prospective guests would get a favourable impression even before they entered the building. Normally, the approach to the hotel, via a wide apron filled with tables, benches and an impressive array of pot plants was highly attractive.

However, before the renovation process commenced, the exterior fittings had been moved to the car park at the rear of the building, and replaced by a quartet of much uglier yellow skips bearing the logo *HSH*, which Nash knew stood for Helm Skip Hire, together with three more anonymous vans that he guessed belonged to the contractors. Nor was the front aspect improved by the more recent addition of blue-and-white incident tape that was fluttering gently in the breeze. This, together with the flashing beacons of a pair of police cars, signalled that something amiss had been discovered in the building. Why, Nash wondered, was it necessary for two cars to remain in attendance? He suppressed the gallows humour instinct that led him to speculate that the control room had allocated one vehicle per finger.

Nash pulled up behind the gaudily coloured vehicles, and he and Clara walked over to a uniformed officer who was standing by the hotel entrance, looking suitably bored. He gave the detectives a nod of greeting and lifted the tape to allow them to enter the building. Inside, another officer was talking to a pair of workers clad in overalls, who Nash guessed were the men who had made the grim discovery.

As he introduced Nash, the police officer's opening remark confirmed this. Nash concentrated his attention on the shovel one of the workmen pointed to, which was lying on the dusty reception counter. 'I picked one of them up because I didn't believe what I was looking at,' the labourer told him, 'but I put it straight back down when I realized what they were. Up to then, I'd thought they were off a dummy, like you see in shop windows.'

Nash peered at the grisly objects. Although they had attracted a patina of dust, plaster, and fluff from the sweeping process, they looked to be in remarkably good condition, although the skin was atrophied and wizened. Despite not being an expert, Nash guessed that mummification had to be the only logical explanation, but that theory would depend on where they had been kept, and for how long. The pathologist would give the definitive answer, but to assist him, Nash needed to find out what conditions were like in the place they'd been found.

'Can you show me where they were, and how you came to find them?'

'It's through there, at the far side of the kitchen. There's a boiler room and storage area. We're waiting for the plumber to arrive so he can disconnect the boiler.' The man shook his head. 'We could have done it, but you know what it's like, each man to his own trade. Health and safety, they call it. Jobs worth, I call it. So to save time, we've removed all the shelving and units. We'd have finished that part of the job by now if we didn't have to wait on the others. We can't move on until they do manage to turn up, and once they've finished, we'll have the kitchen installers to deal with. That'll be another delay.'

As he was talking, the contractor led Nash through the kitchen to the doorway of the room behind.

'Don't go back in,' Nash told the workman. 'The CSI team will get upset if we trample all over the scene.'

The man looked at him. 'More Jobs worth?'

Nash smiled. 'Not in these cases. Have you checked to see if there are any other body parts lying around?' As he asked the question, Nash glanced at the workman, who looked aghast.

'No, I didn't . . . do you think there might be more?'

'It's very possible.' Nash smiled gently at the man's obvious disbelief, before adding, 'You don't imagine they came here by accident, do you?'

'Er . . . no . . . I didn't like to think about it at all.' It was the horrified reaction of someone unused to dealing with the macabre side of life.

'OK, why don't you rejoin your colleague outside while I take a closer look?' As he was speaking, Nash pulled a pair of overshoes from his jacket pocket — not that they would be of much use in a demolition site. But at least they would keep his shoes clean, he mused.

Even with the boiler off, the room was warm, so Nash guessed that when it had been operating the enclosed space must have been extremely hot and airless. His inspection of the area didn't take long, and apart from having to disturb a small pile of debris, which he did using the handle of the sweeping brush, yielded no further unpleasant shocks. He had just finished checking the room and was walking thoughtfully back through to the reception area when the pathologist arrived, along with the CSI team.

Nash introduced the workmen and waited as Professor Ramirez asked them the same questions about conditions surrounding the discovery, before examining the remains. He removed the fingers from the shovel with a pair of forceps, turning them over to look closely at the nails before placing them into a small lined cardboard box. He looked up and saw Nash's questioning expression. 'You must be getting past it, Nash, if the best you can manage is two fingers from an old corpse. These remains have been mummified, so I need to keep them in a dry environment until I've examined them at the mortuary. Now show me this room.'

He confirmed Nash's theory within seconds. 'Hot and dry, perfect conditions for the mummification process. At a guess, I'd say her fingers have been there some years, which leads to the other questions: who was she, and where is the rest of her?'

Nash blinked with surprise. 'How do you know the fingers belonged to a woman?'

'The shape of the nails, the way they've been manicured, and the fact that they contain tiny flecks of nail varnish. Of course, they could be from a drag queen, but I think that's unlikely in a place such as this.'

'Is there anything else you can tell from them?'

'Without closer examination, very little, they appear to have been severed with something like a hatchet or similar. The cuts are too clean for a saw to have been the instrument. I doubt whether I'll be able to obtain a fingerprint, but with luck I might possibly be able to extract DNA, given time. Now, if you'll excuse me, I'd better get on. The CSI team are waiting outside to give this room the once-over.' He glanced at the debris surrounding them. 'I wouldn't hold your breath for them turning up anything useful. Unless there actually is a body somewhere,' he added.

After Nash turned the area over to Forensics, he had a quick word with Clara. 'Take statements from the guys who found the body parts, and when we get back to Helmsdale, we need to contact the new proprietors of the hotel and obtain employment records for all previous members of staff. We must make sure we get details for the manager and those working in the kitchen. They're the likeliest sources of information about someone who went missing from this place.'

Having reported the development via phone to Superintendent Jackie Fleming, Nash left the station and headed for home. He reached Smelt Mill Cottage, which was in darkness until the motion of his car activated the PIR light. Inside, the building was cold. With his son Daniel away at school and as Nash was only in the house for a few hours each day, he'd set the central heating to the minimum setting. Even that had seemed excessive the way his workload had been, but Nash was reluctant to admit that the need to spend extra time at work was in part a device to avoid coming home to an empty house. He'd never been bothered about being alone in the past, but recently the silence and lack of someone to interact with had grown oppressive.

* * *

Next morning, Nash, Clara, and Viv discussed the macabre discovery at the Boar's Head.

'Do you think some woman is missing, Mike? Couldn't it have been an accident? It is a catering kitchen, after all.'

'That's up to us to find out. We should check with the owners and see if they have records of any mishaps in the kitchen. Or it may be an incident where the Health and Safety Executive got called in. But that being the case, I do believe that ambulances are in the habit of taking all parts of the patient to hospital.'

'What do you suggest we should do?' Clara looked at Nash for inspiration, but in vain.

'I've no other ideas. I'd love some suggestions, because right now I'm fresh out.'

'Why not ask Tom's advice? He was in charge back then. He might remember something that will help,' Viv pointed out.

Nash smiled. 'Good idea. I'll give him a ring.'

Tom Pratt had attained the rank of superintendent before a heart attack cost him his job. But he found retirement boring and had taken up the post of civilian support officer, covering both Helmsdale and Netherdale HQ. As such, he was proving invaluable, not only for the work he did, but because of his almost unrivalled familiarity with the territory. His intimacy with police procedures enabled him to use them, or even circumvent them, for the benefit of the detectives. His fund of knowledge regarding the area they covered, when added to that of his long-time friend Sergeant Jack Binns, was close to indispensable.

Having heard the background, Pratt suggested they should check their files for potential victims whose disappearance would fit the timescale provided by the pathologist.

'We've already thought of that. There might be a few,' Nash pointed out. 'Mexican Pete said those fingers could be anything from ten to fifty years old.'

'You know as well as I do that thousands of people are reported missing each year, and most of them turn up safe and well. If I recall, the latest published statistics suggest the number of incidents is between two hundred and fifty to three hundred thousand a year. Admittedly, most of them are resolved quickly,' Pratt continued, 'but some remain unaccounted for.'

Pratt paused before adding another chilling dimension to the equation. 'Of course, those figures can never be totally accurate, because they include only the reported cases. There must be considerably more due to foul play that we never get to know about. I dread to think how many victims died unmissed, un-mourned, and unnoticed.'

After a short silence, Nash replied, 'Then what we must do is ensure that the woman to whom those fingers belonged doesn't become one more of that unknown number.'

He replaced the phone, thought for a moment, and then said to the team, 'Tom's checking out the possibility there was a kitchen accident, just to satisfy you, Clara. But he thinks that's a non-starter. In the meantime, Viv, will you and Clara set about going through every female MISPER file from within a ten-mile radius during the period Mexican Pete mentioned? See if anything stands out. I know that sounds like a lot of work, and maybe it will be futile anyway, but we must make every effort.'

'Why futile?' Viv asked.

'Because the victim might not be from this area. It is a hotel after all. In which case, our task will be all the more difficult.'

He stood up and smiled at his colleagues. 'I'll leave you to it. I've got the easy job. I've got to go through to HQ for a meeting with Superintendent Fleming.'

On his return, Nash asked about the progress of their search for information, provoking a groan from Clara. 'I'm already getting double vision from staring at the computer screen. How Viv manages for hour after hour beats me.'

'Being an expert,' Viv told her.

'Yes, I suppose you have to be good at something,' she replied.

'Take regular breaks,' Nash suggested. 'That will help both your eye strain and stop you simply reading the page rather than taking in all the facts.'

'Sorry, I don't follow that bit.'

'I remember hearing someone talking on the radio about proof-reading. They said that if they study a manuscript continually, they get involved in the story rather than checking for errors. The same thing could easily apply to our job, where the tiniest detail could have enormous significance.'

CHAPTER TWO

Donny Barton was a keen artist; had been almost since he could hold a crayon. When he left school, he had a choice of art colleges, all eager to further his fledgling talent. Five years later, the young artist left college and set off to tour Europe, where his burgeoning reputation was soon enhanced. When his first exhibition drew positive comments from a minor critic, several of his works sold for quite respectable prices. Commissions followed, and he spent the next few years painting successive landscapes of the Greek islands, before moving on to the mainland, and thence to Italy. Eventually, with demand for his work outstripping supply, he instructed his agent not to accept any further commissions for at least twelve months and returned to England.

'I'm tired. I've worked every day for the last two years. Christmas Day, Boxing Day, Easter, the lot, and now I need a break. After I've had a rest, I want to paint something else apart from cloudless skies, white buildings, and blue seas.'

His agent protested. 'But those are the paintings that people are clamouring for. They've become your trademark.'

Donny was adamant. 'They'll have to wait. OK, I might return to them one day, but for now, I want to paint woods and meadows, streams and hills. And clouds, clouds filled with rain — or snow. Sun dappling the mountainsides as the summer greenery begins to turn to autumn gold, and following that, the rich dark colours of a British winter bathed in that soft afternoon light that you only get here.'

The agent warmed to the idea, sensing another collection on the horizon. 'Where will you go?'

'Somewhere I can't be reached — by anyone,' he told him pointedly. 'Somewhere without phones: no computers, no email, text messages or radio and TV. I've found a little cottage in Cornwall that suits the purpose admirably.'

The agent had to be content with that, but extracted a promise for Donny to contact him as soon as he returned to London. As he watched the agent leave, the artist smiled at the thought of the man searching Cornwall for him. He removed the magazine from his desk drawer and read once more the article that had attracted him. It was a monthly periodical that specialized in glossy depictions of country living, a hymn to the idyll of rural bliss. It had been on a routine visit to his dentist that Donny had thumbed idly through the pages, until he stopped at an article about a North Yorkshire country hotel and the estate to which it belonged. Although the reporter had been diplomatic in her choice of words, reading between the lines it seemed that the estate, like many others with grand houses to maintain, was strapped for cash. The owners had therefore decided to turn several of their outlying cottages, disused since mechanization had reduced their workforce, into holiday lets. This campaign to raise funds wasn't scheduled to begin until renovation of the properties was complete, which would be more than a year hence. Donny hoped to persuade the estate manager to allow him the use of a cottage out of season, if he offered a good enough incentive.

He dialled the number and after a short period of haggling, arrangements were completed, but with suitable provisos.

'The only property that is furnished and habitable is one that we won't be putting out as a holiday let until May of next year. However, I should warn you that the cottage is in a very remote location.'

'Actually, that suits me fine. The more secluded and private the better,' Donny responded eagerly.

Several minutes later the deal was done, and Barton promised to send a cheque for the whole sum by first class post that day, in return for which, he would become the tenant of Track End Cottage, Thornscarr, from the beginning of October until the end of the following April.

'I'll arrange for the keys to be left at Newton-on Helm village shop. That's the nearest village to Thornscarr, and the closest town is Helmsdale. The shop doubles as a post office and sells most of life's necessities, so you should be well catered for. I look forward to receiving your cheque.'

Donny repeated the lie about Cornwall to his parents, confident that he would be able to work completely untroubled in the depths of North Yorkshire as everyone imagined him to be at the other end of the country. Then he booked a train ticket to York for the first week in October. He didn't own a car — hadn't even a driving licence, but was happy enough to rely on public transport to get him to his destination. Once there, he felt certain further travel would be the last thing on his mind. He had dispatched his artistic requirements and the bulk of his luggage via courier to arrive at the cottage after him.

Having collected the keys at the shop, he'd sought directions and was shown the road leading to Thornscarr. He was mildly surprised to find that the property wasn't actually in the hamlet. His instructions were to turn off alongside the hotel, apparently camouflaged by scaffolding, and then follow the unmade road, little more than a lane, for half a mile until he reached the edge of the woods. He did so, noting that the hostelry was closed for renovations, so that meant he couldn't be tempted away from his work.

Thornscarr was all that the artist could have hoped for. The fact that the place was more or less deserted apart from the hotel, and that the only pub he had spotted and the shop were almost two miles down the dale also failed to disturb Donny. He wasn't a drinker, and he didn't want to send any mail, knowing he definitely wouldn't be receiving any. The only mild inconvenience being the need to walk some distance to keep his food supplies topped up.

At the shop, he'd bought enough provisions for his immediate needs and had taken the opportunity to check the contents of their twin freezers. They proved to be ideal for his requirements, offering a variety of quick, convenient, ready meals that needed nothing more than unwrapping and popping into the microwave; just the thing for someone who wanted to devote as much time as possible to painting.

Equipped with warm clothing, including thermal underwear ideal for someone intending to pass much of the time outdoors during a North Yorkshire winter, he devoted the daylight hours of the first four days of his stay walking around the narrow, twisting lanes in the surrounding countryside. He was able to identify several superb locations that he knew would provide ideal settings for landscapes and was confident they would command good prices at exhibition. One such scene was a point where the River Helm plunged over Simeon Falls, a spectacular waterfall. Further from the village, the brooding presence of Black Fell and the even more impressive Stark Ghyll would give him ample opportunity to portray their rugged splendour.

As he walked, Donny made copious notes of each of the sites he had found, notes that described the scenes, the light values, time of day, and any elements that he was particularly keen to replicate.

On his return to the cottage on the fourth evening, he dined on lasagne. His concentration was not on the pasta, but on his notebook, and the meal was almost cold by the time he reached the last forkful. His walks had thus far provided almost all he needed to complete what he believed would be an impressive portfolio. But he was lacking an image that he had already formed in his own mind. He needed a setting where a meadow was fringed by a copse of trees, their branches stripped of foliage in preparation for the cold months ahead. If it could include dry stone walls, sheep grazing, a hillside, and a river, that would be even better.

He sighed, knowing that was probably too much to hope for. He would have one last try the following day, but if that was not possible, he might have to move on, find another location. His short-term tenancy of Track End Cottage had not been expensive by London standards, so vacating it early was not going to be financially crippling. One way or the other, it didn't matter too much, for the time being he had plenty of other scenes to keep him occupied. He looked at the pencil sketches he had already made. There was over a month's work in those alone. It didn't matter, he wasn't on a deadline. Other artists might have tried to paint the scene from the image they had dreamed up, but he felt that would be unfair to those who would view the finished object, and even more so to anyone wishing to buy it.

The following morning as he was washing up, sound, and a blur of movement, caused him to glance out of the kitchen window. He was in time to see the cause of the disturbance; a Land Rover was passing the cottage heading towards the main road.

The artist was surprised. He wasn't aware the track led anywhere other than into the woods that surrounded the cottage. Obviously, there was more, and he determined to explore the one area he hadn't so far tried.

The path wound its way for over a mile between high hawthorn hedges, bare at this time of the year, the lack of foliage allowing glimpses of the countryside beyond, which, as with the area near to the house, appeared to be mostly woodland. Eventually, the hedges gave way to a red brick wall, which was in turn supplanted by the line of single-storey buildings. Donny guessed these to comprise nothing more than pigsties and barns, but as he reached the corner of the building he realized he was wrong, and smiled with delight at the view before him.

Set at right angles to the livestock residences was a pleasant-looking two-storey house, larger than the one he had rented, but by no means huge. Possibly part of a farm, he speculated. The small garden beyond the house gave way to a lush meadow that sloped gradually towards the distant River Helm. Framing the field, surrounding the house on three sides, were banks of trees that formed the fringe of a deeper forest, almost exactly as he had visualized them. On the far side of the river, a few sheep were grazing with their lambs on the lower slopes of Black Fell. 'Perfect,' he breathed.

Any plans for leaving the area were shelved. Donny knew there was no way he could leave until he had captured this scene on canvas. All he had to do beforehand was to seek the house-owner's permission to cross their land to where he could set up his easel and commence work. The thought that the property might form part of the estate that owned Track End Cottage didn't enter his mind at that juncture. He walked through the open gate bearing the sign Keeper's Cottage, and crossed the gravel drive. He reached the front door, lifted the heavy brass knocker, and banged it three times on the oak panel.

CHAPTER THREE

Kim Nelson was loading the washing machine, but her mind was elsewhere. Had she thought long enough about her situation, she'd have wanted her mind and body to be elsewhere on a permanent basis. Since losing her job at Helm Plastics, another victim of the cutbacks forced on the company by the state of the economy and the rapidly growing aversion to the use of their products, Kim had been tied to the house. Her efforts to find other work were so far unsuccessful, and to compound the boredom of the long days, the drudgery of housework and the loss of the small amount of independence her income had provided, Kim was forced to endure the company of her husband on an almost full-time basis. Apart from a shopping trip into Helmsdale each week, he was the only person Kim spoke to, and he wasn't a spellbinding conversationalist.

Kim enjoyed those trips, taken on the Dales Village Bus. She often shared a seat with an elderly gentleman from Wintersett. She liked the old man and felt sorry for him. He must lead as lonely an existence as hers, she thought, with only his small terrier for company since the death of his wife. Kim liked the way his eyes lit up when he got on the bus and saw her sitting alone. He always made a beeline for her seat and was happy to flirt gallantly with her, wishing he was younger, or alternatively, simply to gossip about the various villages they meandered through and the characters he'd known who lived there.

Why was it, Kim thought bitterly, that she couldn't have found someone like the old man to marry, albeit a much younger version?

Her actual marriage had been a mistake. A marriage she'd begun to regret almost before the Registrar's ink had dried. Kim blamed her inexperience and loneliness. Her parents had divorced when she was seventeen; her mother had died soon afterwards. Kim's father, already remarried and surrounded by his new family — including two children — didn't want anything to do with Kim, a painful reminder of his first failure in the marriage stakes. Kim, having few claims to academic success, had settled for a production-line job in a local factory to help pay for the tiny, rodent-infested and damp flat she called home. Her life was dreary by comparison with that enjoyed by her peers. Hoping for some excitement, she'd obtained a passport and headed for Ibiza, but the combination of nightlife, booze, drugs, and casual sex were not the sort of cheap thrill she was seeking. So when Elijah had met her, then dated and proposed, Kim had accepted, convinced that married life in a country cottage set in delightful surroundings had to be an improvement. Nothing in that dream could have been further from the reality. She was now trapped in a marriage from which the last vestiges of affection, love or any of the tender feelings had vanished. In fact, at times Kim wondered if they had ever existed.

If Elijah Nelson was aware of his wife's lack of feeling for him, it didn't concern him. If he knew that the marriage had been a mistake, he ignored the fact. When, as happened regularly, usually after a drinking session, he became in turn amorous and violent, he ignored Kim's protests. As far as Elijah was concerned, she was his wife. And to Elijah, the word *wife* equated to *property*. He neither knew, nor cared, that Kim had developed a deep loathing for him and that his touch made her skin crawl. It was her duty to satisfy his demands, no matter how much she detested them, or believed them to be abnormal. When he wasn't affected by alcohol, he was cold, taciturn and sullen, and any emotions he might have felt were kept rigidly under control.

There had only been one occasion when he let his feelings get the better of him, a time several years ago when an altercation in a Helmsdale pub had led to his arrest and conviction for causing an affray. To Kim's surprise, whereas many employers might have seen this as reason to discharge a member of staff who had gained a criminal record, the Harland estate had backed Elijah, even providing such a good character reference that he had escaped with nothing more than a short-term community service order plus a fine, which the estate paid, along with the legal fees that had accrued.

Kim often wondered why the estate had acted in so supportive a manner. Was it nothing more than extreme loyalty to a staff member who had already undergone great troubles — or was there more to it than that? It wasn't the first time they had come to Nelson's aid in a crisis. Nelson had told Kim, albeit unwillingly, about his mother's desertion of the family to live abroad with her lover, and of his father's subsequent suicide.

'I found him in there.' Elijah gestured to the kitchen. 'It was a right bloody mess. Blew his head off with a .12 bore.'

He then told her how the estate had taken care of him, giving him an apprenticeship to the head gamekeeper, and later promoting him after that man retired. The more she thought about it, the more puzzled Kim became about that and other facets of Nelson's life, things that he refused to share with her. What, for example, was so special about the outbuilding that ran at ninety degrees to the house? The single-storey edifice had once been a piggery; that much Elijah had told her. However, to the best of her knowledge, he had never kept pigs. Nor would that explain why the building was always kept locked; the windows boarded over. She often wondered what was inside that made such security necessary. Eventually, she'd plucked up courage to ask — and soon regretted the curiosity that prompted her question. Elijah had glared at her. 'Just a load of old stuff, rubbish mostly,' he'd said, but the look on his face had belied his words.

Later, he'd gone off to the pub, and on his return gave her one of the most ferocious sexual assaults and beatings imaginable. It was as if he was taking revenge on her for having the temerity to ask something that invaded his privacy. Even as she nursed her wounds, Kim realized that there was far more she didn't know about her husband than all the things she'd learned about him.

As Elijah left the house that morning to supervise the shoot day on the estate, he warned Kim that he would not be back until late, and there would be no need to prepare a meal, as he would be dining at the manor house, courtesy of his employer and the shooting party. Kim was at first elated, then fearful. Happy that he would be out of her hair all day and evening; dreading what condition he would be in afterward, and what consequences she might have to suffer.

She had placed the washing tablets in the machine and was about to start the wash cycle when she heard the knock at the door. Kim frowned. By now the shoot would be well under way. Had he forgotten something? The thought that it might be someone other than Elijah didn't occur to her. Stuck out there in the wilds, visitors weren't rare, they were non-existent.

She hurried down the hall to open the door which she had bolted after his departure. Any delay would arouse his suspicions, although what he imagined she could get up to alone in the house, she couldn't guess. She slid the bolts back and flung the door wide; then blinked in surprise when she saw the stranger standing on the doorstep. The man was about her age she guessed, reasonably good-looking, and appeared mildly apologetic.

He smiled. A nice smile, Kim decided.

'Sorry to disturb you.' Then he began to explain the reason for his intrusion. Kim had already noticed the absence of a car on the driveway, which tallied with his statement that he was staying at Track End Cottage. He gestured to the paddock below the garden. 'If you would allow me access, I'd like to set up my easel and paint that glorious scene. I promise not to disturb you, or make a mess,' he ended.

'I'm sure that will be OK. The land belongs to the estate. This is only a tied cottage. My husband is the estate gamekeeper,' she explained.

'Oh, I never thought of that. If that's the case, and if it's all right with you, I'll make a start tomorrow.'

* * *

As he walked back up the lane, Donny thought about the woman he'd just met. She was pretty and had a terrific figure. He'd always concentrated on landscapes, which had disappointed his college tutor who reckoned he could have made a fortune painting portraits. Now, for the first time, he was tempted by the idea. He would have to paint her nude, of course. His artistic eye had already provided a mental image of what she would look like under those less-than-flattering clothes. It was a shame she was married.

That last thought disturbed him. He hadn't really been considering her in that light, but once the notion entered his head, he found it difficult to dismiss. He sighed: she was married, just his luck, probably quite happily married. Although her expression when she mentioned her husband didn't reflect that, he mused. No doubt there would be three or four kids around the place as well. Better to stick to landscapes and keep his mind from straying onto her obvious appeal.

* * *

Donny managed to get an outline sketch of the scene onto paper the next day, but contrary to his normal habit, didn't work on it when he returned to the cottage. That he was subconsciously spinning the task out didn't occur to him until much later. Halfway through the second afternoon, the gamekeeper's wife walked down to the meadow with a mug of tea she had brewed for him.

Over the next week, this became a sort of ritual, and after delivering his drink, Kim would stop and admire the developing landscape. These visits became more protracted as they chatted about their respective lives.

Although Kim didn't say it outright, he sensed her deep unhappiness. Her comment when she learned that he was single had been telling. 'Marriage is over-rated anyway,' she'd said.

He had only one brief encounter with her husband, who he thought to be surly and antagonistic.

It was a surprise to Kim a few days later when Elijah returned home early, nodding abruptly in response to the cheery wave from the artist, who was just packing up his materials. On entering the house, Elijah told Kim, 'I'm going away for a week. The boss has entered his prize sows in a show down south and he wants me to attend and display them. After that, he's taking me to a game fair in Hampshire. Pack me a bag.'

The following day, she sighed with relief when she saw the tail lights of the Land Rover disappear along the lane. An hour later, she glanced out of the window and saw that, ignoring the threatening clouds that were beginning to form over Black Fell, the artist had started work. It was a mild morning. The temperature had risen slightly from the previous days and he didn't feel the need for his jacket. She decided to walk over and talk to him, using the by now habitual mug of tea as an excuse. They chatted for a long time, and for once, they touched on matters that were deeply personal. It was surprisingly easy, merely a chance remark that led to the irreversible course of their relationship.

'I've never done portraits,' he told her, 'I've always concentrated on landscapes.' He paused before continuing; knowing that once he said it, there would be no going back. 'That was until I met you. I'd love to paint you. I'd love to try and capture your beautiful face, your figure, every intimate part of you.'

'You mustn't say things like that,' she told him. 'It isn't fair. I'm going inside.'

He'd blown it, he realized as he watched her returning to the cottage. He'd ruined his chance with her by his own stupidity.

The rainstorm struck suddenly, with a violent squall driven by the strengthening wind. At the first drop, he flung the cover over his canvas and thrust it into the waterproof bag and began folding his easel and stool. Collecting the tools of his trade would take some time, and he was already drenched.

Then he heard Kim call, 'Here, let me help.'

She was as ill-dressed for the weather as he was, having dashed from the house on seeing him struggle. By the time they reached the shelter of the house, they were both soaked to the skin. 'Upstairs,' Kim commanded him. 'The bathroom is the first door on the right. Get those wet clothes off before you catch your death of cold. I'll find you something to wear while I put them in the tumble drier.'

'What about you?' he objected. 'You're as wet as I am.'

'I'll manage.'

Kim had gone into her bedroom and was down to her bra and pants when she remembered that she'd put the bathroom towels in to wash that morning. She hurried out onto the landing and took a bath sheet from the airing cupboard. She paused; gripped by sudden apprehension at what she was about to do. Would she be jumping from the frying pan into the fire? For all she knew, Donny could be as bad as her husband — possibly even worse. After all, she knew nothing about him apart from what little he'd told her. Then her need overcame her fear.

He had stripped off and was beginning to shiver when he looked round and noticed there were no towels. He was pondering putting his wet clothes back on when the door opened. He automatically turned towards the sound, then as quickly turned away as Kim entered the room. 'I forgot I'd put a towel wash on,' she apologized, holding the towel out.

He reached out for it, hoping that she hadn't noticed his instant reaction on seeing her half-naked. She held onto the towel, however, causing him to look at her.

'Kim,' he said, his voice a croak. She took hold of the towel in both hands and began to dry him, every movement a caress that inflamed him further. Then she wrapped the towel scarf-like around his shoulders. She stood back, and he watched, spellbound as she unhooked the bra, and wriggled out of her pants.

'Now you must dry me,' she told him, her voice husky with desire.

He moved towards her, then checked. 'What about your husband?' he said. 'What if he returns home?'

'Forget him; he's on his way to attend an agricultural show and a game fair down south somewhere. He'll be gone for a week, a whole glorious seven days.' She turned her back and waited as he began to dry her hair, then her body, his hands lingering over her breasts before continuing down. He felt a shiver run through her as she reached her hand out and began to fondle him. 'The bedroom's this way. Let's go in there, shut the world out, and pretend we're the only ones left alive.'

* * *

Elijah was supposed to be away. He had told her so, deliberately emphasizing that he would be gone for a week. That had been a lie. There was no agricultural show, only the game fair. His absence from the estate would only be three days. He had even asked her to feed the poultry as part of the deception. He'd spent the night in town, a novel experience, and one he wasn't keen to repeat, but it had certainly proved enlightening, and in parts, deeply satisfying.

The old binoculars from his childhood were essential to his work as a gamekeeper. They had saved him a lot of time and wasted effort. Using them to locate errant birds on the vast moorland slopes had enabled him to reduce the mileage he had to walk dramatically. Today, however, they were being put to a different use. Although perhaps not that different, as their powerful magnification was showing another being who was straying from the straight and narrow. He'd had his suspicions for a while now. Confirming their accuracy brought him no satisfaction or pleasure, quite the reverse.

From his vantage point high above the house that nestled in the valley, the binoculars brought the front of the building into sharp relief. With the aid of the powerful zoom, he could see through the rain right into the house. His house. He could see right into the bedroom. His bedroom. He could see exactly what the woman on the bed was doing. His woman and his bed. And he could see who she was doing it with. He lowered the binoculars, unable to watch the nauseating spectacle any longer.

The prospect of his long absence had given them licence to indulge themselves to the full, and they were making the most of the opportunity. The game fair he was scheduled to attend didn't take place until the next day, so he had this one chance to see if his suspicions were justified. Confirmation that his guess had been correct would bring about many changes, of that he was aware. He would never sleep in that room, in that bed, again. He would certainly never sleep with that woman again.

Faced with a similar situation, many a cuckolded husband would have fallen into despair, or given vent to their feelings with a violent physical rage. He would do neither. He would deal with it in his own way, the calm, logical way. He would take the common-sense approach. The decision made, he felt at once more settled, more at peace with himself.

He would need to resolve things regarding his wife and her lover first, but that would have to wait on his return. Nelson glanced at his watch. His surveillance had yielded results, but it had made him late for the train he was scheduled to catch. He couldn't afford to miss it, or he'd be in trouble with his boss. Still, the journey would give him chance to plan his course of action. In Nelson's eyes, that plan of action meant only one thing — exacting a cruel and terrible revenge for the way he had been betrayed. He would make her suffer.

CHAPTER FOUR

For the occupants of the large Victorian house close to the centre of Netherdale, it was the day their landlord called to collect the quarterly rents due. All the occupants paid a quarter in advance, which, given the shifting population of private tenancies, was a sensible precaution on the owner's part. On this particular day, the landlord was particularly keen to catch up with the tenant of flat number three, a young woman whose occupation was questionable, but who usually paid on time.

The landlord had a shrewd idea how the woman earned her living, but the fact that she might have used her apartment to entertain clients posed no moral issues for him. If she chose to earn her money by offering sexual favours for sale, that was no concern of his. As long as she paid when the money fell due, he had been quite prepared to overlook the dubious legality of her profession.

However, on this occasion she hadn't paid on time, so his interest in the woman became personal, in a totally different way to that of her clients. He hammered on her door, but failing to get a response, concentrated on the occupants of the other flats, asking them, as he collected their rent, if they had seen the young woman. Their replies were unanimous, giving him stronger reason to suspect that she had departed without giving notice, a practice known locally as *doing a moonlight flit*.

Concern for the money owing to him rather than her welfare caused him to use his master key to enter her apartment. It was dark, so his first task had to be to feed the prepayment meter, before being able to switch the light on. He was surprised to see that the flat appeared to be occupied, in the sense that her clothing and belongings were all still in place. He'd expected to find the apartment stripped of all her personal effects, and possibly even some of his property. He was annoyed, but not alarmed. The idea that anything untoward might have happened to her never crossed his mind. His vexation increased when he checked the fridge in the kitchen. The sparse contents were mouldy, the milk sour. His automatic reaction was to reach for his mobile phone. He rang the maintenance man who took care of all his properties and issued terse instructions.

'The fridge needs emptying and cleaning out and all her clothing either sent to the charity shop or binned. Given that she was on the game, I guess most of it will be underwear, and I suggest you wear gloves before touching it; the same goes with the bedding. In fact, I'd keep gloves on all the time you're inside the flat.'

Once he'd given his orders, the landlord locked up and left. He soon forgot about the defaulting tenant, his mind concentrating on finding a new occupant, one willing to pay a higher rent. Had he a stronger sense of public duty, he might have reported the woman as a missing person.

Two weeks later, at Netherdale Police station, a woman was attempting to report her daughter missing. She had hesitated. She knew how her daughter earned her money, knew she couldn't change that, but she was worried. The mother had been alerted by the fact that her daughter hadn't contacted her on her birthday, something that, no matter how bad her life situation was, she had never forgotten previously. Enquiries at the flats and from the landlord merely increased her anxiety over her daughter's well-being. Her alarm reached such a degree that, despite her reluctance, she approached the local police force to make her concern official. She was too distraught to notice that the person who took the details seemed unsympathetic almost to the point of being unhelpful.

* * *

Mike Nash had a problem. It was a dilemma he faced when trying to juggle the requirements of his work as a senior police officer and the demands on his time as a single parent. Under normal circumstances, he was able to fit the two roles together without too much hassle, but in this instance there seemed to be no easy solution. In fact, no solution at all. Nash had been forced to take a week out from his annual leave entitlement to care for his son. Normally, he would have been able to rely on the services of the childminder who looked after Daniel over the school holidays, but she was away during term-time. Unless Nash was able to arrange something, the boy would be without supervision when his father returned to work. Something he would not even consider.

Daniel had been sent home from his boarding school. Although he was coping with the broken collarbone received during a particularly strenuous hockey match, his main concern at his enforced absence was missing the remaining matches of the season.

Nash's quandary was resolved once he discussed it with Clara Mironova. Clara had acted as an unofficial aunt to Daniel ever since the boy had arrived in England from France nearly five years ago as a timid, shy, and nervous six-year-old who until that point had never met his father. It was only after Daniel's mother died, and the boy was brought to Helmsdale by an elderly aunt of his mother's, that Nash learned of his existence. Since that time, father and son had bonded well. Daniel's circle of friends now extended beyond school, and home, to include Clara, who he called Aunt, and her fiancé

David Sutton, a recently retired army officer, now deputized as Uncle.

'I could take him to France, but he'll be going for the summer holidays as usual, and it wouldn't be fair on his great-aunt Mirabelle. He loves it there and she loves having him, but it would be asking too much.'

'Why don't we take Daniel?' Clara said. 'David's at home, and Daniel's stayed with us before.'

'I can't ask that. The doctor said it could take up to six weeks to heal.'

'So? It will stop David being bored, and he'll keep Daniel occupied.'

'But I thought you were off to Spain over Easter?'

'We are, but there's time yet. If we can get a seat on the plane for Daniel, there's no reason he can't come with us. David's hired a villa which sleeps six. There's a swimming pool, which will be good exercise for Daniel's shoulder, and after some of the injuries David's picked up he knows more about physiotherapy than most professionals.'

'I don't think I'll need to ask Daniel, I'm sure he'll be thrilled, but shouldn't you check with David first? If he agrees, and you let me pay for Daniel's share, that'll be fine by me.'

Clara smiled. 'David's army career means that he's used to obeying orders, even the ones I give him.'

* * *

Two days later, Nash went into the CID suite on the first floor as Viv Pearce's mobile was ringing. Nash watched, with amusement, the expression on Viv's face. He couldn't hear the conversation, but his body language told Nash all he needed to know.

Viv jumped to his feet, a look of sheer panic on his face. 'It's coming! It's too soon. What do I do?'

'Don't ask him.' Clara had also realized what was happening. 'He's only interested in the manufacturing process.'

Before she finished speaking, she saw the pained expression on Nash's face and regretted her joke. Nash ignored her comment and took charge of the conversation.

'OK, Viv. This is what you do. First, you calm down. Where is Lianne?'

'Er, at home. She said her waters have broken.'

'Was she panicking?'

'No. But she said we need to go to the hospital.' As he was speaking Viv was trying to get his jacket on, but thought someone had tied the sleeves together. 'I have to go.'

'Hold on. Take a deep breath and calm down,' Nash repeated firmly.

Viv gave up the struggle.

'Now, stay calm. It's only a couple of weeks early. Get your car keys, go to the car park, get in your car and drive home. Slowly! Lianne needs you with her, not in a bed in accident and emergency. Got it?'

'Yes, I'm OK. Thank you.' He set off for the door when he was halted momentarily.

'Viv, give her our best wishes — and good luck,' Nash said.

Viv grinned as the door slammed behind him.

Clara looked at Nash. 'Mike, I'm sorry. I wasn't thinking, I shouldn't have said that about you.'

'What's done is done, Clara,' he replied, with a sad smile that she found distressing. 'You can't be guarding your tongue forever because what you say might offend someone. And before you ask, yes, it still hurts like hell, but there's nothing I can do but live with it.' He headed for his office and closed the door firmly behind him.

Knowing him as well as she did, Clara was convinced that her tactless remark, plus Viv's circumstances, had set Nash to thinking about his own situation, and the losses he'd suffered in the not-too-distant past.

* * *

Detective Constable Lisa Andrews was normally stationed at the force's Netherdale HQ, but with Viv Pearce now on paternity leave, she'd been drafted in to assist at Helmsdale.

While Lisa made coffee, Nash asked Clara if Daniel was OK.

'Stop worrying, Mike. He's settled in fine. David has the painkillers if they're needed, and he reckons a giant jigsaw is on the menu for today.'

The trio sat down to discuss their current situation. 'Luckily, things are fairly quiet at present,' Nash said. 'If they stay that way until Viv gets back, that'll suit me fine.'

'When's he due to return?' Lisa asked.

'In a couple of weeks, give or take a day or so. He had some holiday entitlement left so he's tacked that onto his paternity allowance. It's fortunate for us that Lianne decided to give birth early, and his leave doesn't clash with Clara's forthcoming holiday.'

'I'm not sure Lianne had much say in the matter. It must have come as a shock, but at least both mother and baby are well. Having said that, I can't see Viv handling nappies, can you? Not unless they've invented a computerized, digital version,' Lisa added.

* * *

It wasn't until the following day that Nash was to remember his own advice, not to tempt Sod's Law. That was his expression for the phenomenon that the very worst thing will happen at the most inconvenient moment.

With little to occupy him at work, Nash returned home earlier than usual. He had barely entered the house when his mobile chirped to signal an incoming text. The message was from Daniel. 'I'm OK. Uncle David's feeding me *Toblerone* . . . again!'

Nash smiled a trifle ruefully. Although he already missed his son, a reminder of the separation came as he tackled his next chore, which was to load the washing machine with clothing, most of it Daniel's. Having set the machine going, he took his evening meal from the fridge. Nash enjoyed cooking and always had a stock of available home-cooked meals in the freezer, which, with the aid of the microwave, often saved him time. Ignoring the dining table, he sat down to eat, using a tray in front of the TV, and reflected ruefully on his solitary existence. When Daniel was at home, there was plenty to distract him. But now, the contrast was stark.

Nash's gaze strayed briefly to the large landscape painting that covered two-thirds of the wall over the fireplace. Alondra had painted it as a farewell present after ending their affair. Nash knew the work was extremely valuable, by now worth a six-figure sum, and liable to increase even further with Alondra's growing reputation as one of her generation's leading landscape painters. Despite its worth, he'd willingly have given it away if the artist was there alongside him. Nash had been responsible for discovering the truth about Alondra's past. He'd tried to persuade her to stay, but the darkest reason for her departure was one Nash didn't care to dwell on, because it stirred up emotions he would rather remain buried.

He sighed; dwelling on what he'd lost wouldn't help. In the past, he'd always been able to shake off the feelings of sadness and regret that followed the ending of a relationship, but on this occasion, he was unable to do so. Even with the passage of time, the hurt refused to heal. In fact, it seemed to him that the wound became deeper, more intense. If Alondra had still been with him, she would have looked after Daniel, and Nash wouldn't have had to rely on the good nature of Clara and David. His thoughts turned to Daniel, recalling how well he and Alondra had got on, aware that he wasn't the only one who missed her. When Easter came Daniel would be on holiday, and Nash would really have liked to be there with them, but instead he was going to be condemned to this solitary existence for the foreseeable future. Perhaps this was how a convict felt, separated from those near to him.

He tried to focus his thoughts elsewhere. Possibly concentrating on the television would help, but with little worth watching, it promised to be a long evening.

Later, Nash found sleep difficult to come by, he was too preoccupied with the past and the woman he'd loved — and lost. When he eventually did manage to sleep, he dreamed of her.

The bitter disappointment when he awoke to find that he was alone was a bad start to what promised to be a long day. Perhaps when he reached work things would improve. Let's face it, he thought, they couldn't get much worse.

CHAPTER FIVE

Market day in Helmsdale was always busy, the cobbled Market Place closed to vehicles as it gave way to market stalls. It was also a day when farmers congregated at the nearby auction mart for the weekly sale of livestock. Although the focal point of the action was inside the ring, a considerable amount of buying and selling went on between the farmers and dealers leaning on the perimeter fence. Many of these deals, particularly those transacted by the older generation, were cash sales. The agricultural community has a natural distrust of banks, cheques and other methods of payment they couldn't count in their hand. Deals would be sealed with a handshake, concluded the following week by the delivery of beasts and paperwork in exchange for a corresponding wad of notes. These deals had the added advantage of not being subject to the auction's fees.

One of the farmers, who had particular reason to celebrate, retired to the Cobblers Arms for a late lunch of the liquid variety, which he took along with several of his cronies. An hour and several pints later, he excused himself from the company and retired to the toilet to make room for more beer. His progress down the short corridor at the back of the bar leading to the facilities was slightly erratic, possibly because of the urgency of his mission.

He reached the urinal and began to relieve himself. He was in full flow when he heard the door open. He didn't look round, knowing that sudden movement could lead to disaster. The next moment, he caught a glimpse of a flash of light in his peripheral vision. Simultaneously, something cold touched the side of his neck.

'Keep on doing what you're doing,' a voice in his ear told him. To emphasize the statement, the knife pressed harder on his neck, breaking the skin. He felt a trickle of blood, warm against his skin, escape from the puncture site. Helpless, he sensed the hand searching his pockets, locating and removing his wallet. Then the knife was gone, the door slammed, and he was alone. Alone, but unable to give chase, as he still had unfinished business. At last, trembling with shock, he zipped his flies and staggered out to raise the alarm.

* * *

The pet supplies stall had been doing a brisk trade throughout the day. Around 3.30 p.m., the stallholder, along with several of his colleagues decided it was time to pack up. Had the day not been as successful, he might have considered staying longer, but the takings were good enough to justify the early closure. He told the girl who helped him to start clearing the stall. 'Get the boxes from under the tables and start packing stuff. Take all the gear hanging from the canopy down and collect the pegs into that box at the end. I'm going for the van.'

Before he left, the stallholder removed the notes from the till. There were people who came to buy things as they were packing up, but it was a rare event. He put the notes into the zipped section of the apron he wore around his waist and set off through the archway and down the narrow ginnel leading to the hotel car park. The manager allowed him to park his van in the corner of the yard in exchange for cat food for the hotel's mouser.

He walked swiftly, hoping to overtake the redhead in front of him. She had a stunning figure, and he wanted to see if the face would live up to the promise shown by her rear view. Sadly, she seemed to be in even more of a hurry than he was, no doubt something to do with whoever she was talking to on her mobile. A boyfriend, perhaps? Lucky bugger.

He reached the van, unlocked the door and was about to get in, when he sensed someone behind him. Before he could turn round, a voice forbade him. 'This knife is very sharp. One move and you're as dead as the dog meat you sell.'

The blade glinted evilly in the late afternoon sun. At the same time he saw a flurry of movement, felt the apron strings loosened, the cash belt pulled free. Then he was alone. As soon as he was sure the danger had gone, he looked round, but there was no one in sight.

Had the market trader been braver and looked sooner, he would have seen the man walking swiftly, removing his balaclava, and stuffing it along with the apron inside his jacket, before turning the corner and heading back towards the Market Place.

As the thief walked he reflected on what had occurred, all but oblivious to his surroundings. Had he been less preoccupied, he might have noticed a teenager walking away from near to where he'd robbed the pet food supplier, but even had he done so, he wouldn't have placed any significance on it.

It had been a good day so far. Seeing the look on the farmer's face, and relieving him of the fifteen hundred pounds in his wallet as the old man was relieving himself had been very satisfying. Then the market trader had donated generously; around another five hundred pounds there. He should have been content, but then again, when you're luck's in, there's no point in stopping. Especially as he had another easy target in sight, and he reckoned the cafe qualified as an easy target.

The Market Cafe catered for a different clientele to the more genteel Helm Tea Rooms. There, customers could expect waitresses dressed in black with neatly starched white aprons. They could expect dainty pastries and slices of delicious cakes to complement the tea served in delicate china crockery.

In the Market Cafe, they got more basic food — at a far more basic price. The cafe opened at 7 a.m. every morning, except on market days when it was open an hour earlier. Almost as soon as the sign on the door was switched round, the kitchen became redolent with the appetizing aroma of bacon and sausages on the griddle, the scent of which was carried outside by the extractor fans. The smell attracted market traders, who paused in their task of setting their stalls out to grab a quick bacon and egg or sausage sandwich. They were joined by shopkeepers about to open up, workers on their way to offices and factories on the industrial estate, and early shoppers.

Nor was the breakfast trade the only busy part of their day. While Helm Tea Rooms tended to the more sophisticated needs of visitors, the Market Cafe continued to serve a steady stream of customers throughout the morning, before their legendary *meat and two veg lunches for £5* caused another queue to spill out onto the pavement outside. Once that rush died down, it was easier going for the owner, who doubled as the chef, and her two assistants, one who combined duties as till operator and table clearer, while the other concentrated on delivering food to the hungry diners as fast as she could.

At four o'clock in the afternoon, following the practice that had been established since the day the cafe first opened, the door was locked. The chef took off her apron and retired outside to the small courtyard with a mug of coffee and a packet of cigarettes. This routine never varied, come rain or shine, even on the coldest days of winter. To help her unwind, she had purchased a small picnic table and umbrella to ward off the worst of the weather.

The courtyard was actually the end of a small cul-de-sac of mews cottages which ran either side of the short cobbled back street. It was a tiny haven of charm that had changed little over the two centuries since it was built. There was little evidence of the intrusion of modern life, save some double-glazed windows, a couple of satellite dishes and the large wheelie bin that coped with the cafe's waste.

At approximately 3.50 p.m. a pedestrian walked swiftly down the mews and took up position behind the wheelie bin. Having made a slight adjustment to his clothing, he waited. Before long, the chef emerged from the back door from the kitchen, set down her coffee on the table, returned to close the door and then sat down and took out her cigarettes and lighter from her pocket.

As she crouched slightly to shield the flame of her lighter from the breeze, she noticed a blur of movement in her peripheral vision. At first, she thought it was one of the neighbours' marauding cats that were always on the hunt for food scraps. Before she had chance to turn and investigate, something bright glinted in front of her eyes and she felt a cold, sharp sensation at her throat.

'Stand up.' A voice growled in her ear.

Terrified, the cafe owner obeyed, the lighted cigarette still clutched in her hand.

'Drop the fag and go to the door. Slowly!'

Again she did as she was ordered, her stomach churning with fear.

'Open it and call your friend.'

She did so, shouting for her deputy as instructed.

The woman emerged and stopped suddenly, staring at her employer and the knife held close to her throat. If that wasn't frightening enough, the glittering menace of the attacker's eyes seen through the slits of his balaclava was terrifying.

'All the notes from the till. Now! Do it — or I slit her throat,' he growled.

The instruction was clear enough, but the woman remained rooted to the spot.

'Do as he says, Carol,' the cafe owner told her.

'Yes, Carol. Do it! And be quick.' The assailant moved the knife slightly, drawing a trickle of blood to emphasize his point. 'Oops, careless,' he remarked. The threat was effective.

Within a minute, Carol returned with a sizeable wad of notes, which the attacker snatched from her. In almost the same movement, he thrust the cafe owner violently through the open doorway, where she cannoned into her assistant. As the two women sprawled on the kitchen floor in a tangle of arms and legs, the thief slammed the door. Carol, the first to recover, staggered to her feet. As she did so, she heard a rumbling sound from outside. She flung the door open to give chase; an act that she later realized would have been extremely foolhardy. It was thwarted, however, because her progress was blocked by the wheelie bin rolled in front of the exit. Helpless, she stared down the courtyard in time to see the man disappearing round the corner, removing his balaclava as he went.

* * *

The first call came in at around 2 p.m. Nash took it, listened to what Jack Binns said and then put the phone down. 'Come along, Clara, we're going on a pub crawl.'

'What?'

'Well, one pub to be exact. Somebody mugged a farmer as he was taking a leak in the toilets. Apparently, they've got fifteen hundred pounds from him.'

'Blimey, that's a lot of cash to be carrying around. Where did he get that sort of money from?'

'That's what we'll have to find out. If I'd to guess I'd say he might have been paid in cash for some beasts he sold at mart. Either that or he had a big win at the bookies. Would you hold the fort, please, Lisa?'

It took the detectives no more than a couple of minutes to walk across the market square to the Cobblers Arms, where they found the blustering farmer having a plaster attached to his neck by the barmaid. His collar was spotted with blood, but he assured the detectives he was otherwise uninjured.

They listened to the aggrieved man telling his story, with frequent ribald interruptions from his cronies. After the third of these, Nash turned and told the onlookers, 'Can we just listen to what happened without you lot taking the . . . Mickey,' he changed the ending rapidly, but not before his audience noticed. He waited for their laughter to die down and then nodded to the victim, who resumed his narrative.

'Did you notice anyone suspicious in the bar before it happened?' Nash asked when he'd finished.

'Nobody at all,' the farmer replied.

'That's not surprising,' one of the other men interrupted, 'you were too busy ogling that young lass sitting at the bar. Undressing her with your eyes, you were, not that it would take much doing, seeing she was only half dressed.'

Nash blinked. 'Tell me more.'

'She came in a bit after we did and perched on that stool at the end of the bar. She had a right short skirt on. Little more than a belt, it were. I reckon if she'd sat facing us, we'd have got visions of the Promised Land. Nice legs, too,' he added as an afterthought.

'Anything else you noticed about her?'

'She'd bright red hair. Long red hair. Not natural. It were bright scarlet. Oh, and she spoke funny.'

'Funny, what do you mean?

'Her accent sounded foreign.' The way the man pronounced it made the word sound like "furrin".

'Was she alone?'

'As far as I know,' the victim admitted sheepishly. 'I didn't pay much attention to owt else.'

'When did this scarlet woman leave?'

'A few minutes before he were robbed, I reckon. She made a call on her mobile; then finished her drink and headed towards the toilets,' one of the other men replied. 'Strange though, I never saw her come back.'

Nash turned his attention to the victim. 'What about the man who attacked you? Did you get a look at his face?'

'I did and I didn't. I saw his reflection in the mirror.'

'Can you describe him?'

'No, he was wearing one of those hoodie things across his face. Like the ones the SAS use.'

'A balaclava?'

'Aye, that's it.'

'How was he dressed?'

'I could only see his head and the sleeve of what looked like one of them bomber jackets. It was black, like his gloves.'

'What age was he?'

'I don't know. Not a kid, but not old. Twenty to thirty perhaps, judging by his voice; I'm not sure — he didn't sound local.'

'He didn't?'

'No, sort of foreign-like.'

'Any idea how tall he was?'

'Not right big; about the same height as me I reckon. The arm holding the knife wasn't at an angle like it would have been if he'd been taller. Skinny, I guess, but like I said, all I saw were his reflection. That's all I noticed. I was too busy worrying about having my throat cut.'

'Did any of you see this person pass through the bar?'

They all shook their heads.

'Right, wait here. We'd better take a look at the crime scene.'

The toilet facilities were located at one side of a long corridor leading from the bar, at the end of which was a door to the car park. 'Clara, check the ladies, see if this redhead's in there.'

'You think she's involved?'

'No idea, but I'm not ruling anything out. Not with two "furrin" accents,' he said, mimicking the farmers.

Within moments, Clara returned. 'Empty. Must have gone out the back way.'

'Probably the same with the mugger,' Nash supposed.

Their inspection of the gents revealed nothing to give them a clue as to the attacker's identity, and Nash was in the process of telling Clara to order a CSI team to dust the room for prints, when the door opened.

The customer's face registered horror when he saw Clara. He glanced at the logo on the door and realized he hadn't walked into the wrong toilet by mistake. Nash showed the man his warrant card and told him, 'Use the ladies' toilet. This one is a crime scene and won't be available until our people have finished here.'

Clara was already on the phone to Netherdale when Nash's mobile rang. He listened for a few moments and then said, 'Thanks, Lisa, we'll deal with it. We're about finished here, so we'll go straight round. I'm sending a group of farmers across to the station. I want you and Jack to take their statements about the mugging. Be sure to get all you can from them about a redhead seen in the bar around the time of the robbery. We think she could be in league with the thief. Don't let them dwell on her charms too long though, or you'll have to wipe drool off the interview room table.'

'We need to be on the move,' he told Clara. 'There's been another mugging. Same MO, by the sound of it. Better tell the landlord to put an out-of-order sign here until CSI have finished. Also, apologize to him for taking some of his best customers away and send our bucolic friends across to the station. Lisa's waiting to take their statements. Once you've done that, follow me to the next crime scene.'

'I'll come now.'

'But you've to wait for CSI.'

Clara was trying hard not to grin. 'No, I don't. They're not coming.' She saw Nash's puzzled expression. 'Do you want the exact words — or the polite version?'

'I want to know why they're refusing.'

'OK, and I quote, "tell your boss if he thinks we've got time to print a bloody public convenience on a busy market day, then spend hours analysing the dozens of prints we find, he's got another thing coming".'

'And what did you say?'

'I said I'd tell you.' She grinned. 'But he does have a point. I expect it's well used. And it isn't as though anyone was seriously injured. Besides, we both forgot something.'

'We did?'

Clara was now tight-lipped and trying not to laugh. 'Erm, yes. The assailant was wearing gloves.'

Nash shook his head and sighed. 'Tell the landlord it's business as usual. Leave him a card in case anything occurs to anyone, then follow me.'

'Where will you be?'

'In the car park at the back of the Fleece Hotel — talking to a very unhappy market trader.'

* * *

Lee was on his way home from the swimming baths. He should have been at school but had skived off; hoping his girlfriend Milly would do the same. She'd lost her nerve, so rather than waste the afternoon, Lee had been to the baths. He set off towards the market place intending to arrive home at the same time as the school bus reached Newton-on-Helm. As he turned the first corner, he saw the robbery of the market trader unfolding in front of him.

Lee's first reaction was to run, but then he had a better idea. Reaching into his pocket, he grabbed his mobile and began recording the scene, even managing to capture the thief in the act of removing the balaclava. As the mugger turned to walk towards him, Lee ducked swiftly round the corner, retreated a dozen or so paces, then resumed his original route. So preoccupied was the villain that he didn't appear to have noticed Lee, even when he used his mobile again to take another photo of him, this time much closer to hand.

Lee was about to run for his bus, excited and nervous at the same time, but then had second thoughts. This was really something. Wait till his mates at school saw this. He could post it online, get thousands of hits. This was really going to up his street cred. Having pondered what he'd seen for a few seconds, Lee wondered if he could get more. What if he followed the robber and found out where he lived? Unmasking the villain would raise Lee to the status of super-hero, at least in Milly's eyes.

He realized he was shivering, but he wasn't cold. His breathing was erratic, but surely that was because he'd been running, wasn't it? By the time he reached the bus stop, he'd changed his mind, and began to sprint back towards the scene of the offence. He reached the lane running behind the market place just in time to see the robber disappear into a back yard. Lee knew this was the rear entrance to the Market Cafe. Did the villain work there, or could he be planning another heist? Lee was calmer now, but riddled with doubt. He had to check out what the man was doing, but without exposing himself to danger. Cautiously, Lee reached up and pointed his phone over the top of the wall; the camera set to video mode.

With the zoom on, he soon had images that showed the next robbery taking place. It was then that he saw the knife for the first time, and his earlier bravado vanished. Self-preservation took over. At that point, the gate leading to the back yard opened and the robber emerged. Lee had just been able to conceal his mobile before the man glanced his way. Lee turned and hurried in the opposite direction, passing a young woman with incongruously coloured red hair as he hurried back to the bus stop.

Now he was in a quandary; what to do with the photos and videos he'd shot? If he put them online everyone would know where he'd been and they'd ask awkward questions about why he hadn't been in school. His mother would find out he'd been in town. His teachers would know he wasn't ill.

'Bugger,' he said, as he sat on the bus staring at the screen of his mobile. Then he smiled. 'At least I can show Milly.' It was then another, far more serious thought occurred to him. What if the mugger had seen him? What if word got out and he came looking for him? And he had a knife!

Now he was scared.

CHAPTER SIX

The pet supplies seller told a very similar story to that of the farmer. Although he hadn't been able to see if his assailant was wearing a balaclava or not, there was little doubt in either of the detectives' minds that the attack had been carried out by the same person. Or persons, as it soon transpired.

'Did you notice anything before the attack?' Clara asked him. 'Anything that might be relevant?'

The trader's smile was a little shamefaced. 'To be honest, I wasn't paying too much attention. I walk through the ginnel to the car park twice a week. I've been doing it for so many years it's become like being on automatic pilot. Besides which, I was too busy looking at the girl.'

Nash and Clara exchanged glances.

'Girl? What girl?' Clara asked.

'There was this redhead walking in front of me. Lovely figure, legs that went all the way . . . well, you know what I mean.' He looked at Nash for support. 'She was talking on her mobile and I hoped to catch up with her to see if the view from the front was as stunning as it was from the back. But she was in a hurry, so I never did get a look at her face,' he ended sadly.

Clara continued to question the trader about the incident as Nash answered another call on his mobile. Out of her eye corner, she saw his face change, and when she heard his closing words, realized they had further problems. 'OK, Jack, we'll head there straightaway. Better let Lisa know we're sending her another victim; she'll need to take another statement. No, this one isn't a farmer. It's the market trader. Oh, and, Jack, ask Lisa to get a description of the woman. Tell her it sounds like the same one as the farmers mentioned from in the Cobblers Arms. That could be coincidence, but I—'

'Don't believe in coincidences,' Binns finished off Nash's sentence for him.

After ending his call, Nash asked the victim to go to the police station. 'Ask for DC Andrews, she'll take your statement as soon as she's free. At the moment, she's dealing with someone else who was victim of what sounds like the same thief. Unfortunately, we have to leave now to attend another incident.'

'What is it this time?' Clara asked as they made their way through the narrow ginnel to emerge in the market place.

Nash pointed to his right. 'The Market Cafe's been done over, and it sounds like the same couple. At least, the description fits the man, or lack of description I should say, seeing he had the balaclava on again. But I don't know if the woman was involved. He waited until the owner, whose name is Alison, went into the yard behind the cafe, held a knife to her throat, and demanded all the notes from the till. An ambulance has been called.'

They hurried along the pavement and after the assistant had unlocked the door, found the owner sitting on a chair, holding a tea towel to her neck and in an obvious state of shock. In her trembling hand was a lit cigarette.

'Sod the smoking ban,' she said. 'This is my cafe.'

The lack of information supplied about her assailant sounded depressingly familiar. It was only later in the interview with the woman and her employees that one or two useful facts emerged. Although the proprietor was unable to describe her attacker, her estimate of his age tallied with that provided by the pet stall owner. 'I'd say he was in his twenties. Early rather than late. Certainly not thirty,' Alison told them.

'What makes you think that?'

'His voice. It wasn't as deep as an older man's. Not high-pitched, but young-sounding. I barely caught what he was saying. It was almost slurred. Or it could have been foreign, I don't know.'

'You're holding the left side of your neck. Was he right-handed or left-handed?'

'Right-handed.'

'That tallies. Can you describe the knife?'

'Yes, it was a kitchen knife. I should know. Knives are my business.'

'How much was stolen?' Clara asked.

There was a slight hesitation before the cafe owner replied, and when she did so, Nash noticed a look of slight surprise on her assistant's face. They turned their attention to Carol, and she corroborated her boss's story in detail.

'I was in the kitchen when Alison called out. When I saw the man holding that knife to Alison's throat, I ran in here and grabbed the notes from the till like he told me. As soon as he got hold of the money, he pushed Alison towards me. We both fell over, and by the time I got to my feet, he'd slammed the door. I opened it to run after him.' She saw the look on Nash's face and explained, 'I know it was a stupid thing to do, but I wasn't thinking straight. Anyway, it wouldn't have done any good. He was too far away for me to have caught up with him, even if he hadn't shoved the wheelie bin in front of the door.'

At that moment, the paramedics arrived and checked Alison over. They applied butterfly stitches and a dressing to her neck and, much to her relief, assured her there was no need for a visit to A & E. They suggested she should go home and rest as soon as possible.

It was the third member of staff who provided the more significant information when Nash spoke to her. 'You were in the cafe itself while all this was going on, is that right?'

'That's right, I was wiping tables down.'

'Were there many customers in the cafe at that time?' Clara asked.

'No, there was an elderly couple who had taken afternoon tea, but they left before the trouble started. It was their table I was clearing. The only other one was the young woman who was taking her time choosing a piece of cake.'

'Did you know the customer?'

'No, I've never seen her before. But I would definitely remember her.'

'Why was that?'

'Because of her hair.' The assistant paused, before adding, 'I'm not sure if it was a very good dye, or whether she was wearing a wig. That shade of hair certainly isn't the colour she was born with — or anyone else for that matter.'

'What colour was it?'

'Bright crimson.'

'Where was this woman? Was she seated at a table?'

'No, she was by the counter, looking at the stuff in the display cabinet.'

'Apart from the hair, can you describe her?'

'Early twenties and quite pretty. I say quite pretty, but I didn't get much of a look at her face. Her hair was covering it part of the time, and then, as she was by the counter, she was using her mobile. I thought she was making a call, but she didn't speak to anyone. I suppose she might have been texting, or surfing the internet.'

'Did she select a cake, or did she leave without buying anything?'

'She bought a couple of vanilla slices to take away.' She paused. 'Because she didn't say very much, only a couple of words, I'm not sure . . . but I'd say she wasn't English. I thought I detected a strange accent.'

* * *

Back at the CID suite, as the detectives compared notes, Lisa Andrews said, 'They've done all right for themselves, haven't they?' They had reviewed the statements she'd taken and she had totted up the figures. 'Less than three hours work for over two thousand pounds is pretty good going by any standards. Except perhaps a bank director,' she added.

'I think it's a bit more than that,' Nash replied.

Lisa frowned, his expression puzzled. 'How do you mean, Mike? Have I got my sums wrong?'

'No, going on what they told us, the figures add up correctly. I just don't believe the stallholder and the cafe owner told us the right amounts. The farmer's figure has to be accurate, that's too easy to check up on, but I don't think either our dog food seller or our bacon butty provider gave us the real total they lost. I think they deliberately understated the figure.'

'Why on earth would they do that?'

'Two reasons that I can think of. I was almost sure the market trader wasn't telling the full story, and when the cafe owner stated the amount I saw the surprised look on her assistant's face. At a guess, I'd say one of the reasons is to do with their insurance. If they quote the correct amount when they claim, their premiums will escalate sharply. Either that, or when their policy is reviewed, they might even lose their theft cover altogether.'

'And the other reason?' Clara asked.

'Your friend and mine: income tax. With both businesses being cash-only, I don't think for a minute they declare all their earnings week in, week out. If we catch the thieves and the case comes to court, I bet they'd be scared stiff that the publicity will attract the attention of the Inland Revenue and get some nosy tax inspector curious as to the amount they're actually taking as opposed to what's on their tax return. All they'd have to do is compare the sum they lost with similar figures for other market days and question the discrepancy. The loss of a few hundred pounds would be chicken feed compared with the extra tax and penalties the Inland Revenue would impose.'

'What made you suspicious?'

'They reduced the amount by too much. If you look at the sums they say were taken, and think of what the market trader has to pay for his stall, and add the wage of his assistant, and the cost of his stock, it wouldn't be worthwhile for him to drag himself out of bed. The cafe owner has to find business rates, rent, electricity and gas, plus her own wage and two assistants. Ask yourself how either of those businesses makes a profit if the amounts they quoted us represent their takings on one of the two busiest days of the week?'

'What do you suggest we do about it?'

'Clara, I think I'll leave it to you to suggest tactfully that they might like to revise their first estimate of how much they lost.' Nash smiled. 'I'd say something along the lines of, I know you were suffering from shock at the time, but now you've had chance to think things over and do a more accurate calculation, perhaps you might be able to give us a more realistic figure. We think it might be considerably more than what you first thought.' Nash paused before adding, 'And I'd emphasize the word *realistic*.'

'And what do we do after I've played at diplomats?' Clara asked.

'The rest will be a much easier task. All we have to do is identify a man wearing a balaclava and who might not be English, and a woman with a foreign accent who might not look at all like her description, both of whom have been acting like a modern-day Bonnie and Clyde.' Nash paused before adding, 'One other complication is that they might have faked their accent in the same way as the woman disguised her appearance.'

'Of course, Mike, that makes it much simpler.' There was no disguising the sarcasm in Lisa's voice.

'You're starting to sound like Clara.'

* * *

Harry Johnson, the civilian receptionist on duty at Netherdale Police Station, looked across the desk at the man standing in front him. His appearance was scruffy, his hair tousled and his clothes badly in need of a visit to the laundrette. His expression was troubled, probably by the surroundings he was in. He seemed to be the sort who would be less than happy to visit a police station, even when it was voluntary.

'Can I help you?' Johnson asked. Get someone to help you into a cell, he thought.

'Who do I talk to about a missing person?'

'You talk to me in the first instance, whether it's about a missing person, a missing dog or cat, or your missing lottery ticket with the jackpot winning numbers on it.'

Sarcasm was wasted on the visitor. In fact, Johnson wondered how much of what he'd said had been taken in. Although it was morning, the visitor looked to be worse for wear.

However, when he spoke, the man proved him wrong. 'All right, no need to be sniffy. I'm only trying to help. It's my duty as a citizen, ain't it?'

The receptionist sighed and pulled a pad out from under the counter. 'A missing person, you said. Care to give me some details?'

He was anxious to get rid of the man, less because of his scruffy, unshaven, and generally seedy appearance — more because as his body adjusted to the warmth of the room, he was beginning to give off a strong and unpleasant body odour.

'Her name's Janet, Janet Wilson. I haven't seen her for a couple of days. I asked around, and nobody's seen her.'

'What can you tell me about her? How old is she? Where does she live, and where does she work? And what exactly is your relationship with her?'

As Johnson asked the questions, he was fairly sure he knew at least some of the answers. If his memory was correct, Janet Wilson had been arrested several times for soliciting.

'Don't know her age. Not exact. Mid-twenties maybe. She lives in Hawthorn Street. Number seventeen. I'm her landlord.'

He didn't have the appearance of a landlord, even of a rat-hole like Hawthorn Street, or of anything bigger than a dog kennel. The support officer doubted the description. Pimp, more likely. 'And your name is . . . ?'

'Shane Barry.' The name was issued with great reluctance.

'Thank you. Now, Mr Barry, can you tell me when you last saw Miss Wilson?'

As he continued questioning the man, he wondered if this would prove to be a wild goose chase, a considerable number of those reported missing were never traced, simply because they didn't want to be found.

Would Janet Wilson turn out to be one of these? Had she made a desperate bid for freedom? Was her disappearance an attempt to escape the clutches of this man and others like him? Harry Johnson didn't care to hazard a guess; in fact, he was more than a little disinterested in the welfare of a tart whose pimp was concerned by a drop in his income.

As he took Barry's contact details, which comprised a mobile phone number and, unsurprisingly, the same address as that of the missing woman, Johnson speculated as to what percentage of the police routine had been spent dealing with false alarms. Still, he shouldn't grumble. That was part of what he was paid for, and as long as he went through the motions, he could soon forget about this unwanted intrusion into his working day. He filled the report form in and promptly filed it. He wasn't prepared to utilize his time and that of officers on what would no doubt turn out to be wasted effort.

His action — or lack of it — owed nothing to police procedure, but rather to Johnson's own prejudices, formed from tragic personal experience. All of which did nothing to help Janet Wilson. Even the fact that he had now been informed of two missing women, both prostitutes, failed to trouble him. As far as he was concerned, if anything bad happened to a woman who chose that way of life, it was her own fault.

CHAPTER SEVEN

The morning following the market place robberies, DC Lisa Andrews woke early, far earlier than usual. It was still dark outside, and she knew she ought to turn over and try to get back to sleep. However, her mind was troubled by a thought that refused to go away. The thought that there was something she, Clara, and Nash ought to have done the previous day, something that had been missed in the maelstrom of events.

Alongside Lisa, Alan Marshall, her long-term partner, was snoring gently. She pondered the idea of getting up and making herself a cup of camomile tea. That often helped her to sleep. She glanced at the bedside clock and decided to forego the tea. It was almost daybreak, and elsewhere, for a lot of people, the working day had already begun. In Helmsdale, for instance, the council workmen would already be starting to . . .

Lisa sat bolt upright. That was it! That was what they had missed. And if she didn't get over to Helmsdale quickly, it would be too late to rectify the omission. She got out of bed, switched on the bedside light, and ignoring Alan's sleepy protest, dressed hurriedly. She bent over and kissed him lightly on the forehead. 'Sorry for disturbing you, love, but I've got to go check some wheelie bins.'

An hour later, when Marshall woke up again, he wondered if he'd been dreaming. Had Lisa actually woken him and told him she was going to check some wheelie bins? He dismissed the weird idea. He must have been dreaming; it was far too absurd to be true.

* * *

Although Nash was usually the first of the detectives to arrive at the station, he noticed Lisa's car was already there. Once inside the building, he paused for a quick word with Sergeant Binns before going upstairs to the CID suite. When he entered, Lisa was sitting at Pearce's desk, cradling a mug of coffee.

'Morning, Lisa, what's wrong? Alan kicked you out of your rural love nest?'

Lisa grinned triumphantly, if a little wearily. 'No, I woke up early and couldn't get back to sleep. I was sure there was something we ought to have done yesterday evening, but with everything else that was going on, we didn't think of it. So I had to go check up before we missed our chance, and I was only just in time.'

'Go on. What did we forget?'

Andrews reached over and held up a clear plastic evidence bag. 'I found this in one of the wheelie bins on Daleside Avenue, close to the alley at the back of the cafe. I remembered it was collection day today. They always empty the bins following market day, and a lot of people put theirs out ready the previous afternoon or evening. I thought if I got there before the council, I might find something the thieves had discarded, the balaclava, for instance. I was lucky. I got there with ten minutes to spare.'

Nash stared at the long red wig curled up inside the evidence bag; then at Lisa. 'How about if you swap places with me?' he suggested. 'Because I reckon you might be better at this job. I should have thought of the bins.'

'No thanks, Mike. The huge salary you're on would be welcome, but I couldn't stand the responsibility.' She grinned and added, 'Besides which, I don't think swapping places would work at home, because, I'm sorry to say, you're not Alan's type.'

'Better get that wig across to Forensics and ask them to check it for DNA. I feel sure the wearer will have left some trace. Wearing that thing must surely make your head sweat. If we arrest a suspect, this will provide a good match.'

Nash was about to go into his office, but then paused. 'I suppose we ought to change the description of the accomplice we circulated, and strike out the part about her red hair. She is certainly not going to put a red wig on over red hair. We're going to have to concentrate on her, because the description of the man is far too vague to be of any use.'

Nash sat down behind his desk. Missing the bins had been a basic error, he reflected ruefully. It was extremely fortunate that Lisa had been able to put it right.

* * *

It was a couple of days later before they received news on the cases that were baffling them, and to begin with, all the developments provided was further frustration.

'Forensics has reported on the wig,' Lisa told Nash. 'They said there is no DNA trace, nothing to suggest it has ever been worn. They speculated that if it is the one used in the robberies, the wearer must have had some sort of skull cap between the wig and her own hair or scalp. They also told me the wig is a fairly cheap one, the sort that can be bought fairly easily anywhere online or on the High Street.'

'That suggests the villains are professionals. Anyone who goes to that much trouble to avoid detection must be really determined not to get caught. If that's the case, it stands to reason that they must have done this sort of thing before, probably lots of times. Ring Tom and ask him to run their MO through the computer and see if he comes up with anything.'

'OK, but if we draw a blank with that, we're no further forward,' Lisa said.

Nash looked round the room. 'Any other bright ideas?'

'Actually, I have had an idea,' Clara said. 'I began by wondering how the thieves picked that particular farmer to target. If you remember the statements his cronies and the landlord gave, they said the woman with the red wig made a phone call and then left the bar. To me, it seems obvious that she was telling her accomplice that the victim was about to become separated from his mates, and therefore ready to be mugged. However, she could easily have done that when one of the others went to the loo. Of course, they might have just dropped lucky, but they sound to me too professional to rely on chance. Therefore, they must have known that their victim was the one carrying a wad of cash, and the only way they'd know that would be by watching the activity at the auction mart earlier.'

'I agree,' Nash said after some thought. 'I think one of us should go to the mart and ask the auctioneer and the other officials if they can remember any strangers hanging around during the sale.'

Clara groaned. 'By one of us, I suppose you mean me? I'll go now. One other thing, Mike, regarding those fingers found at the Boar's Head. We've been through the MISPER cases for the years Mexican Pete suggested, but we couldn't see anything from our area that would match the woman, which suggests she must be from elsewhere.'

As she reached the door, Lisa stopped her. 'Clara, hang on. I was wondering, does Professor Ramirez know his nickname is Mexican Pete?'

Clara burst out laughing. 'Of course he does. He's not that dim. Everyone calls him that.'

'I know that, but he's Spanish, not Mexican.'

'Blame the *Ballad of Eskimo Nell*.'

* * *

The landlord of the Black Bull public house close to Helmsdale town centre was due to bank the pub's weekly takings. Conscious of his own safety, and mindful of the warnings issued by the police and his insurance company, he tried to vary the process as much as possible.

In Helmsdale that was more difficult than in larger towns and cities. There were only two routes from the Black Bull to the bank and both of these involved crossing the market place. The landlord's choice was to either exit via the front door, entering the square via Bakers Alley, or by going out of the back door, emerging onto Butchers Alley and from there reaching the market place. Both ginnels were narrow and dark, presenting prime locations for an ambush if one was being planned.

Having reached the main road, there was little the landlord could do to change his route. At one time, there had been six banks and four building societies in the town, but following the banking crisis and the economic downturn, and after a couple of mergers, there were now only three financial institutions represented in Helmsdale.

Apart from choosing the route, the only other variant the landlord could rely on to prevent anything untoward happening was the time of day he set off for the bank. On most occasions, he went in the afternoon, but occasionally he opted for the morning — on one occasion even reaching the bank as their doors opened, much to the surprise of the cashier.

If there was to be an attack, the one place the landlord felt confident that it wouldn't happen was in the pub's back yard. In winter, this area was used to store empty barrels and beer crates. These were cleared away in spring to make room for a couple of tables and some bench seats, the addition of which led to the yard being re-classified as a beer garden. This was in spite of the fact that the only plants growing there were the moss and weeds that sprouted from the crumbling brickwork of the walls.

It was those walls, together with the locked and bolted gate, that gave the landlord confidence for his safety within the yard. The walls were over seven feet high, and at some point, one of his predecessors had enhanced the security by adding the extra deterrent of broken glass set into concrete on the wall tops. Used beer bottles, of course; Yorkshire innkeepers don't believe in waste.

A couple of days after the market day muggings, as the robberies had been categorized by the *Netherdale Gazette*, the landlord set off for the bank, informing his live-in girlfriend of his intention to call at the butchers to collect some meat on the return leg of his excursion. She glanced at the clock, noting that there was ample time before the scheduled hour for opening, and then returned to her study of a Sudoku puzzle that was proving obdurate.

It was only when two regulars, their thirst in need of quenching, arrived and banged on the pub door that she realized her lover had failed to return. She unlocked the door expecting to find him standing there with them, shamefaced and keyless, but there was no sign of him. She ran to the back door, her alarm turning to panic as she opened it to see him lying face down on the concrete. Her screams brought the drinkers hurrying out, forsaking the chance of a pint in their need to find out what was wrong.

* * *

By the time Nash arrived at the pub yard, the victim was seated in a chair brought outside by one of the regulars. A few seconds later, when DS Mironova joined them, having phoned CSI to request their presence, Nash asked the victim if he felt well enough to tell them what had happened. 'Perhaps it would be better if we all go indoors,' Nash began. He gestured towards the newly arrived ambulance crew. 'These guys will help you, I'm sure. Once we're in the warmth, you can explain how you were attacked.'

'Sorry,' the paramedic said, 'you can talk to him on the ambulance.' Then added, 'After we've checked him over and bandaged his head.'

Nash watched as the paramedics assisted the landlord onto a stretcher and wheeled him onboard. The publican was barely able to stand unaided, and when he moved, it was like watching someone of extreme age and infirmity.

'CSI will be about half an hour,' Clara explained. 'I assume that's why you wanted the yard clear, to prevent contamination of the scene.'

'A bit late for that. But, while we're waiting, let's hear what mine host has to say.'

The landlord's opening words were familiar to both detectives. Nash had lost count of how many times he'd heard a victim say, 'It all happened so fast.' Having listened to the tale of a balaclava-clad figure that had appeared out of the hiding place created by a stack of crates containing empty bottles, Nash asked if the victim could describe his assailant.

Nash was beginning to think nothing positive would come from the interview until he asked how the victim had been knocked out.

'I don't know,' the landlord admitted, 'one minute I was grappling with the bastard, the next I felt a burning pain on the back of my neck and I went out like a light. I must have banged my head on the wall or one of the crates as I went down.'

One of the paramedics, monitoring his patient, interrupted. 'There's a mark on his neck that I reckon might have been made by a Taser.' He pointed to the twin circular bruises. As Nash examined the discolouration, he asked the landlord, 'Was he behind you when this happened?'

'Sort of, more alongside me, I think.'

The only other information they elicited was that the cash taken by the attacker had been inside a cotton bag issued by the bank.

The ambulance had gone, and as he watched the CSI team doing their work in the yard, Nash mulled over what the victim had said. Highest among the questions posed by the statement was, how had the attacker gained entry to the enclosed space? And, equally important, given that the gate was still locked and bolted, how had they left?

He glanced at the wall before calling the forensic team leader across. 'I think the thief might have escaped over the wall, so would you make sure your guys check the top?'

The officer sighed and looked at Nash. 'That's probably the only uncontaminated site in this place with Fred Karno and his army having tramped through it,' he said pointedly.

Nash signalled Mironova to accompany him back to the station. 'I think we should leave them to it.'

As they'd left the pub, he said, 'This looks the work of our friends yet again, or at least one of them.'

'You mean the market muggers? I agree, but how he got in and out of that yard is a bit of a puzzle.'

'He must have scaled that wall, there's no other way. What we need to do is step up our search for crimes with the same MO. These people are too good for this to be their first offence, so we should be able to get details of their previous, and possibly even to identify them. Tom was on with that. Let's see what progress he's made, if any.'

The answer to that question, as they soon discovered, was none at all.

'If they've offended before, I can't find any trace of it. At least, nothing with the same MO or remotely like it is recorded on the PNC,' Tom told them when they phoned.

'Maybe they've been arrested or convicted for other crimes and changed their MO to prevent getting caught again,' Lisa suggested.

'If that's the case, they're going to be much more difficult to catch,' Nash said gloomily. 'Let's hope that, like all other thieves, they get greedy and make a mistake, because short of that, we're up against a brick wall.'

Although Nash hadn't intended the last statement as a pun, it was to be the brick wall to the rear of the pub that, together with the landlord's chance remark, that gave the detectives their first clues.

* * *

Nash had travelled to Netherdale HQ for his regular meeting with Superintendent Jackie Fleming. As he was approaching her office, he encountered the head of the CSI team that had attended the Black Bull mugging incident. 'I'm glad I've seen you; it's saved me a phone call,' the forensic officer told him. 'Your idea about that wall top paid off. We found skin and blood traces on two pieces of glass, so if the DNA matches someone in the database, we're in business. It'll take a couple of days before I know, but in the meantime, if you detain someone, check their arms and legs for wounds. Judging by the amount of blood we found, the injuries will be more than scratches. I'll let you know as soon as we have anything for you.'

Nash thanked the officer and went on to deliver this update along with a status report to Jackie Fleming. Their meeting was well underway when they were interrupted by a member of staff. Maureen Riley worked as civilian support officer, and was the widow of an officer killed in the line of duty. Following his death, she had continued working at Netherdale, where her role complemented that of Tom Pratt. This enabled the small detective force to have someone always on hand when needed, and also gave Maureen a much-needed salary. She possessed an uncanny ability to identify minute evidence that others might have missed. One such instance had led to the arrest and conviction of her husband's killer. Since then, she had proved her value many times over.

'Sorry to interrupt, ma'am, but there's been another incident that I think involves the so-called market muggers.'

Nash and Fleming looked at her, their surprise obvious. It had only been a day since the previous robbery. 'They must be on a productivity bonus,' Nash muttered.

Fleming smiled fleetingly, but asked Maureen for details.

'It's a bit complicated, but by the sound of what the uniformed men who attended the scene told us, it happened in Bishopton. It's market day there, and one of the stalls is a caravan stocking cheese, bacon, cooked meats and so forth.'

'Don't tell me they've stolen the caravan?' Fleming looked shocked.

'Not quite, but close enough. According to eyewitnesses a pickup pulled up alongside the back of the caravan and two people, a man and a woman, jumped out. The man had a pair of bolt cutters that he used to cut through the chain securing the generator the cheese van uses for lighting, and to power their refrigerated display units. They switched the generator off, unplugged it, loaded it into the back of the pickup, and drove off. The eyewitnesses thought that because the market was finishing for the day this was the owner loading his unit before hitching the caravan to the tow bar. Likewise, the cheese man thought the generator had run out of diesel, but as he was closing up, wasn't bothered about refilling it. That gave the thieves ten minutes' breathing space to make their getaway. Except that they didn't.'

'You mean they were arrested?'

Maureen shook her head in answer to Fleming's question. Nash waited, guessing that there was more to come. 'No, what I mean is they didn't leave the town centre. While everyone was busy attending to the generator theft they used the diversion to rob the fruit and veg stall at the opposite end of the market place.'

'How did they manage that without drawing attention to themselves?' Nash spoke for the first time.

'The woman, described by an onlooker as a stunning blonde in a short miniskirt with legs that went up to her shoulders, was selecting vegetables from the stall when a man in a hoodie walked up to the stallholder and whispered in his ear, telling him to give the money apron to the woman or he would slit his throat. He gave her the apron, and then the man told him to sit down on the camping chair he uses on the stall. He did so and the man then gave him a quick burst with a Taser, disabling him for long enough to give them chance to get clear before he raised the alarm.'

'Where was the woman while this was happening?' Nash asked.

'The stallholder said he remembered the couple arriving at the same time. The woman started filling a basket with produce, and then the man attacked him.'

Nash bit his lip. Laughing at that point would have been inappropriate, yet the incident did have its comical side. Not only had they taken a good deal of money, but they'd acquired a generator and taken the opportunity to do a week's food shopping into the bargain. 'I'd better get over to Bishopton and see what I can do. Maureen, will you ring Clara and ask her to join me there, please?'

The story they were told by the victims and eyewitnesses in Bishopton was familiar, but added little to the progress of their enquiry. After taking statements from both victims and various onlookers, the detectives returned to Helmsdale, where they compared notes.

'I reckon our best way of catching these two is to get there before them.'

Clara was used to her boss making odd remarks, ones that usually contained more than a degree of common sense — albeit at times well hidden — but this one puzzled her. 'How do you mean, "get there before them", Mike?'

'I reckon we should try to pre-empt their next move; second-guess them and catch them in the act. If we can detain them, we'll be able to prove our case via their DNA. If it matches that from the Black Bull, we've got them.'

'That's all very well, but they seem to strike at random, so how do we anticipate where they're going to hit next?'

'That's a good question, but I reckon I've an idea. I doubt whether they'll return to Bishopton. The mart there is small and barely worth one visit, let alone two. My guess is that Bishopton, like the cheese stall, was a diversion. I think they'll be hoping we concentrate on Bishopton while they strike elsewhere. If I was them, I'd be eyeing up the chances of a bigger target. I think they'll hit Netherdale next Wednesday or Saturday.'

CHAPTER EIGHT

Nash was in his office later when DC Andrews came in. She'd been through to Netherdale to give evidence in a domestic violence case, and in the process collected some useful information. 'The DNA results from that broken glass are back, and we've no match for it on our database. The result did throw up one surprise, though.'

'And that was?'

'According to the lab tech, the DNA pool was matched to an area of Eastern Europe, such as the Baltic region.'

'That is surprising, but without a more positive match, we're almost back to square one.' Nash paused and thought for a second. 'Actually, that's not quite correct, because we can at least eliminate suspects whose ethnicity doesn't tally.'

'There seems to be little more we can do without catching them in the act, unless you've got any ideas.'

'Nothing springs to mind, Lisa, unless we extend the check Tom made of other forces for similar crimes on their patches even further.'

He saw Lisa's puzzled frown and explained.

'The girl in the cafe said she thought the woman spoke with a foreign accent, and we know from the DNA that her partner's probably not British, so it might be worth checking via Interpol. It's a bit of a long shot that they'd provide anything useful. Still, it's worth a try, so get Tom to check it out, will you? No, hang on, give Tom a break. Viv's rung to say he's coming back a few days earlier than expected, on Monday, so let him have the pleasure. Obviously, you won't be needed here until Clara goes on holiday. But, thanks, you've been a great help and we'll see you then.'

* * *

The CID suite door opened wide and Viv Pearce entered.

'Good to see you, Viv. Glad to be back?' Nash asked him. 'Or are you just glad to get away from nappy-changing duty?'

Pearce grinned.

'How are Lianne and little Brian?'

'Both doing fine, although I never anticipated that anything that small could make so much noise — or be permanently hungry. The sooner we get moved, the better. A one-bedroom flat might be great for romance but it's lousy for parenthood.'

'Good point,' Clara commented. 'But can I ask? Why did you choose to name him Brian?'

Viv looked at her, aghast at her ignorance. 'My father was named after a cricketer; I was named after a cricketer. I wasn't about to spoil a family tradition.'

Clara looked to Nash for support.

'Brian Charles Lara, from Trinidad. One of the greatest cricketers of all time,' he explained, while trying not to laugh.

Clara decided on a change of subject. 'Didn't Lianne mind you coming back to work earlier than originally planned?'

'No. I think I was getting in the way. She told me that if I didn't come to work, I'd be making my own dinner for the next month. Faced with that alternative, I really had no choice.'

'Certainly not with your appetite,' Clara interjected, as Nash led him through to his office to update him and ask him to start the Interpol search for the muggers.

An hour later, Clara called through to Nash's office. 'Mike, Viv wants to see you. He has some answers regarding the market muggers. I think he's found something. Far quicker than we could have done.'

The information Viv had was sketchy, but it provided Nash with slightly more insight into the possible identification of the couple, as he explained. 'The French police suspected a brother and sister who they believe were of Albanian origin. Because they had false papers, there's no clue as to their real names, and the authorities had insufficient evidence to make an arrest. Reading between the lines, I'd hazard a guess that the only reason for the suspicion is that they were in the right towns on the dates that muggings occurred. Having said that, there's a distinct similarity in the MO of the French offences to the ones committed here.'

Nash thanked him and read the document Viv had left him. As Pearce had said, the paperwork yielded little useful information. With nothing concrete to go on, they would have to wait for the thieves to slip up. Catching them red-handed seemed likely to be the only possible solution. Once more, although the outcome could never have been predicted, Nash's guess was way wide of the mark.

That night, following a visit to see Daniel and a meal with Clara and David, Nash slept better than he had for some time. But once again, his rest was disturbed. He woke next morning to that familiar feeling of emptiness.

* * *

Samantha Frost was as cold as her name implied. She was also wet. She was also miserable. But above all, she was desperate. The hunger that had driven her outdoors onto the windswept, rain-lashed streets of Bishopton in such filthy weather was only partly hers. And it had nothing whatsoever to do with food.

Samantha had been with her current partner for two years. The attraction wasn't his looks. It wasn't his money.

It wasn't his magnetic personality, or his sex appeal. It was nothing more than a shared enjoyment of illicit substances that forged their mutual bond.

Such guilty pleasures don't come cheap. To fund them, her partner, ever the gentleman, came up with a simple, effective solution. It involved the sale, or more precisely, the hiring out of their only asset, Samantha's body.

She didn't object too strenuously. It wasn't as if sex meant a great deal in her life. It had at one time, but a series of fumbling, clumsy and less-than-proficient partners had quickly turned her off the delights of the physical act. Perhaps if any of her liaisons had been driven by love rather than lust, it would have been a different tale. But great lovers and true romantics weren't exactly ten a penny in Samantha's social circle.

Two years down the line and the twin effects of the drugs and some fairly rough trade enjoyed by a few of her punters were beginning to show. Her face, once reasonably pretty, particularly in the less than brilliant street lights of Bishopton, was now little more than passable. Careless of her appearance, she had run to seed far too early. As the habit worsened her looks, she could no longer charge as much, attracting a worse class of clientele. One of the younger members of her profession, aware of this and Samantha's age, cruelly nicknamed her the Tenner Lady. It was true that she'd to take on far more encounters simply to pay for her drug habit. Not only that, but she was working for two. As Samantha was earning, her partner saw no reason to dirty his hands and join the working class.

The combination of misuses she subjected her body to accelerated Samantha's deterioration. It was the most vicious of circles. One of the consequences of the struggle to provide for them both, a struggle that was more often unsuccessful was the inevitable worsening relationship, which was now categorized by abuse: mutual, verbal, and physical. Never shy of venting her feelings, Samantha gave as good as she got, within her physical limitations. On several of their not-irregular visits, police and paramedics found that it wasn't Samantha but her partner who was in need of treatment. More recently, however, he'd become increasingly reluctant to risk coming second in their encounters. To prevent this, he purchased a set of wickedly sharp-bladed knives which he used to get his point across during their frequent arguments.

Having established his authority as head of the household, he emphasized his superiority by demanding greater productivity from Samantha. Prices of good gear were escalating fast. It now cost as much to feed his habit as they'd paid for both of them only a year ago. The thought that this might be down to their increased usage never occurred to them. But then, neither Samantha nor her partner were heavily into constructive thought.

On more than one occasion in recent weeks, Samantha had returned with barely enough money to pay for his drugs. That meant she would have to do without. As a sales incentive, this approach seemed revolutionary to him, although it was by no means unknown to those in Samantha's profession. Nor did it work every time; at least, not in the way he had intended it to. When Samantha got beyond endurance, she resorted to pocketing her earnings, buying, and using the drugs before she returned to the love nest. She reasoned that although he could take what remained of the money she'd earned, he'd find it difficult to steal the drugs once they were in her system.

As a strategy it was effective, but dangerous. Venting his anger at her duplicity became a frequent occurrence. Retaliation, even self-defence, was no longer an option open to her. Not when faced with an eight-inch blade being wielded close to her face. That night, as Samantha huddled miserably in a shop doorway that smelt vaguely of vomit and strongly of urine, her desperation and misery were compounded by the fact that she had not earned anything. And the way the weather was looking, her prospects of returning home with enough for one, let alone both of them, were somewhere below zero. In fact, the way things were going, she'd be lucky to be able to afford a packet of cigarettes, let alone the stronger drugs she craved.

It was neither her looks nor her less-than-sunny disposition that were to blame for this. Weather such as they were experiencing didn't so much lower her punters' libido, it destroyed it. Even offering vastly reduced rates, or two-for-one deals like the supermarkets were so fond of wouldn't have done the trick, to use a trade expression.

Bishopton's red-light district, which in reality meant that area patrolled by Samantha and her three fellow professionals, stretched from the corner of the Market Square to the bus shelter on the High Street; a district of no more than one hundred and fifty yards.

From time to time, Samantha walked from one end to the other; partly to warm herself up, and partly to avoid missing a lone punter. Neither objective was achieved. Instead, she got colder, wetter, and more desperate. Eventually, long after the pubs had shut, the twin ethnic takeaways had lowered their lights and Bishopton had gone to bed, Samantha huddled inside the bus shelter. She was unwilling to return home. Not unless she had something to show for her night's work, or lack of it. Returning with an empty purse to face the inevitable beating was an option she wasn't prepared to risk.

Samantha was in a pitiful state. Even someone in peak condition with a healthier lifestyle would have suffered outdoors in such weather. Added to her other miseries, Samantha was beginning to feel the effects of her enforced abstinence. The symptoms were visible. Her hands shook uncontrollably in a series of ague-like attacks. Her eyes were deep, red-rimmed sockets of pain. Her face, pale at the best of times, was grey with exhaustion, lined with suffering. She was about to chuck it in, risk her partner's wrath, the message delivered by his fists, when she saw the lights of a car approaching, being driven at a fairly sedentary pace. She moved from the bus shelter to the edge of the kerb. Was this a punter? Or merely someone who was driving slowly because of the vile weather? She struck a pose, one that displayed her legs, still her best asset. Well, almost the best, but she could hardly display the other in so public a place — especially in weather such as this. The vehicle pulled to a halt a couple of yards short of where she was standing. Samantha shielded her eyes with one hand, peering towards the windscreen.

The driver's gaze travelled down from her breasts, taking in the short, tight skirt, glancing at her legs, before he looked at her face. No prizes for what he was thinking. She knew that look. Assessing? How much? Would she be worth it? In her job, you got to recognize the signs. She squinted back at him, screwing her eyes up against the headlight beam. He looked to be the wrong side of thirty, maybe even forty, she guessed. Not that age made much difference. Dirty old men paid just as well as dirty young men. Better in most cases. And as they were usually more desperate to get their end away, they couldn't afford to be as choosy.

The passenger door opened and she walked towards it. As she bent to look inside, she heard him utter her favourite chat-up line.

'How much?'

'A ton.' Better to start high for when he bargained, as they often did.

'An hour, or for the night?'

She was about to ask if he could manage a full night, but insulting a customer's prowess wasn't the way to increase clientele. And she was hardly fending them off with a pole tonight. 'For the night, love,' she replied.

'Get in.'

The tight skirt presented a bit of a challenge, but she made it, giving him an eyeful into the bargain. His expression certainly wasn't one of disappointment. Samantha settled back against the cold upholstery. 'Where are we going?'

'My place.'

Not a talker, then. Maybe his talents lay elsewhere. Well, Samantha thought, she'd have all night to find out. At least that would give her chance to get warm.

CHAPTER NINE

Nash's phone rang. He woke instantly, the bitter realization that he had been dreaming again overtaken by the fear of what bad news the call would bring. He fumbled for the receiver and grunted something that might have been his name into the mouthpiece.

The caller was Sergeant Binns. 'Sorry to disturb your beauty sleep, Mike.'

'Yes, Jack tell me the worst.'

'It's not that bad, except for the victim. The reason I'm calling you is that there's been a stabbing, not fatal or likely to be, but it's right on your doorstep. Well, on the outskirts of Wintersett village to be exact, Lilac Farm.'

By now, Nash was wide awake. He thrust back the duvet and stood up, stretching slightly to ease the stiffness in his back. 'Give me some details, Jack.' As he spoke, Nash reached for the pad he kept alongside the phone for just such emergencies.

Having scribbled the location, which was near the Miners Arms, he asked, 'Any chance you might fill me in with a little more by way of detail? The victim's name and gender, for instance.'

He sensed Jack Binns' grin, but the reply was confusing to put it mildly. 'The victim had no ID, which was hardly surprising seeing he was only wearing his trolleys.'

'What was someone doing out at this ungodly hour with only his underpants on?'

'I've no idea, Mike, that's why I called you. Aren't you supposed to be a detective? Should I get the delectable DS Mironova to help you?'

'I assume you're on call and out of Mrs Binns' earshot, otherwise you wouldn't have referred to Clara as delectable.' Nash enjoyed Binns' gasp of alarm. 'No? Well, if I was you I'd make her a nice cup of tea as a peace offering. And definitely don't call Clara. She's got enough to do without your heavy breathing down the phone at two o'clock in the morning.' Having exacted suitable revenge on Binns, Nash returned to business. 'You could ask the paramedics not to set off before I've had chance to view the victim or speak to him, if that's possible.'

Nash got dressed hurriedly. He knew there would be at least one uniformed officer at the scene, and hopefully, if the ambulance crew got his message in time, they wouldn't have removed the victim yet, not unless it was urgent.

It took less than five minutes to reach the scene. The beacons of a police car and an ambulance guided him up the lane to the farm. That was the easy part. Once Nash had ducked under the incident tape, getting information as to what had happened was far more difficult. The officers explained how they had found the victim in the farm yard. Standing alongside him had been a lady who had applied pressure to the wounds to stop the bleeding and covered the unconscious man with a blanket while waiting for help to arrive.

Having been given permission to interview the victim, who was now awake, Nash climbed into the ambulance and showed the man his warrant card. As he was speaking, Nash glanced casually at the victim, appearing not to notice his facial injury, shielded by a dressing, to the man's cheek, just below his eye. Nash wondered if the eye had been the attacker's target. If so, the victim had been lucky not to lose his sight. He began by asking the man his name. The only response he got to that and all the following questions was a blank stare.

He turned to one of the paramedics who was monitoring his patient and winked. 'I don't think this warrants taking up a hospital bed,' he told the medic. 'Dress those scratches and deliver him to the police station. Tell them to charge him with wasting police time.'

As he spoke, Nash watched the man on the stretcher, heard him gasp and saw the alarm in his eyes. 'Right, so you're not deaf and you do understand English, so enough of the pretence. I need to know your name, your address, and who did this to you.'

It was of no avail, the man lapsed into sullen silence. Once he was out of earshot of the stabbing victim, Nash checked with the ambulance crew, who told him the man also had a wound to his shoulder and another on his side at waist height, none of which were life-threatening. 'I thought I should mention that he also has a grubby bandage on his hand and another on his leg, obviously not relevant to his current injuries. They look like stab wounds.'

'Take him to Netherdale General and ensure the doctors give me precise details of his injuries.'

He turned to the two police officers, who were loitering by their patrol car, obviously waiting to be given the go-ahead to return to their regular duties. 'One of you needs to go with him, and I need one of you to remain here until we get more info. He may be keeping quiet, but he is still the victim of an assault which could have proved far worse. It looks like being a long night, gentlemen. Contact control and find out who reported this.'

Although their faces were in the shadow of the car's beacon, he sensed them wince and hid a smile. It seemed to be his night for upsetting people, and it was far from over yet.

The control room was obviously not overloaded with work, because it was less than five minutes later when the officer's radio crackled, informing him that the woman who made the triple nine call, a lady called Olivia Brook, lived at the farm. He relayed this information to Nash.

'Do you know her? I assume she's the farmer's wife,' Nash asked.

'I didn't recognize her, and I've not come across the name before.' He smiled. 'That probably means she's not been in trouble.'

'OK, let's go and find out what Olivia Brook can tell us.'

The building, a stone-built house that looked as if it had been there for centuries, was obviously the farmer's residence. Backing up their theory about the woman who had made the call, lights were burning in what Nash could tell through the window was the farmhouse kitchen.

He approached the front door and gave it three lusty taps with the iron knocker that the light over the door showed to be in the shape of a ram's head. Only seconds later the heavy oak door opened, to reveal a woman in her mid-thirties. 'Mrs Brook?' Nash asked, displaying his warrant card.

'It's Miss Brook,' the woman replied. 'I thought you might come here. Is he seriously hurt?'

'His injuries aren't life-threatening,' Nash replied. 'What can you tell me about him, and how he came to get those wounds? I tried asking him, but he seemed very reluctant to tell me anything, even his name.'

'He's called Camlo Hajdari. He works for me as a farm labourer, mainly as stockman. He lives there' — she pointed to the tied cottage across the yard — 'along with his sister.'

'Would you mind if we come inside? I need to make notes and my handwriting's hard to decipher at the best of times, and trying to take details down in this light is nearly impossible.'

She agreed, but with obvious reluctance and a good deal of hesitation. 'You can go into the kitchen.' She pointed to her left. Nash and the officer entered the room, whereupon Olivia Brook closed the door and leaned against it.

If Nash thought her behaviour unusual, he didn't comment, despite the questioning looks from his fellow officer.

'Now,' Nash began, 'could you repeat the victim's name and spell it for me, please?'

She did so, and Nash asked, 'And what about his sister?'

'I don't know much about her. Her name is Aishe.' Her answer was hesitant.

'Has this man worked for you long?'

'Only a couple of months.'

'The name is obviously foreign; whereabouts are they from?'

'Albania, I believe, but they've been living in France for some years, from what I remember him saying when I interviewed him.'

'So what happened tonight? How did he come to get stabbed?'

'I've no idea.'

Nash ignored the frankly disbelieving stare of the uniformed man and asked, 'When you rang the emergency services, you told them you'd found him lying in the yard, is that correct?'

'Yes.' The reply was less than forthcoming.

'And the call was timed at two-fifteen, so where were you going at that time of night?'

There was a long, awkward silence, before Olivia said, 'I went for a walk.'

The lack of conviction in her voice made it apparent that she, like her listeners, knew the story was less than credible.

To the surprise of his colleague, Nash didn't press her for details, or attempt to contradict what he took to be an obvious lie. Instead, he asked her, 'One other thing, this man Hajdari, how good is his English?'

'He speaks it well enough, although his accent makes it a bit difficult to understand at times.'

Nash closed his notebook and turned towards the door. 'That'll be all for now. We'll leave you to get a good night's sleep while we go talk to the victim's sister. I take it this girl Aishe also speaks English.'

'I believe so.'

Once outside, as the reverberations from the door still echoed round them, the uniformed man looked at Nash. 'If the names she gave us are correct, that's the only part of her story she didn't make up.'

'That's true,' Nash agreed, 'but what we don't yet know is the reason she lied. Let's see what the victim's sister has to say.'

Nash knocked on the cottage door, which swung open at his touch. Light spilled out, but there was no response when Nash called out the woman's name, following this by identifying himself. He signalled to his colleague to follow him. Then he noticed the blood drops trailing across the floor from the staircase. Nash returned to his car and took two pairs of overshoes and latex gloves from the boot, handing one set to the officer. They entered the building cautiously, both of them apprehensive as to what they would encounter. The officer drew his baton, ready to face any threat from within. Having checked the downstairs rooms, frequently calling the woman's name without eliciting a reply, Nash was about to signal the officer to follow him upstairs when they heard a slight creaking sound from the upper floor.

Nash signalled to the officer, who nodded and took a firmer hold of his baton.

They reached the landing and paused, but could hear nothing. Nash pointed to his right, and opened a bedroom door. He flicked the light on, but the room was empty. It had obviously been the victim's, judging by the male clothing scattered on the bed and a chair.

Nash turned and pointed to the other side of the landing. He opened the second bedroom door and once more depressed the light switch. He stopped dead in his tracks and held up a warning hand, signalling the officer to remain outside the room, stepping through before closing the door on him.

He stared at the young woman for a second before averting his eyes. Assuming the naked girl lying handcuffed by one hand to the iron headboard to be the victim's sister, he addressed her, his voice gentle and reassuring.

'Aishe, my name's Detective Inspector Nash. I'm a police officer. Let me help you.' As he was speaking, he lifted the blanket from the floor and draped it over the girl. As he covered her, he noticed the bloodstains on the sheet, on her body and on the knife she was still clutching in her free hand. He also noticed the blue, black, and yellow blotches on her skin, evidence of beatings he guessed had been delivered over a prolonged period. All the while, he was aware that the girl, who could be little more than twenty years old, was watching him with wide, terrified eyes.

Rather than heighten her fears any more, he spoke again. 'Would you mind if I take that knife from you? Then I'm going to get a female officer to come and help you.'

He gently removed the knife from her hand. She didn't resist but remained still, watching him, her expression still one of fear and despair mixed. Nash smiled reassuringly and turned away.

He exited the room and told the officer to fetch an evidence box. Once the knife had been secured, Nash rang Clara's home number. David answered, his voice drowsy. When Clara came on the phone, Nash told he needed her at Wintersett as a matter of urgency. Then he phoned for an ambulance.

For the detective and the officer, the wait before Mironova arrived seemed like an eternity. The only break in their boredom was when Nash rang headquarters to order a CSI team to the cottage.

As soon as Clara reached Lilac Farm, Nash explained the situation. Mironova's look of horror showed that she understood exactly. She donned a pair of gloves and overshoes as he hustled her into the cottage and upstairs.

'You'll need to find a key for the handcuffs, unless ours fit, which I doubt.'

'Might the brother have them on him?'

'Not likely,' Nash told her, 'when he was discovered in the yard he was wearing nothing more than his underpants. While you're attending to Aishe, I'll look for the keys. We need photos of the scene,' he pointed out. 'I don't think CSI should be the ones to take them, do you?'

Minutes later, he introduced her to the petrified girl, accompanying this by telling her, 'Clara's a very nice person, and she'll take good care of you.'

When at last Clara emerged from the room, clutching a bag of clothing for the woman, her grim expression was evidence enough that Nash's guesses had been accurate.

'I used the camera on my phone.'

Nash nodded his thanks.

'Luckily, my key fitted the handcuffs. I've wrapped her in a blanket, but I don't think we should question her yet. She's told me she stabbed him with that knife you took from her; apparently he's her half-brother. They were the ones who carried out the market muggings and the other robberies. She told me he forced her into helping him and that she had refused to take part in any more. His reaction to that was that she was no longer of any use to him. That's when he attempted to rape her. She was afraid of him and had secreted a kitchen knife under her mattress, and when he attacked her, not for the first time, she fought him off with it. I think it would be best if I take her through to Netherdale to the rape suite and get her checked out. She said there was no penetration, but the medics will give her a thorough examination and will photograph and document her injuries. Hopefully, they might find evidence to support her story. That could be vital, because if we can prove the attempted rape, that would make the stabbing self-defence. I'm not sure what physical damage the beatings and the attempted assault have caused, but I guess the mental scars will be with her for the rest of her life.'

'I agree, and that's very good work on your part.' He turned to the ambulance crew. 'DS Mironova will accompany you. And in this instance, I think a direct route to the rape suite will be better than accident and emergency, where her alleged victim is.'

He turned to Clara. 'We'll wait until she's safely out of the house before we get the CSI boys in. I'll instruct them to pay particularly close attention to the bedroom. Leave me your car keys. I'll get it driven to Netherdale HQ. You can collect it from there.'

CHAPTER TEN

As soon as the tail lights of the ambulance disappeared down the lane, Nash signalled to the duo of waiting forensic officers to enter the cottage and directed them to the bedroom. At the same time, he handed the uniformed officer a fresh pair of gloves and told him to accompany him back inside. They moved from room to room on the ground floor, and their search soon yielded dividends. In the small pantry alongside the kitchen, they found a generator.

'That's a bit odd,' the officer said, 'why keep a thing like that inside the house?'

'At a guess, I'd say because that generator was stolen from Bishopton market, and they don't want nosy people like us catching sight of it,' Nash told him. 'Check the serial numbers and I'll bet you'll find they tally. Especially in view of that,' he added, pointing to the shelf above.

The officer reached out and removed a balaclava and a linen bag bearing the distinctive name and logo of Shire Bank. A Taser tumbled out of the bag as it was lifted down. Nash picked it up and smiled at his colleague as the officer removed a biscuit tin from the same shelf. Inside was a large quantity of cash. 'I think this haul means we've just solved the recent spate of muggings that were committed in the dale. I believe this Taser was used to subdue the landlord of the Black Bull and the market trader before they were robbed. And this' — he tapped the tin — 'is the ill-gotten gains. It will be interesting to see what our stabbing victim has to say about this lot when he's shown them. They might help him remember how to speak — in either English or Albanian. However, I think robbery charges are the least of his worries, although I doubt whether he'll know that yet.'

When they had informed the CSI team of their findings, Nash followed this with instructions to the officer, who by this time had given up hope of a mid-shift break, that he was now required at Netherdale General with his colleague. 'Go up there and arrest the bloke on suspicion of attempted rape and burglary. And, if necessary, handcuff him to the trolley, or whatever they've got him laid on.'

The officer got back into the patrol car. This was not the sort of night he had been anticipating.

Nash thought for a moment and rang Netherdale control room, advising the duty sergeant of his instructions to the patrol officer. 'There's a patient been admitted to Netherdale General with stab wounds. I need the officers to arrest him — and for you to put him on bed watch. If he becomes suspicious about the trouble he's in, he might leg it.'

Nash listened to the sergeant's complaint about staff shortages and then told him, 'They've spent most of their shift doing nothing, so they'll be in practice. If he gets discharged, put him into detention. If not, leave somebody on it until the end of their shift and then find a replacement. By my reckoning, you've a couple of hours to allocate the manpower.'

He ended the call, leaving the duty sergeant staring at the receiver. Nash's tone and abrupt speech were totally unlike his normal laid-back attitude. 'It's not my fault you're not getting any,' the officer muttered, unknowingly putting his finger on Nash's problem with devastating accuracy.

Unaware that he had upset yet another person to add to his growing tally, Nash returned inside the cottage. Once the

CSI team had completed their work, the house would have to be secured. He found a bunch of keys, one of which fitted the front door, another was a car key. He looked out towards the farmhouse and saw the woman he'd interviewed earlier about to step outside. He waited, noticing that she locked the door behind her, and then called her across.

'Just to let you know, the man who was stabbed is likely to face some serious criminal charges as a result of what we've found in the cottage. Speaking of the building, it remains a crime scene, so on no account must anyone enter it until I give the all-clear, understood? I will be locking the house as soon as the scientific officers leave. They will probably be back tomorrow. Does your stockman have a vehicle?'

'I allow him to use the farm pickup on his days off. Why do you ask?'

'No particular reason.' As he was speaking, Nash looked beyond the woman to the farmhouse. He thought he saw a curtain at one of the upstairs windows twitch, but in the dim light of dawn, it was difficult to be certain.

By the time the CSI crew reported their work done for the night, it was almost daylight. 'So much for a good night's sleep,' Nash muttered as he watched their van trundle down the farm track, followed by Clara Mironova's car, which was being driven by a member of their team. It was far too late to consider going back to bed. He might as well return home, have a shower, breakfast and then go into work.

Despite taking his time over his ablutions and morning meal, Nash was still the first to arrive at Helmsdale, even beating Jack Binns, who was normally there before any of the detectives.

Having brought the station sergeant up to date with events, Nash asked Binns, 'What do you know about the woman who owns Lilac Farm?'

'Is that where that bloke and his sister with the unpronounceable names were living?'

Nash nodded, and Binns asked, 'So you met Olivia Brook, did you? I'll bet you didn't meet her twin brother, though.'

'I didn't even know she had a brother; I thought she ran the place on her own. Why did you say I wouldn't have met him?'

'John Brook doesn't meet people. He stays out of sight when somebody calls and never ventures outdoors in daylight.'

'Why not?'

'Poor John suffered a terrible accident when he was no more than a toddler. He wandered into the kitchen when his mother was on the phone. Being inquisitive, as most youngsters are, he grabbed hold of a pan handle and pulled the pan off the stove — it was filled with hot oil. That was over thirty years ago, when plastic surgery was nowhere near as advanced as nowadays; the accident left him terribly disfigured. He went to school when he was old enough, but the other kids were less than kind to him, so his parents kept him at home and hired a string of tutors to give him a decent education.'

'What a very sad story. I suppose he doesn't work, given what you've told me.'

'Actually, you're wrong. He's a very clever bloke, and although he lives like a hermit, he designs computer software and sells it. I believe he's very successful and well thought of within the industry. When their parents died, Olivia took over running the house and the farm. She does all the cooking, because John won't go anywhere near the kitchen. Olivia's a good woman. She sacrificed her own happiness for her twin brother. She was engaged to be married, and as far as I know still is, but she won't leave John to fend for himself.'

It was hardly the brightest start to the day, Nash thought as he climbed the stairs to his office. He hoped things would improve.

* * *

It was mid-morning before Mironova phoned from the rape suite at Netherdale General, to update Nash and ask for instructions. He listened to a brief outline of what she had learned and then suggested that they should interview the girl where she was. 'I'll drive over when she's available. In the meantime, explain to her how the legal system works and see if she wants a solicitor.'

Immediately after he ended the call, Binns phoned through to tell Nash that he had a visitor. 'Miss Brook is in reception and would like a word with you.'

Nash went downstairs and showed her into an interview room. 'What can I do for you?' he asked.

'I wanted to know what's happening about my farm-hand. You suggested he might be in serious trouble. That means I'd have to find someone else to work the farm. I also wondered what's happened to his sister.'

'I can't reveal anything regarding enquiries that are ongoing,' Nash replied, 'but I can tell you that your employee will be facing serious charges which, if he's found guilty, could result in a prolonged term of imprisonment. The same might apply to his sister, but there is a measure of doubt in her case. It might well transpire that she will not be charged with any offences, but that decision won't rest with me, it would be the responsibility of the Crown Prosecution Service. Forgive me for mentioning this, but you seem to be taking a great deal of interest in what becomes of them, unusually so for an employer of casual labour. Is there some specific reason for your concern?'

'As far as the man's concerned it's simply a matter of making sure I have someone reliable to help with the farm. However, I have a brother, John—'

Nash interrupted, 'I'm aware of the circumstances.'

Olivia smiled and nodded. 'Thank you, that'll be down to Jack Binns, I suppose. I wasn't very open with you last night at the farm. I was returning from walking with John when we found Camlo. But we are worried about the young woman's situation. John has taken a liking to her, and has asked me to intercede on her behalf if that proves necessary.'

'I appreciate that, but I wasn't aware he knew the young woman. I was given to understand that your brother doesn't socialize.'

Olivia's smiled, but without much humour. 'He doesn't as a rule, but he made an exception for Aishe. It came about almost by accident. On occasion I need to go out, and John doesn't like to be left alone, so I asked her, through her brother, if she would mind sitting in the house for the evening.'

'And her brother agreed to this?'

'He did, sort of, but only if he was allowed to be present as well. John wasn't too happy about it, but he had no choice. When this happened, John said afterwards that although he liked the girl, he wasn't at all keen on the man.'

'Thank you. That might prove more useful than you know. I'll try and keep you up to date with developments, but at present we're only in the very early stages of the investigation.'

After Olivia left, Nash went back to his office and made a couple of phone calls. The first was to Superintendent Fleming, the gist of the conversation being the potential solution of the crimes that had been nicknamed the market muggings. He also briefed her on the stabbing incident and what they'd discovered at the victim's house.

His second call was to the CPS, and in it, he put forward a hypothesis, asking for their advice as to how to proceed. The answer was less than satisfactory, and it caused Nash to remain in his office, deep in thought, until Clara Mironova phoned to say the doctors in charge of Aishe had given the go-ahead for her to be interviewed, and she didn't want the duty solicitor or need the services of an interpreter.

Nash drove through to Netherdale and instructed Clara to tell Aishe they would start the interview shortly, but first he had to make a phone call.

Ten minutes later, Nash entered the small room and smiled at the girl, who was looking understandably nervous. He nodded to Mironova before turning to Aishe. 'I think Clara has explained that we need to record a formal interview. This is as much for your benefit as ours. In the event that you face any criminal charges, there should be a record of the questions we ask and your answers. You must also inform us if you require a solicitor at any time during the interview, should you change your mind. DS Mironova will conduct the interview along with a senior woman police officer, Superintendent Fleming. They will ask the questions. I will attend purely as an observer, and will only intervene if I believe there is something they might have missed. Is that all clear in your mind?'

Aishe's voice was quiet, subdued and a little nervous as she replied, 'Yes, I understand everything. I will not need a lawyer yet.'

'We have to wait until Superintendent Fleming arrives before we begin, so in the meantime, have either of you had anything to eat?'

Both women shook their heads. 'In that case, I think we should order sandwiches all round, because I for one am ravenous.' He smiled at Aishe. 'What would you like?'

He nodded to Clara to follow him out of the room. 'Will you look after her and get us all a drink while I go to the bakery down the street. When you interview her, just ask Aishe to describe everything that happened. If there's anything you've missed, either Jackie or I will remind you. Otherwise, the ball's in your court. Oh, by the way, try and make the coffee somewhere near drinkable. We don't want to be accused of police brutality!'

CHAPTER ELEVEN

They had just finished eating their sandwiches when Superintendent Fleming arrived. After introducing her, Nash set up the tape machine. He turned to the girl and explained the technical side of what was about to happen. 'Now, once this tape is running, I'll do the introduction, which is also a legal requirement, then Clara will begin asking you questions. Don't forget that should you want to stop at any time, all you have to do is ask. The other thing to remember is to speak clearly.' He smiled at her. 'The tape machine can't interpret a nod or shake of the head.'

Nash set the tape rolling before sitting behind and to one side of Aishe as the DS commenced asking questions. His purpose in positioning himself so precisely was to remain out of Aishe's direct line of sight, which he gauged would be less intrusive should she have to reveal intimate details. He listened attentively as the tale unfolded, his anger at what the young woman, little more than a teenager, had been made to suffer, and marvelled at her resilience in the face of some inhumane treatment. The fact that this had been inflicted by a member of her own family simply made matters worse. He could tell by his colleagues' body language and the increasingly gentle tone of Clara's voice as she put the necessary questions to Aishe that both she and Fleming were deeply affected by what they were hearing.

As soon as Clara nodded to him, signifying that she had nothing further to ask, Nash stated the time and switched the machine off. Only then did he speak to the girl. 'Regrettably, Aishe, because of what you've told us, we must formally charge you with assault and with complicity in the robberies.'

He paused, and when he saw the look of dawning horror on the girl's face, added swiftly, 'However, that is purely to comply with regulations. Do you understand?'

Aishe nodded as tears began to spill down her cheeks.

Nash tried to calm her. 'I will be making urgent representations on your behalf to ensure that those charges remain nothing but a formality.'

'Inspector Nash is correct,' Jackie Fleming added. 'I will be pressing the Crown Prosecution Service to comply with his instructions. If that isn't sufficient, I will ask my superior, the chief constable, to take the matter up with the Home Office. Believe me, Aishe, every effort will be made on your behalf.'

As DS Mironova was completing the charge procedure, Fleming and Nash discussed the revelations in the privacy of another room. 'What that poor girl has been through is beyond belief,' Jackie said. 'To have been more or less abducted by her half-brother within days of her mother's death, forced to act as decoy for him in a string of robberies, held prisoner in a small room, beaten up on a regular basis, and then finally the attempted sexual assault, is depravity that matches anything we've seen before. I'm surprised the girl had the courage to act as she did, and I will fight every step of the way to ensure she doesn't suffer any longer. I would suggest the stabbing is a clear case of self-defence, and if necessary, I'll reveal what she told us that animal said to her as a threat to force her compliance, even though I can barely believe it myself.'

'It is difficult to comprehend that someone could be so evil and do such things.' Nash shook his head, the outrage apparent on his face. 'To threaten her with rape, and then say that he would have to kill her, because, according to their culture, she would no longer be a virgin and therefore an un-saleable commodity . . . it's hard to credit, but that's the twisted way abusers operate, I'm afraid. One other point we should consider is the possibility that when Hajdari is fit enough to make a court appearance, he could easily get bail and if that happens, Aishe could be at risk. We could keep her in the cells, but I think it would be better if we should find somewhere safe for her to stay.'

'I agree, Mike. Will you tell her that?'

'I'll get Clara to do it; she's built up a good rapport with the girl.'

'Anything else to report?'

'Only a total lack of progress on the fingers found at Thornscarr. That case might remain unsolved, because we've no idea who they belong to. I've put that on the back burner until we've wrapped this up. It's a question of prioritizing due to lack of manpower, and after all this time, a few days isn't going to make much difference.'

* * *

Back at Helmsdale, Sergeant Binns was struggling to complete the remand process of a man who had been detained earlier. He was proving to be a difficult customer. He had been arrested for attempting to rob a woman in the car park behind Good Buys supermarket in Bishopton. Unfortunately, the attempted mugging had taken place under the watchful eye of a couple of police officers who were in their patrol car eating sandwiches in their mid-shift break when the offence occurred. Although patently guilty, the arrested man had proved difficult to detain, and through the custody procedure was even less cooperative.

'OK, let's try again,' Binns said patiently. 'I need your name and address for the record.'

It didn't help that the man he was trying to question was all but out of it. Despite Binns' considerable experience, he initially failed to recognize the symptoms that denoted the sudden withdrawal from a Class A substance.

'You're not going to get me to talk. I know you're working for *them*.' The man struggled to free himself from the officers' grip.

'What are you talking about?' Binns was alarmed by the man's eyes, which were rolling around in their sockets.

The prisoner looked behind him, to where the two arresting officers were standing in close proximity, in an attempt to prevent him falling over. 'You're all working for them,' he added, trying to gesture towards the uniformed men. 'They kidnapped me.' He paused and then looked round, his expression one of total fear. 'Who said that? Where are you?'

His head turned from side to side. He leaned forward, so only Binns could hear. 'There, I told you they were after me. You heard that. They've brought me here to kill me. You've got to help me escape. Those two,' — he jerked his head towards the officers — 'they're all part of it. They want me dead. It's not their fault. They're only obeying orders.'

His expression changed suddenly and he tried to step away. 'Why am I telling you this? You're part of it too. You all work for them. Don't think I haven't guessed what you're up to. They found out I'd been asking questions, didn't they? That's why those two were sent to kidnap me. I know what will happen next. I'll just vanish — disappear without trace just like all the others, just like she did. Do you know why they're doing it? Do you? No, then I'll tell you.'

He looked round again. Seeing the amused expressions of the two arresting officers simply increased his agitation. 'You think it's a joke, do you? That's because they haven't told you what they're really up to. If you knew, you'd never have agreed to take part in it. How many others have you taken? I bet they didn't tell you what they intended to do with the people they ordered you to snatch.'

He fell silent, and in the pause, as Binns was trying to decide what to do next, one of the patrol officers said, 'We certainly shouldn't go hungry tonight, not with the fruitcake here.'

Suddenly, without warning, the prisoner launched himself towards the speaker. Despite the restriction of his handcuffs, he succeeded in landing several painful kicks, and with his long, talon-like nails, inflicted a series of scratches down the officer's face before they pulled him off. Even then, he writhed and squirmed his way clear and raced towards the door, only to be brought down by the second patrolman with a tackle that would have been applauded at Twickenham.

He held the prisoner down by the simple process of sitting on him while Binns unearthed a pair of ankle restraints from the supply cupboard and secured the detainee with them. They picked him up and carried him to the cells.

If the officer was expecting sympathy, it didn't happen. 'Try explaining those to your wife when you get home,' his colleague told him. 'She already thinks you've got a bit on the side.'

'Can we please concentrate on the job in hand? Will one of you go into the office and phone for a medic? I reckon this guy's deranged.'

As one of them went to call the police surgeon, Binns and the other officer watched the prisoner, who, it seemed, had lost the will to fight, and was sitting, head bowed, sobbing quietly and muttering unintelligible words to an unseen audience.

The prisoner had lost interest, it seemed, and was staring down at his manacled hands in horror. 'Help me, I've got to find her, got to find Sam,' he said, his voice no more than a whisper.

Binns and the officer exchanged glances.

The other officer returned and informed them that the police surgeon was on his way. 'I described the man's behaviour and the doc believes he's possibly suffering from withdrawal symptoms, from either alcohol or drugs. Either that or he's schizophrenic — or a combination of both.'

'Well we can't identify him, so the doctor can't access his medical records to discover what the man's suffering from. That also means he probably won't want to give him a tranquillizer, in case that makes his condition worse. Did you search his pockets when he was arrested?'

'No, because he kicked off so violently we were busy trying to restrain him and get him safely into the back of the car.'

Binns glared at his subordinates. 'So much for proper procedure, I'll speak to you two later. Now get on with it.'

'Yes, Sarge,' they both muttered in response.

The man began shouting again. As his threats and accusations grew wilder and more incongruous, centring round the mysterious people or creatures he believed were trying to abduct him, they succeeded, but their search had them none the wiser. The prisoner was carrying nothing that could be used to identify him. They tried to think of a way out of the impasse. Their thought process was not helped by the detainee's continued outbursts.

Much as Binns had predicted, the doctor was unwilling to administer a sedative until he knew more about the patient and his medical history.

In the end, it was Jack Binns who provided the solution. He turned to the arresting officers and asked, 'What about the mugging victim? The woman he tried to rob?'

'What about her?'

'Did you ask her if she knows this man? Bishopton is only a small place, and I can't for a minute think he drove there to attack and rob her, so perhaps she can identify him.'

'We didn't get chance to ask her,' his colleague replied. 'We were too busy dealing with him to do more than get her details.'

'OK, give her a ring and see if she can tell us who he is.'

Ten minutes later, the officer returned from the office brandishing a slip of paper. 'You were right, Sarge, she does know him. To use her words, 'He's a low-life by the name of Tyler Swift.'

'Sounds like an American singer,' his colleague muttered.

'I ran the name through the PNC and I've got his address. Seems he's been arrested before — possession of a

Class A substance, but not on our patch, which explains why we didn't recognize him.'

The doctor, on hearing this, interrupted, 'Do you know what the substance was?'

'Cocaine, it said on the file.'

'That would explain his behaviour. The symptoms are typical of rapid withdrawal. Obviously, for whatever reason, his access to the drug has been abruptly halted and the reaction is what's commonly known as "cold turkey". Like in the film *The French Connection.*'

'What can you do to keep him quiet?'

The doctor considered Binns' question for a moment. 'I can give him a mild sedative now I know the likely cause. It won't put him to sleep, but it will prevent his extreme behaviour. He needs long-term treatment, though.'

'Should I call an ambulance?'

'There's not much more can be done at the moment. He'd need your officers with him if you do. Can you spare them for however long it takes?'

'Not really. Let me think for a minute.' Binns turned to the officers. 'When the doc's dealt with him, you two had better go to that address and see if you can find a relative or next of kin. Given the state he's in, there ought to be someone to look after him.' He glanced up at the wall clock and grimaced. It was going to turn into a long shift. He wouldn't be transferring him to Netherdale and locking the station at the usual time. Before he did anything, he'd better tell his wife he'd be late home for dinner — and possibly supper as well.

As the medic was administering the sedative — no mean task, as his patient thrashed about in a violent but futile attempt to avoid the treatment — one of the officers trying to hold him down commented, 'You'd think with his history, Swift would enjoy being injected.'

His colleague's laughter all but masked Swift's protest, which was directed at Binns. Although Binns heard it, the statement made no sense.

'What about Samantha? What are you doing about her? Where's Sam?'

The most important decision to be made was what to do with Swift. Technically, Binns knew he should be charged, but the complications thrown up by his medical condition made it difficult to choose the best way of handling the situation.

The doctor made a suggestion. 'There's a drug dependency unit in Netherdale that might take him and treat him until he's coherent,' he said. 'How that ties in with your arrest, I've no idea.'

'Neither have I, Doctor, and I think the decision is above my pay grade. I believe the American expression is "passing the buck", and in this instance, I'm more than happy to get rid of the problem. Will you hang on here until I can raise a decision maker? If they agree, I might need you to arrange for him to go to that unit.'

Binns set about trying to contact a senior officer willing to accept responsibility for the decision. Both Nash and Fleming were unavailable, so in desperation, Binns' only resort was to speak to Gloria O'Donnell, the chief constable. Having listened to Binns' graphic description of Swift's hallucinatory behaviour, she agreed the plan, but with the proviso that Binns should formally charge him before he was moved. 'Even if he doesn't understand what you're saying at the moment, you can insist he is given one of those cards used to charge people who are hard of hearing. Give it to the doctor with instructions to pass it to the patient once he's *compos mentis* again.'

Half an hour later, Swift, whose behaviour had calmed down to a more manageable level, was in the process of being transported by the arresting officers to the drug dependency unit. Before they left, Binns told them he would ensure that Swift's next of kin were informed the following day. 'By the time you've got him installed there, your shift will be all but over, and you've still the arrest paperwork to do before you sign off. I'll get someone round there in the morning. They're probably used to him going missing.'

CHAPTER TWELVE

At around the same time as Binns was locking up the Helmsdale station, Mike Nash was seated in the lounge at Smelt Mill Cottage, staring again at the painting that occupied the wall over the inglenook fireplace. His thoughts were on the artist and his recurrent dreams about her. Somewhere in the time he spent looking at the landscape, he came to a decision. He knew what he wanted, and now realized that the dreams were the result of his frustration at being unable to be with Alondra.

There was only one way to resolve this, and it was a radical one. He would go and see her. He would beg her either to return with him to England, or if she was unwilling, ask her to allow him to move and live with her. That would mean quitting his job, and that would be a huge upheaval, but he now appreciated that the work he did, although valuable, paled into insignificance compared to his peace of mind. But what of Daniel? How would he handle the situation? Nash rubbed his eyes. He had never felt like this, only knew that he was sinking lower than ever before.

His spirits were at such a low level that he had no confidence in his ability to convince Alondra to change her mind. On the positive side, they had never quarrelled, or disagreed to any great extent. Her reasons for ending their relationship had been more because of her own perceived inability to give Nash what she believed he needed from her.

Although Nash would have welcomed the opportunity to persuade her that her reasoning was totally wrong, he had been denied the chance. Alondra had returned abroad, to her home, after refusing all his efforts to speak to her. Knowing that, caused Nash to refrain from making contact then, or in the two years since — until recently. He had phoned, but met with no answer. His only hope was that she would recognize the number on her phone and call him. Now he was determined not to wait any longer before confronting the woman he loved — the woman he wanted to spend the rest of his life with.

Making the decision to visit was one thing; implementing it wouldn't be straightforward. It certainly couldn't happen in the immediate future. There was no chance of him being able to take leave. Clara was going on holiday, and once she had returned to work, Nash would still have to spend time getting Daniel off to school, assuming he was fit enough. Only then could he think of making one final effort to rescue some part of his personal life.

* * *

Whether it was Nash's resolve to take pre-emptive action, or simply the fact that he was exhausted, he slept well that night. When he woke next morning, he felt more refreshed and optimistic than he had for a long time.

His cheerful mood contrasted sharply with that of Sergeant Binns. When Nash arrived at Helmsdale, Binns was in the process of issuing instructions to a couple of uniformed officers. He responded to Nash's greeting with a scowl, accompanied by a slight wave of one hand, before turning back to the men.

Nash continued upstairs. Viv Pearce was already in the office, and was speaking on the phone when Nash walked in.

A couple of seconds later, he replaced the receiver. 'Morning, Mike.'

Clara walked in as Nash said, 'Morning, Viv, I'm going to introduce myself to the coffee machine.' He grinned at the DS. 'Would you both like a mug? It's so much nicer now than when we had to rely on the snake venom you produced.'

Clara stared at Nash in surprise. His cheery disposition and light-hearted comments were so at variance with his recent downbeat mood that she wondered why. Once Nash had vanished into the small kitchen, she muttered to Viv, 'I'll bet Mike got his leg over last night, and that's why he's so happy this morning. He always used to be this way after he'd scored.'

Viv grinned. 'Yes, and it shows.'

Clara continued staring at the closed door until she heard Nash returning, and then she and Viv hurriedly began rustling papers and trying to look busy.

* * *

Days before the end of term, as his school friends were busy packing their belongings ready for the Easter holiday, Daniel sat in the back of his father's car as Nash took him, along with Clara and David, to the airport. As he hugged his father before leaving, the boy was unaware that in addition to caring for him and giving him a good holiday, his Aunt Clara had a hidden agenda in spending time alone with him.

Nash watched as they queued at check-in and waved farewell before they disappeared towards the security checkpoint and departure gates. Glancing back at her boss, Clara saw the expression on Nash's face, the one she disliked. It was a look of sadness compounded by loneliness, and nothing like that of the cheerful, upbeat character she was used to. She looked at Daniel and noticed that the boy was biting his lip, as if hiding a powerful emotion. It strengthened Clara's resolve to try and set matters right. Once they'd boarded the plane and were airborne, Clara turned to her unofficial nephew, who was seated between her and David and explained about her plan.

Daniel's eyes opened wide with surprise as he listened to her idea. As a solution to the problem she had identified, one that worried him, it would be ideal — if it worked. 'How are we going to do it?' he asked.

'*We're* not, you are; this has to come from you. But that's only if you're sure you want to. It has to appear to have been your idea from start to finish. Otherwise, it won't work. Believe me, I know the people concerned, and because I do, I can guess what the reaction would be if it came from an outsider. So what do you think, Daniel? Is this something you want to happen?'

Clara felt confident that Daniel would understand her logic and would agree to the scheme. Although he was only ten years old, Daniel was mature for one so young.

'I wanted it all along, but didn't think it could happen. It's a great plan — but I don't know how to do it.'

Clara gestured to the tablet computer resting on the fold-down table in front of Daniel. 'Why not start with Mr Google? You've enough information about the subject to use as input.'

'Brilliant, but I'm not allowed to do it here.' Daniel gestured to the plane's interior. 'I'll try as soon as we've landed and I can get a Wi-Fi signal.'

* * *

Later, at Helmsdale police station, Sergeant Jack Binns was awaiting a report from the officers he'd sent to Tyler Swift's flat in Bishopton. He'd all but forgotten the task he'd sent the two local officers to perform earlier but remembered it soon after lunchtime; then dismissed it as unimportant. Tyler Swift was in safe hands across at the Drug Rehabilitation Clinic in Netherdale so the job of informing his next of kin, or similarly interested persons, could wait until more pressing matters had been dealt with. He knew from a brief report that the officers' visit to Bishopton had been delayed when they'd been diverted to attend a road traffic accident where at least two of the people involved had life-threatening injuries. That, as far as Binns was concerned, took priority over a drug addict-cum-failed-mugger.

Nash was being optimistic. 'Right, we seem to have wrapped everything up nicely. Hopefully, we'll be able to relax a bit. Let's call it a day.'

His complacency was shattered when, as they walked out through reception, Lisa reminded him of unfinished business. 'We've still got the okra to deal with.'

Binns overheard, but was puzzled by the reference. 'What's she talking about?'

'She's referring to the remains found at the hotel at Thornscarr. Ladies fingers, in case you didn't know, is a term used for the vegetable okra.'

'Oh, very droll. It's all right for you part-timers in CID to be disappearing early, but some of us round here still have work to do.'

The remark was by no means original, but on this occasion, Binns delivered it with little of his usual humour.

Nash eyed him with mild concern. 'Is something wrong, Jack?'

'I'm not sure,' Binns replied. 'I was told something a while back and I have a feeling that it might be important, but I can't for the life of me think why. On the other hand, it might be nothing more than my imagination working overtime. I suppose that's what comes of hanging around with CID types.'

Nash smiled wickedly. 'More likely down to getting old,' he retorted.

Binns waved a dismissive hand. 'Go on, get out of here, and spare a thought for us poor, elderly uniform blokes while you young whippersnappers are sitting with your feet up.'

* * *

The spate of muggings had made headlines in the local media. When the anchorman on the evening news introduced the topic, announcing the arrest of a suspect believed to be responsible for the assaults, Lee gasped, audibly enough to disturb his mother.

'Something wrong?' she asked.

'Er, no.'

She looked at him. He seemed to have paled in the reflection from the screen. 'Come on, Lee. Something's worrying you, I can tell.'

'It's OK, Mum, honestly.'

'Yes, and I'm the Sugar Plum fairy. What is it?' She knew him too well for him to get away without telling her the truth.

Lee gestured to the screen, hesitated, then said, 'I was in Chapel Street on the way back from the swimming baths when one of those muggings took place. The owner of the pet food stall was being robbed, and I actually saw the man attacking him. Not only saw it, but I took photos and a video on my phone.'

'You did what?' His mother was aghast.

'I got the whole thing, and I got a good shot of the attacker's face. I followed him and got more footage when he stole money from the Market Cafe.' Lee bit his lip. 'Then I forgot about it,' he muttered.

'No, Lee, you couldn't forget something that dramatic. So why keep quiet?'

He looked at her for a few seconds before replying. 'Er, it slipped my mind because the minute I got home, I had a load of homework.'

'Oh, they give homework out at the swimming baths, do they now? What exactly were you doing at the baths on a school day?'

'Hmm, I wasn't feeling well that morning. And, hmm, I felt better by the afternoon and thought a swim might help.'

His mother sighed. 'We'll deal with that later. Have you still got those photos and the video?'

'Yes, they're in my phone.'

'Let me have a look at them.'

Lee opened the camera gallery and passed the mobile to his mother. After examining both sets of stills and the video clips she told her son, 'I think it would be a good idea to tell the police about them, but first, I'll phone them and explain.'

'But I can't do that!'

'Why ever not?'

'He might try to find me.'

'You're not scared are you?'

There was a slight nod of Lee's head.

'Oh, Lee. Do you think he'd have let you walk away if he knew you were filming him? Let you catch the bus and come home?'

'Er, well I suppose not. But what if the police want to take a statement from me? Or do a line-up ID.' Lee was panicking. His eyes were like saucers.

Suddenly he thought of the street cred he'd lost earlier; now, it could be resurrected. He tried not to smile. 'Er, I think your right, Mum. They might need my witness account to back up the images. It's called being a good citizen, isn't it?'

His mother sighed again. 'Yes, Lee, it is. You'll have to go to the police station. I'll come with you.' She reached for the phone.

'I suppose that would be all right.' His shoulders rose and the grin he'd tried to conceal emerged as he grabbed his mobile.

'What are you doing now?'

'Just texting my mates.'

His euphoria ended when his mother told him, 'And then you'll have to think up a more convincing reason for skiving off school. One that your headmaster will believe.'

* * *

Next morning, Nash asked Viv Pearce, 'Have you checked to see how the stabbing victim is? The last I heard he was on the mend, so perhaps we should ask the doctors when they think he'll be ready for release. Then we can swap his ward for a nice comfortable cell.'

'No, Mike, I haven't, but I'll get onto it straightaway.'

Lisa had just walked in, heard the instruction, and looked at him, her expression like a teacher with an unruly pupil to control. 'And what will you be doing?' she asked.

'I'll be thinking,' Nash replied, 'something I haven't had much chance to do recently.'

'You weren't planning on doing anything useful, like making coffee, I suppose?'

'I could probably fit that into my crowded schedule. And when you're both done, come through to my office. I've got some interesting photos and a couple of videos to show you.'

Having provided the coffee, Nash retired to his office and closed the door. Lisa eyed it for a few seconds. Obviously, Mike intended to do exactly as he'd said.

'What's he up to, Viv? He's got something on his mind, don't you think?'

'Hasn't he always?' Viv replied.

Nash was concerned about the safety of Aishe, should her half-brother be released on bail. She needed somewhere to stay, a refuge where he couldn't reach her and inflict further abuse, possibly even carry out his threat to kill her. In larger towns and cities there were centres where women could seek shelter, but in a rural area such as this, no such places existed. He was still pondering how to overcome this difficulty when a solution was offered, from a most unlikely source.

The phone rang. The call was an internal one, from Sergeant Binns. 'Olivia Brook is here again, Mike. Shall I ask her to wait?'

'No, Jack, I'll come straight down. Did she say what she wants to see me about?'

'No, just that it was important.'

He greeted the visitor. The farmer looked at him, and for once seemed less than her usual confident self. 'It's about the girl, Aishe,' she began, 'I wanted to know how she is, and what's going to happen to her. I realize you might not be able to tell me everything, but I . . . er . . . we thought we'd like to help if we can.'

'By we, I take it you mean you and your brother?'

'That's correct, as you know John doesn't go out, except occasionally after dark, and there are times when he's working and I'm on the land when he could do with someone else in the house. It's a big task taking care of him and doing the chores, plus the farm work, so I thought, or we thought, that Aishe might suit the role of housekeeper for us. She'd be well paid and have her own room. That's what I came to ask you, but if it isn't practical, please let me know now rather than later.'

'It isn't quite as straightforward as that,' Nash told her. 'I shouldn't really say at this stage, but as it happens, you've offered a possible solution to a problem I was mulling over when you arrived.'

He reminded her that unless the Crown Prosecution Service cooperated Aishe could well face criminal charges. 'However, I've made it perfectly clear that I will be opposed to that and will provide ample evidence of the mistreatment she suffered and her predicament when we found her. With all that in front of them, I doubt whether they'll proceed against her and even if they do, I don't think a jury would convict, especially if she has a competent defence counsel who can present the facts in a sympathetic light. That's for the future, but at present, I'm concerned about her safety. Hajdari has already threatened to kill her, and I must ensure she's kept in a place where he can't reach her until the trial is over. There's little doubt in my mind that he'll be convicted, sentenced and then deported. That leaves another problem for Aishe, in that she could also face the threat of deportation, but again I've asked my superiors to look into the possibility of giving her asylum, citing the danger she would face back in Albania. Meanwhile, do you think the farm would be a suitable place to shelter her? My doubts centre round the fact that Hajdari might head there if he's given bail.'

'Well, he won't be welcome if he does,' Olivia looked horrified at the thought. After a moment, she said, 'There is one other solution that might serve, but I would need to ask first. My aunt and uncle live in Bishopton and they have spare rooms in their house. I think they'd be more than happy to look after Aishe for a short time, I can find out and let you know if you wish.'

'You seem to be going to a lot of trouble for this girl,' Nash said, his tone deliberately neutral.

Olivia smiled. 'You said that last time I was here, and the answer's the same. There are very few people John is comfortable with, and Aishe is one of them. Actually,' she added confidentially, 'I think John's taken quite a shine to her. Aishe isn't put off by his disfigurement, which is most unusual. Added to which, I like her enormously and what you've told me about the abuse she's suffered merely confirms my opinion. Together, John and I are determined to try and help give her a better future, and let's face it, that can't be too difficult.'

'I'll keep you up to date with developments as and when they occur, but it might not be for a while. We're a bit short-handed at present and we've quite a case load. Some of it going back years.'

'That sounds intriguing.'

'Unfortunately, there isn't enough evidence to tell whether it's a criminal case or simply a terrible accident. Some workmen at Thornscarr found human remains while they were renovating the hotel. Only fingers,' he added, at her shocked expression. 'Unfortunately, beyond knowing that they belonged to a woman, we've no other clues.'

'It had a strange reputation, that place, as I recall, not that I know much about it. The man you need to talk to is a neighbour of ours in Wintersett, Jonas Turner.'

Nash looked surprised. 'I hadn't thought of asking him, but I will now you've mentioned it. I know Jonas well. In fact, he helps me by doing some gardening.'

'Of course, Inspector Nash, I'd forgotten you live up the road from the village.'

He thanked Olivia, and before leaving she promised to let Nash know as soon as she'd spoken to her aunt and uncle. In return, he reiterated his promise to keep her up to date with any developments regarding Aishe's case and that of Hajdari.

Before Nash returned upstairs, Jack Binns stopped him. 'I've got one of my lads coming in to cover the desk. There's something I need to do.'

'That's not like you, Jack. Running errands during working hours,' Nash laughed.

Binns did not look amused. 'It's work, not personal, and I won't be long,' he growled, before he turned and went through to his office.

Nash looked surprised. Something was obviously a problem, but no doubt he'd hear in good time if it concerned CID. He headed for the stairs.

CHAPTER THIRTEEN

When Lisa and Viv entered Nash's office they were expecting to see nothing more exciting than some holiday snaps sent through by Daniel. They certainly weren't prepared for the images that proved conclusively the identity of the mugger who had attacked the market trader and the cafe owner.

'Blimey, Mike, where did you get these?' Viv asked.

'A sixteen-year-old who was playing truant.' Nash laughed. 'He happened on the scene and, as most of the younger generation seems to do, filmed what he saw. Having captured the first incident, he had enough courage to follow the mugger and shoot the second instalment. It's only just come to our attention because his mother found out and contacted us. Reading between the lines, I think the young man was scared by what he'd seen and that, coupled with the fact that he was skiving off school, made him keep quiet until his mother convinced him to do the right thing. She rang in last night and then emailed them through. She's bringing him in this morning to make a statement.'

Nash continued, 'Far more importantly, these photos and his eyewitness account will make a great bargaining tool when we interview our market mugger, as you insist on calling him.'

'You can do that today, Mike. He's just been released from hospital and is on his way to custody at Netherdale,' Viv told him.

'That's good, because now I have these to back up my argument. I reckon I can persuade Hajdari via his brief to make a full confession. If he does that, we might be able to keep the girl out of it entirely. She's had more than enough suffering to contend with.'

'Do you think the solicitor will go for that? Wouldn't he be more likely to want the girl implicated to lessen the weight of guilt on Hajdari?' Lisa asked.

'Not if I also show him another photo, the one Clara took of Aishe handcuffed and naked on the bed, and explain that if his client cooperates we'll overlook the sexual assault charge. However, if he fails to play ball, we'll throw the book at him, and instead of a possible five-year sentence he'll be looking at a much longer term inside — and moreover, one where he'll be branded as the worst kind of pervert. My guess is that if we had to do that, Hajdari's life won't be worth living once he's inside.'

* * *

As Lee had hoped, his mother received a call requesting that she and Lee attend Helmsdale Police Station that morning for him to give a formal statement.

On arrival, they were escorted to an interview room where Nash greeted them, shaking hands before thanking Lee for his cooperation and introducing him to Lisa. 'DC Andrews will take your statement, but I hope it will be no more than a formality and that you won't need to testify, because with all the other evidence at our disposal, we intend to persuade the offender, via his solicitor, to plead guilty to these offences, rather than face more serious charges relating to another offence.'

Lee's mother was curious as to why the detective seemed so confident, but was reluctant to ask. She was more anxious to get the proceedings over and leave before anyone from the village saw them. Gossips were never kind.

Lee, however, couldn't wait to get to school and entertain his mates with the story, in which, within his mind, he had already become the star witness — and even more important, to tell Milly.

After he'd signed the statement, countersigned by his mother as appropriate adult, Nash accompanied them to the door. The laughter in Nash's voice was reflected in his eyes as he bade them goodbye, aware that the pleasure the boy had got from this was written on his face.

Lee heaved a huge sigh of relief once he was clear of the building.

* * *

Once they had Lee's statement printed and copies of the photos, plus the revealing one Clara had taken of Aishe, Nash was ready to tackle Hajdari.

Nash thanked Lisa and said, 'I've decided to take Viv on this one. I don't want Hajdari ogling you during the interview. He doesn't know how English law works, and he could be intimidated by us. I think two men might just put the wind up him. Before we go, I want you to find out the name of the solicitor appointed to defend him. If we know that beforehand, we can plan our interview strategy better. Will you also fax that statement from our truanting photographer through to Maureen, so that she can have a copy of it typed up to give to the defence brief? Meanwhile, I'm going to check with Jackie Fleming and get her approval for what we're proposing to do, and that she'll have some time spare for us to update her afterwards.'

If Lisa was disappointed, it didn't show. She knew Nash had good reason.

* * *

Having learned which solicitor had been allocated, Nash decided on his line of approach, which he outlined to Viv as they drove to Netherdale.

Viv commented on the variation to previous interviews he'd witnessed. In response to which, Nash explained, 'I've met this solicitor before. Having recently seen one interview technique, he'll most likely be expecting something similar, so by changing tactics we should be able to catch him unawares and thus gain the upper hand. From my experience, if you can gain control in the early stages of an interview, you're far more likely to retain command of the situation. Otherwise, you get the suspect reverting to the old "no comment" routine.'

It was another example of the meticulous approach Nash took, and Viv reflected that Clara had often mentioned this. It was certainly true that Nash rarely went into an interview unprepared, and for suspects to rely on 'no comment' was all but unheard of.

Having obtained Superintendent Fleming's go-ahead for his line of attack, and collected the typed statement, Nash and DC Pearce sought out the solicitor. Nash invited him in to a second interview room and indicated to Viv to load the tape recorder and set it running.

'Your client, Mr Hajdari, is next door, but, in the interests of accuracy, for full disclosure I am taping this interview to avoid any misunderstanding.' Nash smiled at the solicitor. 'Your client is charged with having committed a series of attacks comprising robbery with violence. Before we continue, I think you ought to take a look at several photographs, of which DC Viv Pearce has copies for you.'

Nash signalled to Pearce, who produced the snaps culled from Lee's phone and laid them side by side on the table facing the solicitor. He paused as Nash had instructed him beforehand, holding the envelope in front of him, ensuring that it was directly in the solicitor's line of sight as he awaited his cue.

'As you can see, those photos clearly show the robbery of the market trader and that of the Market Cafe owner taking place, and the video clearly identifies Mr Hajdari as the perpetrator. Not only that, but when we searched the suspect's house, we found a bank bag identical to that taken from the landlord of the Black Bull pub, which we expect to carry the landlord's DNA. Concealed within that bank bag was a Taser, bearing your client's fingerprints, and a balaclava on which we await DNA results. Together with a large quantity of cash, there was also a generator, the serial number of which tallies with the one stolen from Bishopton market.'

Nash paused, not only because he was about to change topic, but to let these facts sink in. 'However, that is not all, far from it, and the next piece of evidence relates to a much more serious matter, concerning which, we have another witness statement and photograph to show you. There is sufficient evidence in our possession to warrant arresting your client and charging him with an extremely unpleasant offence.'

He nodded to Pearce, who drew from the envelope another witness statement, the one signed by Aishe, together with the photograph Clara had taken of the young girl lying handcuffed and naked on the bed. 'This young woman was found in this situation in the suspect's house, having stabbed him to ward off his attempted rape. We also have documented evidence of DNA taken from her skin at the Netherdale rape suite which matches your client. The fact that she was able to defend herself does not negate the charge of sexual assault, which is accentuated sharply by the fact that the victim is the suspect's half-sister.' Nash saw the look of dismay on the solicitor's face turn to one of revulsion at his final comment. 'I suggest we leave you to confer with your client before we begin the interview.'

He turned, switched off the tape machine, and handed a copy of the cassette to the solicitor. 'For you,' he said.

As he and Pearce were leaving the room, Nash turned and addressed the solicitor again. 'Perhaps when you have consulted with him, we can discuss the best way forward. By the way, don't be fooled by his dumb act. I have it on good authority from his employer that his English is perfectly adequate.'

* * *

Later, as they returned to Helmsdale, Viv Pearce reflected on the satisfactory outcome of their afternoon's work. Having been made aware of the more serious charge his client was facing and the overwhelming weight of evidence in both cases, the solicitor was more than anxious to see what sort of a deal he could obtain for Hajdari. He eagerly accepted their proposal that his client should give a full and frank confession to the robberies, and at the same time, completely exonerate Aishe from any involvement in all of those crimes.

In return for this, Nash agreed that they would dissuade Aishe from pressing the sexual assault charge. The outcome would be that after serving his sentence for the lesser crimes, Hajdari would be deported back to Albania, which would ensure Aishe's continued safety and freedom from oppression and fear.

As they approached the outskirts of Helmsdale, Nash glanced at the Range Rover's fuel gauge, then at the clock. 'I need to get some petrol, so I'll drop you at the station. If you take the paperwork up to the office, there's nothing to stop you going straight home. Tell Jack I'll be in first thing in the morning, and not to bother ringing me unless there's a treble murder before then.'

As he passed through reception, Pearce delivered the message and saw Sergeant Binns frown. 'Is there something Mike should know about?' he asked.

'I was hoping to have a word with him, but I don't suppose it's anything that won't wait until morning.'

* * *

That night, Nash was restless and unwilling to cook for himself. Nor was he prepared to sit alone all evening occupied only by a fruitless search for something worth watching on TV. With Daniel away, the washing and ironing baskets were all but empty, and he had already completed other household chores. On a whim, he decided to walk the short distance to the Miners Arms, Wintersett's only pub, which offered a better-than-average selection of bar meals and snacks. With luck, he'd be able to kill two birds with one stone, by following up on Olivia Brook's suggestion.

On arrival, he was greeted with wild enthusiasm by one of the regulars, a small but energetic Jack Russell terrier. Nash bent down to stroke the dog, whose grey whiskers were the only sign of his advancing years. 'Hello, Pip, where's your boss? Waiting for me to buy him a pint, I'll bet.'

Sure enough, Pip's owner, Jonas Turner, was seated by the window, his glass almost empty. Nash made the signal notifying a refill and was awarded by a wide smile, swiftly followed by the glass being emptied. Having obtained two pints, Nash walked over and sat with the old man. 'No, Pip, I didn't forget you,' he placated the dog, who was sitting at his feet watching him with wide, appealing eyes. He pulled a packet of crisps from his jacket pocket and was rewarded with an acrobatic display of pirouettes.

'Cheers, Mr Nash, that's reet good o' you. 'Ow's things down at t' nick? An' 'ow's that lovely Sergeant Miniver? By, she's a crackin'-looking lass, that one.'

Nash chuckled at his reference to Clara, which came from some confusion at their first encounter and had stuck. 'Don't let her fiancé catch you saying that. He's ex-Special Forces, so you'd be in real bother. Anyway, they're looking after Daniel at the moment, and taken him to Spain on holiday with them.'

He explained the reason for this, and Turner shook his head sadly. 'It must be a bugger of a job fittin' looking after t' lad wi' a full-time job like yours, wi' no regular hours. Tha' needs to get thisen a missus to help wi' minding, fer when young Daniel's not at that fancy school of 'is.'

'No chance of that, Jonas,' Nash said, his expression darkened with sadness, 'and I think you know the reason.'

'Aye, well, sorry t' rub it in. Still hurts as much as ever, then?'

Nash shrugged. 'I suppose so, but there's nothing I can do about it. Most days I don't get chance to dwell on it. I'm kept too busy for idle thoughts.'

'You've a lot on, then?'

As they sipped their pints, Nash told Turner as much as he could about the cases he was handling. Having mentioned the market muggings, he added, 'There's also a strange case up at Thornscarr. Builders working at the hotel found some body parts that have been there for years. I was talking to Olivia Brook about it, and she suggested I have a word with you, because you might know more about what went on up there.'

Turner sniffed disdainfully. 'There's nowt that 'ud surprise me about that place. Reet bandit country out there, it is.'

'Rough, is it?'

'One way or t' other, aye.'

Over the course of that pint and the one that followed, Nash listened with mounting interest as he ate his meal and Turner explained his cryptic comment. He talked about the horrible goings-on when there'd been a suicide, before launching into a fascinating monologue about the former owner of the Harland Estate.

'Old man Harland, up at big 'ouse, were a reet 'un for t' lasses, took after 'is father, and when he'd had his fill o' t' locals 'e started usin' t' imported labour. But 'is son were reckoned t' be a different kettle o' fish, that's afore 'e turned up wi' a young Eyetalian lass, a reet eyeful she is, an' must be twenty year younger than 'im. That settled a few people's hash, ah'll tell thee.'

'In what way?'

'Well, when 'e weren't married, rumour 'ad got round that 'e preferred tradesman's entrance, if ye get me meaning.'

'People thought he was a homosexual?' Nash was amused at Turner's use of the local euphemism.

'Aye, and it were only after 'is bride produced first o' their five bairns that they stopped believing it.'

'Anything else interesting about Thornscarr?' Nash's question was a flippant one, but Turner's answer was highly revealing.

'Aye, there's that place ye mentioned at t' start. Boar's 'ead 'otel,' Jonas laughed scornfully. 'I ask yer, 'otel, they call it! It's not what they called it round 'ere, more like Whore's Bed. Ah reckon that's cos they weren't allowed t' tell folk it were a knocking shop.'

'A what?'

'Oh aye, that were one of t' best kept secrets round 'ere. Even your lot never found out. Like I said, t' old squire, Harland were a reet tearaway. 'E'd fettle owt in a skirt apart from a Scotsman, and ahm not too sure abaht that. Anyroad, it used t' be t' old coachin' 'ouse, an' it started as a place for 'im and 'is cronies to bring their totty for dirty weekends, but then, when Harland ran short o' brass, 'e turned it into a business. There was them as reckoned all t' lasses as worked there were on t' game. Local joke were about Gobblin' teas maids. Rumour was it were doin' reet well 'til old man Harland snuffed it, four years back, an' then 'is son leased it out. Med a reet bugger o' it 'e did.'

The old man lowered his voice, leaned across the table and asked Nash, 'Did ye hear 'ow t' old man died?'

Nash shook his head, intrigued and repelled by the revelations. 'Talk were that 'e died on t' job, 'ad a massive heart attack as 'e were fettling one o' t' lasses there. Course, there were unkind folk med lots o' nasty snide comments. One bloke said the lass told 'im it were t' best t' old man 'ad ever performed, and another said summat abaht rigor mortis doin' trick. That aside, I know fer a fact they'd t' get one o' t' estate cars t' cart him back t' Grange where 'is body were "found" next morning.' Turner chuckled.

CHAPTER FOURTEEN

The morning after Nash's visit to the Miners Arms, he walked into Helmsdale Police Station as his mobile alerted him to a new text message. This one was from Daniel. He read it and smiled. Clearly, his son was enjoying his holiday, and reading between the lines, being thoroughly spoilt by Clara and David. The last part of Daniel's text puzzled him. It read, 'Going for a trip tomorrow. You'd like it.'

What was that all about? Nash gave a mental shrug; no doubt he'd find out in due course; probably some new water park or similar attraction.

Sergeant Binns was on the phone, and judging by his expression and tone of voice, the usually amiable uniformed officer was less than happy. Nash thought it better not to interrupt, so he waved a hand in greeting and mouthed 'morning,' but Binns lifted a hand, signalling him to wait. Nash halted, listening to Binns' valedictory message.

'You'd better get someone to bring them here immediately. Don't get distracted or find something else with a higher priority. This situation should never have been allowed to happen. I dread to think what Inspector Nash will say when he hears about it. And as for the chief constable, if she wants to see you, I'd wear two pairs of underpants.'

Binns slammed the receiver down and glared at the phone for a second. He looked up as Nash spoke. 'My detective skills, which you've occasionally called into question, lead me to deduce that something or somebody has upset you, Jack. So tell me, what it is that I'm going to be angry about?'

Binns took a deep breath before he began. 'I was booking a guy a couple of days ago, a druggie who had tried to snatch a woman's handbag. Well, he was drugged up, and making no sense. It was so bad that the doctor had him moved to the rehab clinic.' After noticing the expression on Nash's face, he added, 'With God's agreement,' using the chief constable's nickname derived from the initial letters of her name, Gloria O'Donnell, as much as from her position of authority. 'Anyway, during the course of his ramblings he mentioned a woman's name. He kept repeating something along the lines of 'what are you doing about finding Samantha'. That name rang a bell when I linked it to his address. That led me to send a couple of men to the place just to check that she was there. Her full name is Samantha Frost and she has a string of convictions for shoplifting and prostitution. The officers reported back that according to the neighbours she hadn't been seen for a good while.'

'Go on, Jack, where is this leading?'

'That's where I went yesterday morning, to the rehab clinic to talk to Swift. It seems if you need something doing right, you have to do it yourself,' he added, the anger in his voice unmistakable. 'Swift was no longer talking gibberish, and he confirmed he hadn't seen her for well over a week or so. Then he told me one of his mates in the pub had been drowning his sorrows, and when he got talking, it turns out he knew another woman that was missing, had been since early in the year. It was then that I remembered one of the lads mentioning he heard of a woman who had gone missing at Netherdale a few weeks back, another prostitute by the name of Janet Wilson. It was only hearsay, and he assumed that it had been reported. Then I looked on the system, couldn't find anything, so I got on to Netherdale and asked Tom to check the files in reception and to look further back. He did, and found them, along with a third case back in January, an exotic dancer who worked at Club Wolfgang, among other places, and who supplemented her income by entertaining clients.'

'In other words, she was also on the game?'

'Exactly. She went by the stage name of Suki, but her real name is Susan Farmer. There appears to have been little or no investigation carried out into these cases. As far as I can judge, no proper MISPER file has been instigated, and CID have certainly not been informed of the disappearances, let alone given any details. For whatever reason, someone on the desk there seems to think that because these are working girls, their fate isn't worth what they see as a waste of resources. That's why I've demanded that the files be brought across, because I knew for a fact that you'd do something about it. You'll care about what's happened to these unfortunate women, even if nobody else does.'

'You're damned right, Jack, and well done for spotting it. Do you know who's responsible? Which officer it is?'

'It may not be an officer.'

'Civilian?'

Binns nodded. 'Leave it to me. I'll deal with him, whoever it is.'

Nash thanked him, then shook his head. 'It's alarming that there are three such cases within our area in such a short space of time. What I'll do is alert Jackie Fleming that we might have a potential problem, and ask her to widen the search parameters for any similar cases to include neighbouring forces. If these women have been abducted, which seems more than a possibility, then the perpetrator might have extended the range of his activities. Let me know as soon as you get those files.'

'I will, Mike, but don't place too much reliance on them; from what Tom told me, their contents will be sketchy at best.'

'Yes, we'll probably be better off starting again from scratch.' Nash sighed. 'Just when I was congratulating myself that the workload had eased and how well we'll be able to cope without Clara.'

'How long is it before she's back?'

'Jack, she's only been gone three days.' Nash grinned. 'Are you missing her already? Of course, when they do get back, I'll have to sort Daniel out ready for his summer term, assuming he's fully recovered.'

'How is my little friend Daniel?' The relief of passing the information to a senior officer had lightened Jack's mood, somewhat.

'Not so little, anymore.'

'How old is he now? He must be what, eight, nine?'

'Are you nearing retirement, Jack?'

'Why?

'Because Daniel's nearly eleven years old.'

'Well, that just goes to show how time flies then, doesn't it? He'll be a young man before long. Then you'll really have your hands full — especially if he takes after you.' Jack couldn't suppress a laugh.

'You're probably right. Talk about no rest for the wicked.'

'You'll manage. Anyway, it's Lisa I feel sorry for; she has to contend with you and Viv,' Binns said, with a flash of his old humour.

Nash gave him a vulgar one-fingered gesture and headed upstairs to his office. His priority was the phone call to Superintendent Fleming that would set the ball rolling.

Fleming's reaction was as horrified as Nash's had been. 'Let me have the names of the missing women, then leave it to me. I'll make doubly certain things are dealt with properly at this end, and I'll also put an urgent alert out to all surrounding forces. Initially, I'll extend the time to a six-month timescale, but I won't make any mention of how the women earned their living. This doesn't sound like coincidence, Mike, and if they have been abducted and harmed, as seems highly likely, we can't be certain the person responsible concentrated purely on prostitutes. Once I've cleared my desk, I'll join you at Helmsdale, because I want to thank Jack Binns in person. That's as good police work as what happened at Netherdale was bad.'

* * *

Binns had been right, Nash thought as he skim-read the files Jack had just delivered; in fact, the description 'sketchy' was an exaggeration. He finished his perusal just as DC Andrews arrived. One glance at her face told Nash that Binns had already warned her what to expect, and her opening words merely confirmed that.

'I was going to say good morning, Mike, but in view of the things I've just heard, I reckon that would be highly inappropriate. At first, I thought Jack was pulling some kind of elaborate sick hoax. Sadly, that doesn't seem to be the case.'

Nash handed her the thin sheaf of papers he'd taken from the files, plus Binns' report regarding Samantha Frost. 'The missing women all worked as prostitutes. Susan Farmer vanished sometime during January, Janet Wilson possibly in early March and Samantha Frost approximately ten days ago. Jackie Fleming's looking into the possibility that there might have been other disappearances in neighbouring areas. Once she's dealt with that and a problem relating to the mishandling of the reports, she's coming here so that we can devise a strategy for tackling the problem.'

He watched as she read the files, noting that it took her no longer than it had taken him, and awaited her comments.

'Have you any ideas, Mike?' Lisa gestured to the paperwork, what little there was of it, and shrugged helplessly. 'I mean, where and how do we start? After all this time, it's going to be a nightmare trying to find anyone willing or able to give us reliable evidence of where and when these women were last seen.'

'My first reaction is to ignore the first two of those files and begin as if we'd only learned about the women vanishing this morning — which, of course, is quite true.'

'OK, so would you like me to set up brand new MISPER files?'

'That will do for a start, and once they're in place and logged onto the computer, we need to organize a team to do the legwork, door-to-door, et cetera. We should also check places such as hospitals, clinics and rehab centres, in case any of the women have been admitted or checked in there. Apart from that, all we can hope for is that by some miracle there is CCTV footage that will be useful. I very much doubt it, certainly in the first two instances, because of the time that has elapsed and the uncertainty of the time factor. It would be impossible. Besides, my guess is that any images will have been erased long since. There might just be an outside chance with Samantha Frost, but she was working in Bishopton, and to my recollection, the CCTV coverage there is next to non-existent.'

'That doesn't sound at all promising.'

'It isn't, and although standard procedure in MISPER cases is to look for proof of life, sadly I'm of the opinion that in this instance, if there is a common denominator to these disappearances, that would only be holding out false optimism. It would also send a totally incorrect message to family or friends.'

'What about media involvement? You made no mention of getting the press behind the story?'

'One thing at a time, Lisa. Let's see what Jackie has to tell us from her dialogue with neighbouring forces before we even consider going public. When we do contact the media we need to provide a complete picture of what we suspect we're dealing with.'

It was over an hour later when the sound of vehicles entering the car park caused Lisa to glance out of the window. 'Viv's arrived,' she told Nash, 'and Jackie's car's just come in behind his.'

'Sorry I'm late, Mike. Lianne and I have been up half the night. The baby just wouldn't settle.'

'Don't worry about that for now, just read these before Jackie comes in.'

The conversation ceased and the mood changed abruptly when Jackie Fleming entered the room. It was apparent to all three waiting detectives that she wasn't the bearer of glad tidings.

'I've been talking to Jack Binns,' she explained. 'If it hadn't been for his diligence, this matter might have gone undetected for far longer and more vulnerable women put at risk. Sadly, that's the only piece of positive news I have for you. Following the calls I made to neighbouring forces, I now believe there are five women unaccounted for, five unsolved disappearances — all within the past six months, every one of them involving a woman working in the sex trade.'

She removed files from her briefcase and placed them on the centre table. 'Two of these cases have been properly investigated, sadly not by our force, but one each from West Yorkshire and Teesside. Despite the effort and hard work of both forces, they have been unable to come up with a single scrap of evidence, apart from one grainy CCTV image of what looks like a Land Rover-type vehicle. The car was on the edge of a camera shot taken about the time and in the approximate location where Brianna Fairburn was last seen, late in the evening she vanished. The assumption is that the vehicle belonged either to one of Brianna's punters — or, as I suspect, more likely to her abductor. Unfortunately there is no chance of identifying the exact model of the car from that image, let alone picking up the number plate or any distinguishing features of the driver. There is even less evidence in the other instance, a girl by the name of Tamara Atkinson, known to friends and clients alike as Tammy.'

Fleming paused for breath before turning to events closer to hand. 'I've been looking into the mishandling of the two earlier MISPER cases reported to Netherdale, and as a result, I've placed Civilian Support Officer Harry

Johnson under suspension pending a full, formal disciplinary inquiry. Johnson came to Netherdale when he moved from the Midlands and applied to join when we were recruiting civilians. After checking into his background, I now understand the reason for his action, or should I say inaction, in not recording the details. That doesn't mean that I in any way condone what the inquiry might regard as misconduct.'

'Are we allowed to know why he misbehaved or is that sub-judice?' Nash asked.

'I see no reason not to reveal it — as long as the information stays strictly with those of us in this room. The facts will be presented at the inquiry, so it's merely a matter of time before they become common knowledge. Johnson had a younger brother. Apparently they were very close. When his brother's wife died following a long illness, he sought company from the local prostitutes and took up with one on a regular basis. She had a pimp, a nasty piece of work. He'd beaten her up on several occasions, got her hooked on drugs and he then discarded her. The brother felt sorry for her, but at the time he wasn't aware that she'd contracted HIV. It wasn't until he showed signs of the illness that Johnson became involved. When it got too much, the brother committed suicide by slashing his wrists, then to make sure it worked, he tied a plastic bag round his head. I cannot think of many more painful or unpleasant ways to die. Johnson found him. It tends to explain why he lacked sympathy and wasn't interested in making a report.'

The look of horror on the faces of her listeners was sufficient reassurance that the story would remain secret, so Fleming immediately changed the subject and suggested they examine the MISPER files together. 'Now we have a fuller picture, we might be able to plan a coherent strategy for dealing with this case.'

'I agree in principle, Jackie. But before we do that, I think it would be advisable to set about back-filling those two mishandled cases, plus the most recent one that led Jack to his splendid deduction. That way, we might find something pertinent which we'd otherwise overlook. That will mean door-to-door enquiries, plus all the usual contact channels, friends and family, neighbours, co-workers and even, if possible, punters. After we've compiled as complete a range of information as possible, the comparison will be more meaningful — and following that, we might consider alerting the media, which in turn will help make others involved in the sex trade aware of the potential danger.'

'Good thinking, Mike. How do you want to play it?'

Nash smiled ruefully, 'I assume that means you're putting me in charge of the investigation?'

Fleming nodded her agreement.

'I think we should take one case each and concentrate on amassing as much data as possible. I'd say one detective assisted by two uniformed officers ought to be able to gather all the available facts within a couple of days. Once we have them, we can decide which facts might be relevant or potentially useful.'

'Good enough, I'll see to allocating the uniforms and get them to report to you. When do you want to make a start?'

'As soon as they report here. Lisa, will you take the Susan Farmer file, and Viv, concentrate on Janet Wilson? I'll handle the Samantha Frost investigation. We're going to focus our attention on those groups I've already listed during the day, and this evening we'll need to seek out and interview other sex workers. If we're able to get some of those girls to open up about their punters, we might be able to discover if they've been approached by anyone they felt scared by — or by anyone driving a Land Rover.'

CHAPTER FIFTEEN

Having approved Nash's enquiry guidelines, Fleming got on the phone and spoke to the uniform branch inspector at Netherdale. 'When the two o'clock shift starts, I want three patrol cars, each manned with two officers, to report to Helmsdale as soon as possible. With the exception of a major incident or serious RTA, those officers must be available to Detective Inspector Nash, and warn them they will be working late. Yes, I am authorizing overtime.' Fleming shook her head in exasperation. 'And if they're needed, I want the same officers detailed tomorrow.' She listened for a moment. 'Well it isn't their day off now! Do you understand? Sergeant Binns will monitor their activity during the day and later the overnight duty officer at Netherdale will liaise with Inspector Nash, DC Andrews, and DC Pearce.'

It was obvious that the inspector had raised one or two objections from Fleming's response, which was pithy and direct. 'We're investigating five linked disappearances of vulnerable young women who might have been the victims of malicious activity, possibly as grave as homicide — and in answer to your other query, yes, this does have to do with the reason I've placed CSO Harry Johnson under suspension. I did so with the agreement of the chief constable. I'll brief you on that when I return, which will be very shortly.'

She put the receiver down carefully and then looked at the trio of detectives. 'I'm afraid our colleague at Netherdale needs to be put straight about his lack of oversight of the men under his command. That situation with Johnson should never have been allowed to happen. However, that's for the chief to deal with. As far as you're concerned, the assistance you require will be available within the hour.'

'In that case, we'd better grab something to eat and drink, because we're going to be working late — very late. I'll go for some sandwiches and biscuits, while you two ring home and warn your partners not to expect you until possibly the early hours.'

'What about you?' Fleming said without thinking. She cursed her tactlessness as she saw the shadow that crossed Nash's face.

'I'm afraid there's nobody at home for me to ring. Daniel's away with Clara and David.'

Once they'd eaten their lunch, the detectives went down to reception, where the uniform officers assigned to them were assembled. It was obvious from the discussion Nash overheard as they entered that the men had no idea what the task ahead of them was, so he began by explaining what was required. He watched as the other teams set off, then turned to the men allocated to him. He smiled as he recognized the officers from the incident at Lilac Farm. 'Right, guys, we're off to Bishopton. A prostitute by the name of Samantha Frost went missing about ten days ago. We need to find out all we can about the circumstances surrounding the event.'

'Are the others involved in the same investigation?'

'Yes and no. They're looking into two linked disappearances, those of Susan Farmer and Janet Wilson.'

'You think all three are connected?'

'We do, plus one from West Yorkshire and one from Teesside.'

The officer whistled with surprise, but his colleague focussed on one name, the subject of their inquiry. 'I know Samantha Frost,' he told Nash, 'I arrested her a few years ago for soliciting. She's a bit past her best now, mostly because she's a user.'

'Do you know Bishopton well?' Nash asked as they got into the patrol car.

'I do. I worked out of the old station there before it closed.'

'What about other working girls? We'll need to talk to as many as we can find to try and get more background info.'

'There are three others that I know of, but there may be one or two more that I don't, especially if they've started on the game since I was transferred.'

'Now that's given me a thought,' Nash said. He took his mobile out and phoned Binns. 'Jack, will you contact Viv and Lisa? Ask them to check into the possibility of any prostitutes who might have disappeared and not been reported missing. Asking the other girls about anyone who hasn't been seen on their usual patch might be the best way to pick up such information. Just to be on the safe side, get Maureen Riley or Tom Pratt to check on the computer. I need a list of any girls convicted or charged with soliciting in our area in the past five years, and I want someone to check on the welfare of every one of them. I appreciate it might prolong our task, but it's necessary, I'm afraid.'

Nash thanked the uniformed officer. 'I might not have thought of that without our discussion. Shows how easy it is to miss something that could prove vital.'

* * *

It wasn't until late the following morning that the detectives re-convened at Helmsdale. All three had been working until well after midnight. Nash had advised the officers they would not be needed any further, and hoped they enjoyed their shift break. Both Andrews and Pearce had eagerly accepted Nash's suggestion not to come in early, but when they arrived their boss was already at the station.

'I just saw Mike's car. How long has he been here?' Viv asked Binns as he and Lisa entered reception.

Binns shrugged. 'No idea, he could have slept here for all I know. He was already in his office when I arrived.'

The de-briefing session lasted until early afternoon, extended partly by the need to sift through the information Tom Pratt had faxed through from Netherdale. It was the list Nash had asked for, compiled from the women charged with soliciting. Together, Nash, Lisa, and Viv ticked off names against those prostitutes they'd managed to interview. At the end of the process there were only three outstanding. Nash phoned the details to Jackie Fleming, who promised to get an officer to visit the addresses at once.

Having finished that task, they next compared notes on the previous day's inquiries. 'Did you get anything useful, Viv?' Nash asked.

'Apart from the offer of a blow job and a freebie, you mean?' Pearce grinned.

'Yes, I think we can ignore them. I had a similar invitation. Entertaining, but not exactly useful.'

'You two are lucky, all I got was a load of abuse and being told by one girl "I don't do lessies, love, grow yourself a dick and come back then". A real charmer, she was. Mind you, the attitude changed sharply when I told them who I was and why I was asking, but no joy with anything really helpful.'

'One of the girls I spoke to mentioned a punter with a Land Rover Discovery,' Viv chipped in, 'but all I could get from her was a vague description, the name Eddie and the fact that he paid well and just wanted straightforward sex, no weird frills, as she put it. Oh, and one other thing, she said he'd been circumcised. I thanked her for that, but pointed out that I didn't think we could get a suspect to drop his trousers for an identification parade.'

'Now that is really interesting,' Nash responded, 'not the circumcision bit, I mean the name and the vehicle type.'

He flipped over the notes he'd made. 'One of the girls I spoke to described a punter named Eddie, but she knew a bit more. When they went back to her place he asked to use her bathroom. Apparently he told her he'd recently returned from India, where he'd picked up a stomach bug. That could be worth remembering, maybe we're looking for someone who travels a great deal. Anyway, while he was otherwise engaged, she checked his wallet which had apparently "fallen on the floor".'

'How fortunate.' Viv rolled his eyes, his disbelief obvious.

'Yes, and luckily, she's got a fairly good memory. She said his full name is Edward G Clarke and he lives in Bishopton, which is where Samantha Frost worked.'

'I also talked to a woman who had a punter called Eddie,' Lisa added, 'but that was all she knew about him, same as yours, Viv.'

'OK, now this looks like a live prospect to me,' Nash said, his tone slightly more optimistic. 'Viv, will you work your magic on the computer and find out everything you can about Mr Clarke while Lisa makes coffee. Meanwhile, I'm going to phone Jackie and tell we've identified one possible suspect. Before I do, though, is there anything else? Are there any other possibilities to consider?'

Both Andrews and Pearce shook their heads, signifying that neither of them had come up with alternative leads.

'OK,' Jackie said in response to the information Nash gave her. 'I'll leave it to you. The chief has all the facts and has given you more or less *carte blanche*. Make Mr Clarke the focus of your inquiries, and when the officers I've sent to the addresses of the other working girls have reported back, I'll update you.'

* * *

Viv didn't take long to report his findings. 'All I could discover about Edward Clarke was the entry in the voter's roll.

That in itself is interesting. He lives at number 47 Rothwell Road, Bishopton, and is the sole occupier of that property. The part I said was interesting is that Rothwell Road is only a couple of streets away from where Samantha Frost lives. Clarke's name doesn't show up on the PNC, so he's obviously never been convicted of a criminal offence, not even a motoring misdemeanour.'

'That means little or nothing. Many of the worst offenders have no previous — otherwise, our job would be far simpler. We're going to have to begin by paying Mr Clarke a home visit. Jackie has laid the facts before God, and she's given approval for any action I deem necessary, and for us to concentrate on this case at the expense of any other enquiries we have running, which principally means what Lisa refers to as the "okra case".'

Pearce was puzzled by the okra reference, so between them Nash and Lisa apprised him of the facts.

Given the potential gravity of their inquiry, all three detectives went to Clarke's Bishopton address. There was no response to their knock, so they made enquiries of the neighbour on the immediate right of Clarke's house. All the properties in Rothwell Road were similar, small semi-detached houses that reminded Nash of the old Pete Seeger song *Little Boxes*.

The woman who answered the door, who they later categorized as probably being the town gossip, was as informative as they could have wished for. 'Poor Eddie, he spends as much time abroad as he possibly can these days. He tells me it's because of the demands of his job, but I reckon that's only an excuse, and the truth is that he doesn't like to stay in the house for too long at a time, now that he's alone. I think the place is too full of sad memories for him to cope with.'

She noticed their interested expressions, which was more than enough encouragement for her to continue. 'Lynda, Eddie's wife, was a lovely woman. She died a couple of years ago, and Eddie's been like a lost soul ever since. I reckon it's a mercy he has that job at Helm Engineering. It not only occupies his mind, but he's no sooner finished one project than he's off on his travels again, and ends up in some fairly exotic places. One week he's off to India, then it might be any of a dozen African countries, even sometimes to South America or Australia; literally wherever they send him. I haven't seen him for a week or two, so I reckon he must be away at the moment. To be honest, these days I'm more surprised when I *do* see him than when he's absent, but Mrs Bagshaw across the way might be able to tell you more than me, except that she's visiting her daughter in Leeds for a couple of days. Eddie leaves his spare house keys with her so she can look after the house when he's off on his travels.'

She sighed dramatically and added, 'I remember Eddie telling me it was a mistake to get romantically involved with anyone, because that way when one of them dies, the other one dies with them.'

They thanked the garrulous gossip and returned to the car. 'I reckon that's why Clarke uses call girls,' Lisa suggested, 'after having experienced such a sad loss, he's frightened of the emotional upset of losing someone else close to him. So what do we do next, Mike?'

'I think we should visit his employers and find out where Clarke is and what his travel itinerary has been over the period these girls went missing. If I go alone to talk to the MD at Helm Engineering, at least that won't send as strong a message as it would if we all descend on him. That could be counter-productive if it gives his employers the impression that he's suspected of some heinous crime. Clarke might seem to fit our profile in several ways, but I'm beginning to think we might be barking up the wrong tree here.'

His interview with the chief executive was brief but illuminating, if only in a negative way. 'I'm here to check up on one of your employees,' Nash began. 'A vehicle similar to his was seen near the site of a series of incidents, so we've been tasked with checking the whereabouts of all such car owners on the dates in question, purely for elimination purposes.' He explained who the employee was and gave details. 'I tried at his house but there was no response, so a neighbour directed me here. She seemed to think he is away at present.'

'Eddie Clarke? He's not in bother, I hope. He's very valuable member of our team here, and the poor man's had more than enough to contend with over the past couple of years.'

'No, like I said, this is purely a routine enquiry. If we know Mr Clarke's work itinerary, it will enable us to rule him out of our investigation.'

'OK, I'll get his work rota from our technical director and we can compare that with your dates.'

When Nash emerged from the building, both his colleagues guessed that the outcome had been less successful than they'd hoped. After he climbed into the driving seat, Nash told them. 'My feeling that we were following up a dead end was right. We can cross Eddie Clarke off our list of suspects — not that we have a list. He's in South Africa at present, and has been since before Samantha Frost vanished. Clarke supervises the installation of heavy plant that Helm Engineering export worldwide. Added to the South African visit, he was in Canada when Janet Wilson disappeared and Italy at the time Brianna Fairburn went missing. Now I'll have to tell Jackie the bad news — that we'll have to start again from scratch.'

* * *

'So we're back to square one,' Jackie said, once Nash had informed her that their prime suspect was no longer either prime or suspect. 'Where do we go from here?'

'Quite honestly, Jackie, unless something unexpected turns up or we get a further incident report, which I'm dreading, I haven't the foggiest idea. Assuming the five women were all abducted and harmed by the same person, which I believe to be the case, where does he keep his victims? Unless he's got his own private graveyard or crematorium, or drops them down a disused mine shaft, what does he do with them?

I'm assuming that they're all dead, but unfortunately that's an assumption we have to make.'

'Let's hope for a miracle, then. I do have one piece of positive news. Those three women who hadn't been accounted for have been traced and they're all safe and sound.'

It might have been of some consolation, but Nash regarded it only as cold comfort. The fact that those three were unharmed did little to offset the probable fate of the other five.

CHAPTER SIXTEEN

The school bus meandered through the dale, dropping pupils off at villages and farms alike, ending its run at Newton-on-Helm village, where it delivered the last two passengers.

They had just got off the vehicle which had brought them from Helmsdale Secondary School when Lee told his companion, 'I've had an idea.'

Milly looked at her fellow pupil, her interest showing in the sparkle in her eyes. She had been friends with Lee for several years, long before his witnessing of the market muggings raised him to the status of a minor celebrity at school. For some time now they had wanted to be far more than just friends, but in a tiny village such as theirs, that was far from easy. Even had their purpose not been one of physical intimacy, their chances of being alone and unobserved were next to nil.

'Tell me,' Milly encouraged him, her tone one of suppressed excitement.

Lee pointed to the far end of the village, where the road beyond Milly's house wound its way towards the head of the dale. 'I reckon there's a perfect place in Thornscarr.'

'You mean one of the holiday cottages?' That was a safe guess, because there was little else in Thornscarr other than the hotel, which at present still resembled a building site.

'Why not? There's one that fits the bill perfectly. I happen to know it's habitable because I remember seeing an artist bloke who was staying there. He moved in last autumn, but I've been watching the cottage and I reckon he's moved on. As far as I can tell, the house is empty. And because of its location, there's no danger of anyone peering through the windows at us.'

'How will we get in? Surely it'll be all locked up, won't it?'

'No, that's why it's going to be dead easy. I had a look round yesterday evening. Someone's left a window open on the ground floor. It'll be a doddle.'

'On Saturday, my Mum and Dad are off to Sheffield to see some eighties pop star who is appearing at the Arena. I've never heard of him, but apparently he was mega back in the day. Anyway, that means they won't be back until the early hours of Sunday morning.'

'Perfect. My Mum's on nights this weekend, so it couldn't be better.'

They looked at one another. Even the thought of what they were planning was beginning to excite them. As they parted outside Milly's gate she touched his hand fleetingly. 'See you tomorrow morning, Lee,' her voice was a husky whisper. 'And you will be prepared, won't you?'

That and the touch of her hand were sufficient to set Lee wondering how he'd contain himself until then.

On the pretext of going to the library, on Saturday morning Lee caught the bus to Helmsdale. There he spent the best part of an hour deciding on his options while pacing up and down the High Street. He had two choices. The first was the supermarket, but he could be spotted at the checkout by people he knew, or even worse, who knew his mother. The thought of being seen buying condoms scared him witless. The chemist was another matter. As he reached for the handle, he'd looked through the glass door and seen an attractive young woman serving at the counter and lost his nerve, hence the pacing. At lunchtime he saw the female assistant leave the shop. One quick peek was all it took to spot a man serving and Lee was in. He tried to sound as if this was a purchase he made regularly, tried not to stammer. It was fortunate he did not see the smile on the face of the chemist when he left.

When he reached home, he stammered again when his mother enquired why he was carrying the same library book. He wasn't sure she believed his excuse: that it was so good, he wanted to read it again.

* * *

The arrangement was for them to meet up outside the holiday cottage at 7.30 on Saturday evening, by which time Lee hoped that his mother would have given him his tea and set off for work. His parents were divorced, and his mother worked as a nurse at Netherdale General. Although she alternated shifts, this weekend she was on night duty. As their house was directly opposite the village pub, any attempt to sneak Milly in and out was fraught with danger. In a village where everyone knows everyone else, and the favourite pastime is gossip, a chance sighting would cause wagging tongues to go into overdrive. It wasn't that Milly's parents disapproved of Lee, or that Lee's mother frowned on his friendship with Milly, but all three of them would have taken exception, in the strongest terms, to how they were planning to spend the evening.

Saturday seemed to pass slowly for both of them. Once Milly had waved her parents off in the late afternoon, she spent an hour getting ready, ensuring she looked her best. The fact that Lee saw her every day on the bus and at school never crossed her mind. Once she was satisfied, she spent further hours wandering around the house, occasionally pausing to switch the TV on, only to switch it off a few minutes later, unable to settle to anything.

For Lee, the nervous anticipation was equally stressful. He bolted his tea, before waiting anxiously for his mother to finish hers and set off for work. Eventually, after what seemed far longer than most weeks, she was ready.

'Will you be all right?' she asked.

Lee smiled, she asked the same question every time she left him alone, despite the fact that he was now over sixteen. Only just, but in his mind that made him an adult. 'Yes, Mum, I'll be fine.'

'Is there anything on telly for you to watch?'

'There's a film on, and footie.'

She reached out and caressed his cheek. 'I hate having to leave you on your own on Saturday night. You know that, don't you? I wouldn't do it if we didn't need the money.'

'I know that, Mum, don't worry about me. I'll be OK.'

She kissed him and rumpled his hair.

Controlling his impatience with an effort of will that was almost painful, Lee waited after his mother's car drew away. It was by no means unknown for her to return a few minutes following her original departure, having forgotten some essential item. Her reading glasses were the favourite to be left behind, but Lee had taken the precaution of reminding her about them shortly before she set off.

When he was certain that she wasn't about to reappear, he sent Milly a text telling her he was on his way to Thornscarr. He grabbed his torch before he switched the hall light off, then slipped quickly out of the front door and locked it behind him. It would be just his luck to be found out if someone were to break in and steal something, or even if a neighbour knocked on the door, wanting to borrow a cup of sugar, or something equally trivial. He edged along the pavement, head down and keeping close to the wall, to lessen the chance of any early-evening drinkers catching sight of him. The April evening was starless and with a cloud covering, so by the time he reached the holiday cottage, the darkness was almost total. As his eyes adjusted to the gloom, Lee could make out the shape of the drystone wall alongside the cottage gate, a darker mass in the darkness surrounding it. He was slightly startled by a sudden movement as Milly emerged from alongside the wall.

Lee put his arms around her, clasping her in the embrace he'd dreamed about for so long. As he did so, he thought he could feel her body tremble — or was it his? 'Are you all right?' he asked. 'I mean, are you up for it?'

Milly put her hand on the back of his neck, pulling his head forward to kiss him. 'I am now.'

'Let's get inside.'

They held hands as they walked slowly down the path.

'Over there,' Lee gestured with his free hand, unwilling to let go of her for even a second. 'On the left of the front door, there's a small window I think must be the hallway. I brought a torch for when we're inside, because I guessed the electric would be off, or it might be one of those prepayment meters. In any case, it would be too risky putting the main lights on. I checked their advert online and there are two double bedrooms.'

'Oh good.' Milly squeezed his arm. To have thought all that out, gone to all that trouble, it showed how much he wanted her.

The window was not so much open as off the catch. It was reluctant to move, the wood swollen against the frame. Eventually, with both of them at work, they managed to get their fingers under the lower sill and push it up. Then Lee climbed inside and pulled the window down behind him. He turned to the door, let Milly in, and then closed it quietly. The chance of anyone disturbing them was remote, but better not take any risks.

'We should check the place out first. Make sure no one's staying here.' Lee flicked his torch on, and taking hold of Milly's hand, guided her along the passageway heading for the lounge door.

Milly was the first to notice it. 'Ugh!' she exclaimed. 'What's that smell?'

Lee sniffed. 'Dunno, but it's a horrible pong.'

Lee strode across the hall and opened the door opposite the lounge, revealing the cottage's dining room. The smell was much stronger in there. Without conscious thought, Lee stepped inside. Milly followed, albeit reluctantly. This wasn't going to plan, wasn't what either of them had hoped for. Lee pointed the torch beam towards the back of the house, highlighting a door. 'I guess that's the kitchen, and I bet that's where the stink's coming from. Probably the last tenant left something to go bad.'

He walked towards the door. Milly hung back. Suddenly she felt afraid. Partly because of what they were planning to do, partly because they had already broken into someone else's property, but mainly due to an unidentifiable dread of what might be on the other side of that door. Which was nonsense, she told herself, probably it was as Lee had said, that the last tenant had been too idle to take the rubbish out or empty the fridge.

Except that this smelt worse than rotting food. Far worse.

Lee had paused by the kitchen door, and in the backlight from the torch, Milly could see that his head was bent, as if he was listening.

'What is it?' she whispered.

'I thought I heard something. A noise. Coming from in there.'

She joined him and they listened together. After a few seconds, she heard it too, a faint, rustling sound. It was almost as if someone had moved something. Paper, perhaps, or plastic. Milly saw Lee's hand reach for the door handle and her panic spiralled almost out of control. 'Don't, Lee. Don't open that door. Don't go in. Let's get out of here. Let's go back to my house. I don't care anymore if someone finds out about us. I don't care if the whole county knows what we're doing. I just don't want to stay here. Please?'

'It'll be all right, trust me,' he reassured her. 'We'll just have a quick look, then we'll go.'

He opened the door.

Instantly, they recoiled in revulsion, both at the swarm of bluebottles that surrounded them, and the appalling stench from within the room. As the insects dispersed, the sound of their buzzing anger was replaced. Into the silence, they heard the sound of footsteps. Small, faint, scampering, scrabbling steps, as tiny paws tried for a grip on the tiled surface of the kitchen floor.

Lee recovered and shone his torch inside. At the edge of the beam, they could see light reflecting from several pairs of bright, beady, avaricious eyes. In the centre of the room was a table that was swamped with what appeared to be dried blood. On the centre of the surface was a large joint. The meat was covered with hundreds upon hundreds of bluebottles and their junior partners; a colony of writhing, squirming maggots.

Strangely, the meat on the table was not the focus of the rats' attention. Lee moved his torch, the beam reflecting his shaking hand. As it illuminated the quartet of black bin liners in the corner of the room, they could see that the rats had been tearing with frantic urgency at the plastic, their sharp claws ripping the bags and allowing some of the contents to spill out.

The young couple looked on in horrified fascination as one of the bags moved from the stress of countless creatures inside, each competing for their share of the rations. The movement caused a further item to slip into the entrance hole the rats had created. At first, Milly thought it was a bunch of sausages that the tenants had thrown away. Then, with a fresh level of horror, she saw them more clearly, and realized that sausages don't wear nail varnish.

Milly began to scream, the sound of her hysteria disturbing the diners, who began diving from the sacks, scurrying in all directions.

By now, the torch was almost beyond Lee's control. As he swung round to leave the kitchen, Milly clutched his arm. Her screams grew louder. Then Lee saw what had terrified her. Picked out by the torch beam, in gut-churning clarity, was the kitchen sink and its contents: heads. Four human heads, their cheeks scarred by the rodents' claws as they gouged for the tasty morsels provided by the eyeballs. As Milly vomited noisily on the dining room carpet, Lee's final vision of the kitchen before he slammed the door shut was the eyeless horror of those heads.

CHAPTER SEVENTEEN

Mike Nash was watching TV. Or rather, the set was turned on but he wasn't paying the screen any attention. The after-effects of a long and stressful week had been, in part, alleviated by a walk along the banks of the River Helm near to Smelt Mill Cottage followed by a good meal, and had combined to send him to sleep in the armchair. As he had volunteered to be on call, he had foregone the chance of even a single glass of wine. Nevertheless, soon after settling to watch a promising programme, he was asleep. The shrill tone of the telephone woke him.

'Mike? Jack Binns, sorry to disturb you, but we've got a really bad one.' It had to be bad, Nash thought, otherwise Netherdale Control would have phoned him. Binns must already have been called to open Helmsdale station, which meant they were anticipating trouble.

'Go on, Jack, tell me the worst.'

'A couple of teenagers in Thornscarr broke into an empty holiday cottage and found a load of body parts in plastic bin liners. Mike,' — Binns gulped, emotion threatening to overcome him — 'it's so bad we can't even tell how many corpses there are, but so far we've found four heads.'

'Four? Did you say four?'

'Yes, apparently the kitchen is like a meat market. The only reason they can be certain there are at least four is because they found the heads in the sink.'

Nash felt his stomach churn. Some things you never get hardened to. He wondered what state the youngsters who made the grim discovery were in. 'Give me the details.' His voice was calm, which was far away from how he was feeling.

Binns recited the address, before adding, 'I've raised Mexican Pete. He's organizing a forensic team to go out there. Will you call DC Andrews?'

Nash thought for a moment. With Detective Superintendent Fleming away at a weekend conference, he would have to brief the chief constable on the event. 'I'll do that, and I'll also phone God and let her know.'

* * *

Obtaining the address from Binns had hardly been necessary. As Nash approached the outskirts of Thornscarr, the cluster of blue flashing lights illuminating through the trees would have guided him better than any directions. Even sat-nav couldn't have pinpointed the crime scene more accurately. A patrol car was parked on the main street, near the entrance to the lane, beyond which Nash thought he spotted DC Lisa Andrews' car. She lived closest to Thornscarr and had obviously headed straight there. Nash recognized a reporter from the *Netherdale Gazette* talking to another man he didn't know. 'Didn't take them long,' he muttered to himself.

After entering Nash's name on the log, an officer directed him along the track. Nash noted the property was on the Harland Estate. Not only that, he thought, but the cottage was only a short distance from the hotel where the fingers had been found.

He neared the cottage and saw two more gaudily-painted patrol cars had been pulled round so their headlights illuminated the front of the building. Nash pulled up behind and took his bag from the boot. He ducked under the incident tape and headed down the path to the front door, where two uniformed officers were standing. Both men looked pale, and the younger of the two appeared badly shaken.

'Have you seen DC Andrews?' Nash asked.

'Yes, sir. She's down the road looking after the kids who found this lot,' one of them replied. 'She's going to try and get them to tell her exactly what happened. Apparently she knows one of them, but they're both in such a hysterical state I doubt she'll get much sense from them. Not that I blame them for that,' the man added, jerking a thumb towards the building, 'not from what I saw in there.'

'Did DC Andrews go inside?'

'Only briefly.'

'Jack Binns only gave me the barest detail. Is it bad?'

'Oh yes, it's bad, right enough,' the older officer told him. 'It's the worst I've seen by a long chalk, even after twenty years dealing with RTAs and the mangled remains from them.'

'Right, I'd better get kitted out and have a look.' He took a protective suit from his bag and began to put it on. 'The pathologist and the CSI team should be arriving shortly, and I asked Binns to invite DC Pearce to the party. I wouldn't want him to feel left out.'

* * *

'Madre de Dios!' For Ramirez to lapse into Spanish, Nash thought, things were really bad. The pathologist looked up from where he was crouched in front of the bin liners. Shaking them to remove the last of their uninvited guests had been his first chore. He reverted to English. 'Whoever has done this is totally insane.'

'I'd sort of guessed that,' Nash acknowledged. He flinched and screwed up his face, not just at the spectacle in front of him, but at the appalling smell that accompanied the terrible sight. Even the decongestant smeared liberally beneath his nose behind his facemask did nothing to block the overpowering stench.

After viewing the crime scene for the first time, Nash had barred Pearce from entering what he had heard one of the constables refer to as 'Hell's Kitchen'. He'd found Pearce struggling into his protective suit and told him not to bother. He explained, pointing out that there would be less risk of contaminating the scene and adding that the fewer people forced to endure the grisly sight, the better. 'Believe me, Viv, you really don't want to see what's in there — or smell it, for that matter.' He hadn't noticed that the smell now permeated the air around the cottage.

Even the CSI expert who was taking the crime scene photos had emerged from the house to deposit a large portion of his evening meal into a rose bush before bracing himself to re-enter the building.

Instead, Nash told Pearce to go and help Lisa Andrews talk to the youngsters who had discovered the body. 'I want you to keep an eye on all three of them,' he explained.

Viv blinked in surprise. 'All three?'

'Lisa saw what was in there as much as the kids. More so, I guess, because she would have followed her training and checked the room over. I can only begin to imagine what they're going through. I've seen more than my fair share of revolting spectacles in my time, but I can't think of anything to equal the gruesome sight that's in there.'

'What about you? Will you be OK?'

'I'll have to be — that's what I'm paid for.'

He had just sent Pearce on his way when one of the CSI team approached him.

'This scene might look as if there would be plenty of trace evidence about, but I wouldn't hold your breath,' the forensics officer told the detective. 'Actually, I *would* hold your breath, but not in the way I meant it. Having given the room the once-over, all we've spotted is what appears to be a partial print on the table, but I doubt that it's going to be enough for a potential match; besides which, it could belong to one of the victims. I should warn you not to get impatient, because it could be a long job going through this lot. One thing that might be important is that there's no sign of forced entry other than the window that the kids used tonight, and it looks as if that had been left open. I believe that the only way the killer could have got into the house is with a key.'

'Is there any sign of someone living there? It is a holiday cottage, and although it's early season, there might have been a tenant.'

'Apart from what was in the kitchen, there was absolutely nothing to indicate that anyone has used the house. There were certainly no items of clothing or other personal possessions that you would expect if there was a sitting tenant.'

As he finished speaking, the pathologist emerged. Until Ramirez spoke, Nash assumed that he had merely come outside for a breath of fresh air. Not that he could be blamed for that. However, even if that had been his prime motive, he was also able to update Nash on his preliminary findings. 'There were four victims; all women in their twenties or thirties, by what I can piece together.'

'Is that a joke? If so, it's about the sickest I've ever heard.'

'Maybe you should contact the local toyshop,' Ramirez continued. 'I could do with a jigsaw expert to assist at the post-mortem.'

'If you've finished polishing your stand-up comedy routine, could you tell me if you found anything useful in there?' Nash asked pointedly.

The pathologist sighed. 'At first glance, I'm assuming dismemberment was achieved with the assistance of a chainsaw,' he explained. 'At a guess, I'd say that meant it was done during the daytime, when the noise would be less likely to attract attention. Judging by the blood spatter in that room, I'd suggest the victims might have been alive when they were operated on, but if they were, they must have been sedated heavily, perhaps with something that lowered the blood pressure dramatically before the killer commenced carving. Tests at the mortuary will confirm all this. Again, I'll have to do more work before I can establish when they were killed, but judging by the advanced stages of decomposition of at least two of them, I'd say they all died between one month and six months ago. In one case, possibly a little longer.'

He paused and stared at Nash for a while, his expression grave. 'I know you've had to deal with your fair share of evil characters since we've known one another, Mike, but watch out for this one. Based on what's inside there, it doesn't take a psychiatrist to work out that whoever is responsible is way off the charts as far as human behaviour is concerned. If you get close enough to tackle him, make sure you have all the protection and body armour you can put on. Either that, or talk to him from inside an armoured personnel carrier.'

It wasn't only the message that conveyed the depth of Ramirez' concern, but the fact that he'd used Nash's Christian name.

'Don't worry, I'll be extra careful.'

'Think of all the grieving women should anything happen to you. The funeral cortege would stretch for miles,' Ramirez added.

* * *

The attention of the driver approaching Thornscarr was attracted by the blue lights in the distance, much as Nash had been earlier. These had now been supplemented by emergency lights powered by generators.

He pulled his Land Rover to a halt and reversed into a field gateway to observe proceedings. As he stared towards the hamlet, he frowned with mild annoyance. He wondered briefly how the police had become alerted to the contents of the cottage. Not by a tenant, of that he was well aware. But, if not a tenant, who had told them?

That was of less importance than how the police operation would impinge on his plans. 'This rather alters things, my dear,' he murmured. His companion didn't answer or give any indication that she either heard or understood what he'd said.

'I hadn't counted on this. Obviously, someone has alerted the authorities to the presence of your colleagues. I'll have to come up with an alternative scheme. Let's call it Plan B, shall we?'

Again, the driver's comments failed to evoke a response. He pondered the unwelcome development for some time. It had been his intention to place all the remains in Track End Cottage, ensuring the activity ceased by the end of April, but this idea had now been thwarted. However, with all trace of the previous occupant's presence having gone, the remnants of the plan still remained in place — indeed, the pivotal section of the scheme could still work.

'Good news, my dear, all is not lost. That evil man who preys upon other people's property is still going to be blamed — and there is a measure of retribution in that. All we must do is to ensure suitable alternative arrangements can be made for you.'

He thought for a moment, and then added, 'I have the solution. I was concerned that you might be lonely, but my new idea will ensure that you'll still have company. Indeed, there is already someone waiting there to greet you — and I can easily find you more like-minded friends.'

Yet again the driver's remarks elicited no response. This was hardly surprising, as Samantha Frost had been dead for several days.

* * *

Nash waited outside Track End Cottage, pondering what the pathologist and forensics officer had told him. He had little doubt that the remains would prove to be the women who had gone missing over the past few months, but where was the fifth victim? His other immediate priority had to be identifying the person or persons who had keys to the property and had been able to gain entry without forcing a door or window. As the place was a holiday let, that would mean involving the estate management.

Nash got on his mobile and rang Jack Binns. 'I need you to contact the Harland Estate. I want the owner or estate manager here pronto, and I need them to bring details of anyone holding a key to this place. Forensics told me the doors and windows weren't forced, so the killer has to have access to a key.'

Ramirez rejoined Nash. 'I've done as much as I can inside there for the moment. I need my assistants.' The pathologist gestured towards the house as he ripped his gloves from his hands. 'I'll also need them to move the bodies to the mortuary, but that will have to wait until tomorrow at the earliest, when Scene of Crime has finished. I think it would be advisable for anyone who was unfortunate enough to view that scene to be referred for counselling, where they can be interviewed by a psychologist specializing in post-traumatic stress disorder. I'm particularly referring to those who came upon the horror without prior warning as to what to expect. That would include not only the kids who found the bodies, but those traffic officers who were first on scene, and DC Andrews. It might be that you will also need to talk to someone about it, but you were at least forewarned as to the ghastly nature of what was inside beforehand.'

'I'll be OK. I wouldn't say I was expecting anything this bad, but I had a growing suspicion that something terrible had happened to some women who had been reported missing. That being the case, identification could be conducted by DNA matching.'

'That would be advisable in any case, because I don't think any relative or acquaintance of these poor unfortunate souls should be compelled to witness the state of the remains. What can you tell me about the victims?'

'Actually, there have been five disappearances notified within the past seven months or so, all women of about the age you suggested, and all involved in the sex trade, which means that one victim still remains unaccounted for. That concerns me, as does the identity of the person responsible for all this. However, as the locks and windows weren't forced, we should have a reasonably short suspect list. That, in turn, should enable us to wrap up the whole sorry mess reasonably quickly. I'll get the MISPER files sent through to you as soon as I'm able, and then I'll have to start the process of identifying next of kin.'

He was still dwelling on this when Pearce returned. 'How's Lisa holding up?' Nash asked.

'Bloody well, judging by what she must have seen. She's just finishing up trying to question the kids who found the bodies, not that she's been able to get much sense from them. I think she wants to know what to do next. The girl's parents are at a show in Sheffield, so we can't contact them; their mobiles are off. The boy's mother works at Netherdale General, and Lisa's trying to get hold of her. She's met her before. Guess who the boy is?'

'This is no time for games, Viv.'

'You won't believe it. Lee, our young cameraman from the market muggers.'

Nash shrugged. 'Never mind that, we can work out why, and what they were up to, later. Get Lisa to take them both up to the General and meet his mother there. They're likely to be in shock and need checking over after what they've seen. Mexican Pete recommended it. I reckon it would be best for Lisa to be kept busy. There's bound to be a reaction, but if we can defer it, the outcome might be less traumatic.'

It was another two hours before Ramirez and his team left. Ramirez told Nash and Pearce, 'We'll be back first thing. I'll keep you posted as to when the PMs will be. Unfortunately, regulations still require an officer to be present during the process, but I'll leave it to you to decide who should have that unpleasant duty. It might be sensible not to place the onus on one person, though.'

There was still no sign of anyone from the Harland Estate when the pathologist left, and Nash was becoming irritated by the delay. Five minutes later, Nash and Pearce saw the approaching headlights of a vehicle travelling quickly, either governed by familiarity with the country lane or by the urgency of the situation, or possibly both. Moments later, a Land Rover Discovery pulled up alongside Nash's car and a man emerged, heading directly towards the waiting detectives. As he walked across to them, Nash noticed that he was carrying a folder, and guessed his identity even before he spoke.

'Inspector Nash?' the newcomer enquired. 'I'm Louis Craven. I'm the estate manager. Sorry it's taken me so long to get here. I was out and have only just picked up the message and rang the station. Your officer told me something about what happened here. What exactly went on?'

'I can't tell you much, but suffice it to say that human remains have been found inside the cottage.'

'That's absolutely appalling. What can I do to help?'

'I need details of anyone who had a key to the property. That includes estate employees, present or former tenants, plus any tradesmen who have worked inside the building.'

'That's simple enough. There is one key that remains permanently locked in a safe in my office. That key only leaves there when work is required to be carried out on the interior. Before I came here, I checked my records, and the last time that happened was over eighteen months ago. Work was planned to start on refurbishment next month, but that's been cancelled. The only other key is that used by the renters, usually only for one or two weeks at a time. Although I suppose someone could have had a spare cut,' he added.

He opened his folder and produced a sheet of paper. 'That's a list of the holidaymakers who rented the cottage during the course of last summer, but they all returned the key. At present, that key is in the possession of the current occupant.'

'There is someone renting the cottage at present?' Nash glanced at Pearce. 'The place looks unoccupied.'

'There certainly is; name of Barton, Donny Barton. He's an artist by profession. We check our tenants out beforehand to establish that they are bona fide. He rented the cottage from last October, took a long lease. His tenancy is due to terminate at the end of this month.' Craven delved into the folder again and took out a couple of sheets of paper. He handed these to Nash, 'Those are Mr Barton's details, including his home address in London, plus a copy of the tenancy agreement.'

Nash examined the papers, with Pearce looking over his shoulder as he held a torch for them to read by. 'Thank you, Mr Craven,' Nash told the manager. 'There is one other question I have to ask you, but perhaps it would be easier when you've had chance to consult your diary. There are certain relevant dates on which I need to know your whereabouts.' He saw Craven's horrified expression and explained, 'These are purely for elimination purposes, as you hold one of the only two keys to the cottage.'

'When are you thinking of?' Craven's harassed look hadn't diminished, despite Nash's reassurance.

'There are several, all within the past seven months. Going from memory, one is during February or early March, another sometime in January. The rest I'm unsure of without my file.'

'It depends when exactly in February and March you're talking about,' Craven replied. If he looked more relaxed, it was barely noticeable as he continued, 'I was on holiday in Barbados sometime around then. If you let me have those dates and any others, I'll check my diary for them as well.'

Nash thanked the estate manager, and before he left, told him, 'The cottage will remain a crime scene for the foreseeable future, so if you have any tenancies lined up, it might be advisable to suggest that the potential lessees find alternative accommodation. Not that anyone will want to stay here for some while, I guess, given the publicity that's sure to surround the place.'

'Fortunately, we haven't arranged for any early season lettings. As I explained, work was planned. What should we do about securing the property?'

'Uniformed officers will remain at the premises for several days. Although our forensics team have conducted a preliminary search of the property, they will be carrying out more in-depth investigations, and during that time the cottage will remain a no-go area. It might be as well to let them have your key, and we can ensure it is locked up until such time as we release it to you and you can arrange for cleaners to come in, followed by decorators. You might also want to ensure pest control inspectors are on hand to deal with the extensive rodent and insect population.'

Craven's expression reflected the horror of what he had just learned. As Nash and Pearce watched him climb into his vehicle and drive away, Pearce murmured, 'There goes an unhappy man. I guess he's planning how best to tell his employer about what's gone on here. Still, the Barbados alibi would seem to discount him, which only leaves us with Donny Barton.'

'I'm not taking anything for granted,' Nash replied. 'It's interesting that the vehicle Mr Craven drives is similar to the one on that CCTV image, so I definitely don't think we should rule him out just yet. Overall, though, you're probably right. Barton seems to be our prime suspect, so we need to find out all we can about him.'

CHAPTER EIGHTEEN

It was almost dawn by the time Nash pulled up outside Helmsdale Police Station. He wasn't in the slightest bit surprised to see all the station's lights on; nor was he taken aback when he noticed the chief constable's car alongside the building. O'Donnell was in the reception area talking to Sergeant Binns when Nash entered. They both looked at Nash, concern in their eyes.

'It's about as bad as you can imagine, and then a whole lot more,' he told them, in answer to the chief's enquiry. 'So much so, that I ordered the youngsters who made the discovery to be taken to hospital. Professor Ramirez advised it. He also stated that the two traffic officers who responded to the call should be referred to the police welfare medic. It's precautionary, but he suggests they will all need counselling. I sent Lisa Andrews with the teenagers and said she should also arrange to speak to someone.'

'What about you, Mike? You must have seen as much as the others, more so, probably.'

'I have two advantages; first and foremost, I've seen far more of that kind of thing. Although, I have to admit, rarely as bad as this one. And, thanks to Jack here, I was forewarned what to expect. My only concern is getting this bastard locked up and out of harm's way before any other women are attacked. By what I saw at the cottage, this guy is a total psychopath. I think we'll find he's UTP,' he added, shaking his head.

'Unfit to plead? We'll let the lawyers and doctors fight over that. We've got to find him first,' the chief replied.

'It would help enormously if he's on our system, but I suppose that's too much to hope for, especially as, thus far, Forensics have only come up with a partial print, which they're not confident will be sufficient to identify anyone. However, they've the rest of the house to go at yet. By the sound of it, there seems to be one outstanding suspect.'

Nash explained about the missing tenant, Donny Barton. He'd just finished speaking when Pearce walked in.

'Good morning, ma'am,' he greeted the chief, before turning to Nash. 'It's a good job the traffic guys were otherwise engaged, otherwise you might have collected a ticket.'

'I was in a hurry,' Nash said briefly, almost curtly. He didn't notice O'Donnell look sharply at him, but told Pearce, 'Get on the computer and find out all you can about Donny Barton: age, address, occupation, what car he drives, relatives, the works. I know Craven told us Barton was an artist, but that might have simply been a front.'

Pearce looked taken aback at Nash's response. 'Yes, boss.'

O'Donnell waited until Pearce had gone up to CID then told Binns, 'I could murder a coffee, Jack. Would you make me one, please?'

No sooner had Binns departed when the chief constable rounded on Nash. 'Are you lying, Mike? Did this affect you more than you're prepared to admit? Because your attitude to Viv, just now, was most unlike you.'

Nash shook his head, puzzled by her question. 'No, it's not that, ma'am; put it down to sleep deficiency. I know the cure, though. As soon as this is over and done with, and after Daniel's back at school, I'd like some time off. There's something I need to sort out.'

He didn't offer an explanation, and before O'Donnell could ask what he was referring to, they were interrupted by Binns, who returned bearing two coffee mugs. No sooner had he handed them their drinks than the phone rang. He listened for a long time, during which they could tell more than one person was speaking, then said, 'OK, I'll tell him — and the chief constable.'

Eventually, he put the receiver down. 'That was Alan Marshall, Lisa's partner; well, it was until she took over the conversation. Apparently she spent most of the night at the hospital comforting the teenagers who found the bodies and attempting to reassure their parents. When she told Alan everything about where and why, he insisted she stay home and rest. She was in bed when he rang. That was until she heard him on the phone and took it from him. She's coming in, because as she put it, "Mike and Viv need all the help they can get at the minute. My personal feelings can be put on hold. Above all, we have to get this psycho behind bars. No woman is safe, whether she's a prostitute, housewife, or police officer". Then she handed the phone back to Alan. He said you might have the courage to argue with her, but he doesn't.'

'What about the teenagers who found the bodies?' O'Donnell asked.

'According to what she just told me, it took two hours before the girl's parents arrived. Control passed word to the Arena and they put a call out for them. Security explained to them why they were needed. The boy's mother was already there and Lisa had been able to contact her straightaway. She was working on the night shift in A and E, but she still got a hell of a shock when her son was brought in and when she saw the state of him and the girl.'

'What were they doing breaking into that place? They surely didn't think there was anything worth stealing?' the chief asked.

Nash smiled. 'No, apparently, they needed a secluded spot for an evening of passion.'

Binns nodded. 'The irony is, from what Lisa just told me, after she spoke to both sets of parents, it doesn't seem as if they'd have been overly concerned if the pair had been doing it at home. They are both of age. From what the girl's mother told Lisa, they'd already guessed that it was only a matter of time before the youngsters became intimate. They were less concerned than would otherwise have been the case, because the two had been friends for such a long time that they knew it would be much more than a casual fling. The girl's mother said she was much happier thinking that when Milly became involved with someone it was with a nice lad like Lee, rather than some tearaway who might be into booze or drugs. The boy's mother said much the same about Milly.'

'Lucky for us the kids weren't aware of that,' Nash pointed out. 'That holiday cottage doesn't have a booking for when Barton's lease is up. Without an inspection, if it stayed empty until June, say, the killer could have filled every room in the house with body parts.'

'Right,' O'Donnell told them, 'I'm going to leave you to get on with things. As Superintendent Fleming has swanned off on this conference lark, keep me up-dated on any developments. I'm ordering Jackie to come back early.' She glanced at the clock and frowned. 'However, I'll leave that until a less antisocial hour. I suggest you speak to Lisa Andrews when she gets here, make sure she's OK,' O'Donnell added. 'And if you're not one hundred per cent happy, pack her off home, understand?'

She headed for the door, without so much as a farewell, leaving the two men staring at each other.

* * *

The morning was spent checking computer records regarding the missing tenant of Track End Cottage, Donny Barton, who was now their only suspect. Their searches resulted in a quick briefing Nash held over the phone with the chief constable. After confirming that Barton was still their sole person of interest, Nash said, 'Despite the evidence so far, there are some anomalies that I'm not happy about. A couple of these arise from what we discovered at the crime scene, another from the results of our computer inquiries.'

'OK, Mike, tell me what you know about this man so far and your concerns.'

'Barton is a reasonably well-known landscape artist. Certainly not a Constable or Gauguin, but quite popular, judging by the prices his work fetch.'

O'Donnell was aware that Nash was reasonably well versed in the artistic field, but knowing that this was a touchy subject, still remarked, 'Well you would know.'

Nash was momentarily taken aback at her comment, but continued, 'Barton specializes in landscapes set on the continent, and in particular, around the Mediterranean, mostly depicting village life. That does raise the question as to what he was doing in North Yorkshire, I suppose. However, it also makes me wonder that if he is the killer, why someone with a seemingly good level of intelligence should fail to cover his tracks so completely.'

'You're going to have to explain that, Mike.'

'What I mean is that if he was intending to use the cottage as a slaughterhouse, why did he use his own name and personal details instead of assuming an alias?'

'It could well be that he took the tenancy with no intention of committing murder, but somewhere along the line he could have suffered some form of traumatic incident. I believe they call it a psychotic break. What else have you discovered?'

At that moment Pearce entered Nash's office, waving a piece of paper at him. 'Mike, Mike.'

'Excuse me a moment, ma'am, Viv seems to have found something.' He covered the mouthpiece. 'What have you got?'

'Barton has an agent, I've just spoken to him. Barton told everyone he was going to Cornwall.'

Nash returned to his conversation with the chief and explained what Viv had said. 'I think that adds more to our suspicions. We have his permanent address. It's an apartment block in West London, so it might be an idea to ask our colleagues in the Met to do a home visit. If, as we suspect, Barton isn't there, they should be able to gain entry with the cooperation of the landlord, but that will probably require a search warrant. If they do that, I'd like them to take a forensic officer along. It would be extremely helpful to have a set of Barton's fingerprints.'

'What you're really saying is that you want me to set this up.'

'It would certainly carry more weight coming from you, ma'am, and thanks for offering.'

Nash grinned as he heard the chief constable mutter what sounded like, 'smooth-talking devil'. But more clearly, she responded, 'You mentioned concerns, which I assume means that the use of Barton's own name isn't the only one.'

'Certainly not, ma'am, there are two other matters I find puzzling. One of them is the shortage in the body count.'

He heard O'Donnell spluttering before she said, 'Shortage? What do you mean, "shortage"? Isn't four corpses enough for you? Is Ramirez right about your Dracula complex?'

'Not if, as I suspect, the victims turn out to be the missing prostitutes from this region. We have five extant MISPER cases — so where is the fifth body?'

'I don't think that's necessarily anything to be alarmed about. Quite obviously, the fifth victim was murdered and her body dumped elsewhere — if indeed there is a fifth victim and she hasn't simply done a runner, moved to another area, or become victim to some other crime.'

'Any of those could be true,' Nash conceded. 'But I have one more overriding concern, and that is the matter of transport. I can't understand how Barton achieved it — if he actually is the murderer. I'm speaking of the abductions and the bringing of the victims to that remote location and if he did dispose of one elsewhere, how did he do it?'

'I don't follow you. Explain it in simple terms.'

There was a testy edge to the chief constable's voice which showed she didn't share Nash's concerns. 'According to what Pearce found from his computer research with DVLA, Donny Barton doesn't own a motor vehicle of any type; never has done, and doesn't even possess a driving licence.'

'Inspector Nash, if this man is happily going around abducting women, slaughtering them and cutting them up into little pieces, I certainly don't think stealing a car or driving without a licence is going to hold any terror for him.'

'Again, I go back to his supposed intelligence. Nobody in their right mind is going to ride around the countryside in a stolen vehicle without a driving licence, with a woman's body and a bloodstained chainsaw in the boot.'

'I absolutely disagree. We've already had ample evidence that this character is definitely *not* in their right mind, so I think those reservations you hold are totally spurious. Just to put you fully in the picture, I'm waiting for Superintendent Fleming to return today. She's left the conference and should be back soon. I intend to discuss this case with her, your reservations included, and if she's of the same opinion as me, I think we should get hold of a photo of Barton as soon as possible. Obviously not from his driving licence, as he doesn't have one, but if he's been roaming the continent painting, he must hold a current passport. Then I intend to hold a press conference to go public, announcing him as our prime suspect. I'm planning that media event tomorrow, and I want you to attend.'

'I'm afraid you'll have to excuse me from that, ma'am.'

'Why? Because you don't agree with our actions?'

'Not entirely, ma'am, more because I already have a date. As of eight thirty tomorrow morning, I'll be playing jigsaws with Professor Ramirez.'

'Jigsaws? Did you say jigsaws?' There was a pause before O'Donnell realized what Nash was referring to. 'I see. You're attending the post-mortems. Then deputize someone else to do that.'

'I could, but I'm not going to. As the senior officer in this case, it's not fair to expose either of my subordinates to a further harrowing experience such as the sight of those dismembered corpses. That would not be good leadership, passing the most unpleasant tasks to someone else.'

'Well in that case, we'll just have to manage without you.'

Nash was surprised at her attitude, but asked, 'I'd be obliged if you can inform me when the Met have visited Barton's flat. I've no doubt that won't happen until tomorrow, but for today, I'm about to pack Andrews and Pearce off home. Once they've gone, I'm going to write up my report, and then I've arranged to visit Thornscarr. The CSI team are there, going through the rest of the house.'

* * *

Despite Lisa and Viv's protests, Nash insisted that they take the rest of the day off. 'You've already lost the best part of the weekend; better to make sure it isn't completely wasted. Tomorrow morning, I want you both to concentrate on finding blood relatives of those missing women. We will need to contact them in order to provide DNA samples for comparison purposes, so getting their location will be a good start. We need to know if they can provide a recent photograph.'

He saw the look of disbelief on their faces. 'For the file. It wouldn't help identify them, but they don't need to know that. Oh, and check if the women had any distinguishing marks, tattoos and the like. One more thing, if Jack Binns is still downstairs when you leave, tell him to sling his hook as well. I'm quite capable of locking up.'

When Nash reached home it was early evening. He took a frozen pizza out and stuck it in the oven, far too weary to attempt anything more challenging. Given the loss of a full night's sleep, he felt certain once he got to bed he'd be dead to the world, but it didn't happen that way. All night, he was tormented by dreams, governed by the gruesome discoveries he'd had to witness.

Next morning he was up and about early, despite feeling jaded and stale. He took a much-needed shower and shave, shuddered at the thought of breakfast, and set off for Netherdale General Hospital. He parked at the rear of the building outside the mortuary that now contained the remains of all the butchered victims. With a few minutes to spare before Ramirez was due to conduct the post-mortems, Nash took the opportunity to phone his superintendent, Jackie Fleming.

'The CSI boys went over the rest of the house and lifted a load of fingerprints, some of which I feel sure will belong to Barton,' he told her.

'We should be able to confirm that soon, Mike. The Met are making an urgent application for a search warrant for Barton's flat. Given the gravity of the case, they're making it a high priority. Once they've lifted prints from the flat, they're going to email them straight to our Forensic department.'

Nash told her about his instructions to Andrews and Pearce to find families of the missing women. 'Mexican Pete said we should use DNA to identify the victims. There's no other way an ID could be made. We certainly can't allow them to view those remains. Some don't even look human.'

Jackie Fleming shuddered. 'Having just read the report you emailed me, I quite agree. It read like an excerpt from a Gothic horror novel. Will you be OK attending the post-mortems?'

'I have to be. I explained as much to the chief, but I'm not sure she agreed with me.'

'I don't think she did, but I do.'

'I'll have to go, Jackie. Mexican Pete's just arrived.'

* * *

Out of habit, Nash switched his phone off during the post-mortem examinations. When he emerged late in the afternoon, following completion of the second procedure, he immediately switched the mobile back on and called

Helmsdale CID. 'How are things going, Viv?' he asked Pearce.

'So far, we've succeeded in locating blood relatives of three out of the five missing women. Lisa's still working on the others. How are you doing with the post-mortem marathon?'

'Mexican Pete's managed two so far. He's called it a draw for today. His excuse is that he's getting backache, but I think it's more emotional overload for both him and his assistants. I've never seen him this distressed before, even though he's had some bad stuff to deal with. He said there's no rush as they're not recent deaths. The fact that that each of the bodies was in a separate bag made it easier to assemble the parts. And the matching decomposition of the heads enabled him to marry them up along with the angle of the cut on the neck. As for ID, he's extracted DNA, and we've now got height and hair colour for each victim.'

'How about you, Mike? How are you bearing up?'

'I'm OK. Fortunately, my interpretation of the regulations came to my assistance.'

'How do you mean? I don't understand that.'

'The regulations stipulate that a police officer has to be present at any autopsy. It doesn't say that they have to watch — or listen.'

'That's a point worth knowing, Mike. Actually, I was about to message you with a video clip I downloaded onto my phone, but if you're coming back here, I can show you it when you arrive.'

'I'll be back in half an hour or so. Have you heard anything from Jackie?'

Surprisingly, Pearce laughed.

'What's funny?' Nash asked.

'I think she's been a bit too busy to talk to us. That's part of the video clip. I was going to caption it *Media Circus* if I'd sent it. The majority of it is footage of the media conference the chief held at eleven o'clock this morning. I'd best describe it as a shambles.'

'That bad is it?'

'Bad, and a bit worse, if you get me. I think you'll particularly enjoy the part when God was asked why you weren't there. Her reply was that you had other matters to attend to. She didn't sound or look very happy as she said it, made it sound as if you were investigating a petty theft instead of concentrating on the murders.'

'She's so convinced Barton's the killer that she wouldn't listen to the flaws in her theory. I was pondering calling in at HQ, but after what you've told me, I'll head straight back.'

CHAPTER NINETEEN

Nash was almost at the outskirts of Helmsdale when his mobile rang. This should be interesting,' he muttered when his caller display showed the identity of the person.

He pressed answer on the dashboard. 'Hello, Becks,' he greeted her, using his pet name for Becky Pollard, his former lover, and now a long-term friend who was editor of the *Netherdale Gazette*. 'What can I do for you today? Do you want an update on the region's crime statistics, or is it a social call?'

'Give over, Mike, you know as well as I do why I'm calling. Aunt Gloria implied you've lost the plot, and I wanted to get your slant on things before I publish.'

'That's good of you, but if you write an article giving my take on things, your godmother might not approve. It's happened once before, if you remember. And you know I won't discuss details with you.'

The fact that the chief constable was Becky's godmother had often proved difficult from both sides of the fence, and had once caused a major upset. 'I'll take that risk, Mike. Is it true that you were off investigating other crimes when the press conference was on?'

'No, I was busy watching Mexican Pete.'

'Oh, you were the attending officer at the autopsies, were you?'

'Correct, but obviously that didn't rate a mention.'

'You must have upset her. What did you say that she took exception to? You're usually her blue-eyed boy.'

'I told her I didn't agree with her. That I'm far from convinced that Barton is the murderer. She doesn't take kindly to people defying her, and so she more or less told me I was talking nonsense. I advised against going public with so much emphasis on one man, but she'd have none of it.'

'Here's what I'll do. I'll write the article myself and email it to you in an hour or so for your approval. Could I go far enough to insinuate that there might be a dissenting voice among the officers involved in the investigation?'

'Why not? If what I hear about the media conference is correct, that's already been implied.'

Becky laughed and rang off. Minutes later, Nash joined his colleagues in CID, where he watched the recorded media conference with dismay. Although he might have been most upset by the oblique inference that he was other than convinced of Barton's guilt, he was more concerned that both O'Donnell and Fleming seemed to have pinned their faith to the mast of this one suspect. 'I think Gloria's just struck me off her Christmas card list,' he muttered.

The rest of the clip Pearce had recorded was the lunch-time news, which, as well as containing footage of the media briefing, also showed a photo of Barton, whom the anchor said the police wanted to question as a matter of urgency. The reporter also stressed members of the public were warned not to approach him.

At that moment, the phone in Nash's office rang. He signalled Lisa to answer it, commenting, 'I haven't returned from Netherdale yet.'

She returned a couple of minutes later with a message from Jackie Fleming. 'The Met obtained a warrant for Barton's flat this morning and searched the place. They lifted several sets of identical prints, which they assume to be Barton's, but nothing else pertinent to the enquiry. The prints have been emailed to our forensic team for comparison.'

'OK, here's what I want you to do. Phone Jackie back in ten minutes or so and tell her that just after she rang, I called in. Say that I was deeply upset by the autopsies and that I was going home and wasn't to be disturbed — by anyone or anything. You can say that the pathology showed the two victims examined so far showed signs of prolonged drug abuse and high levels of sexual activity, which tends to confirm our belief as to their identity. You can add that I have to go back tomorrow for the other two examinations, following which, if I feel up to it, I will be contactable — but not before.'

Nash waited a moment while Lisa absorbed what he'd told her, then turned to Pearce. 'Viv, you know one of our CSI blokes quite well, don't you? I mean apart from work, isn't he a neighbour or something?'

'That's right. In fact, I was talking to Alf only a few days ago.' Pearce grinned. 'He was complaining that he couldn't sneak home for lunch in the CSI van while I was on leave, in case I caught him skiving.'

'OK, give him a bell and ask what they can reveal about the prints at Barton's flat, and how they compare with the bloodstained partial taken from what one of our uniformed men referred to as Hell's Kitchen.'

Nash listened to Andrews repeating the message he'd given her for Fleming. After ending the call, Lisa told Nash, 'Jackie says she quite understands, now that she's seen photos of the crime scene.'

Ten minutes later, just after Nash had finished reading Becky Pollard's email to him, and sent his approval to the draft of the article that would appear in next morning's paper, Pearce reported back on his conversation with the scientific officer.

Nash looked at Pearce, who appeared to be containing his laughter as he said, 'Do you think the chief might be interested in a recipe if I can find one for her?'

Both Nash and Lisa looked puzzled, until Pearce continued, 'I think she'll need one for humble pie when she gets the preliminary forensic report. I managed to contact Alf, and, assuming the prints lifted by the Met from Barton's flat are his, they match those taken from the sitting room and bedroom at Track End Cottage. However, according to what Alf said, there is absolutely no similarity between Barton's prints and the bloodstained partial found in the kitchen. He went on to talk about whorls and loops and stuff that I only vaguely understood, but there was sufficient to provide a match had they been at all like Barton's. By the look of it, I'd say you were right, Mike, and that Barton isn't the killer.'

* * *

It was with real reluctance that Nash drove to Netherdale early the following morning. His attendance at the mortuary owed less to his position as a police officer than a sense of duty towards the victims of the butchery. In Nash's eyes, it was his responsibility to give them what closure could be achieved by bringing their killer to justice. He'd scarcely parked the Range Rover in anticipation of Ramirez' arrival when he was surprised to see a car he recognized as that driven by Superintendent Fleming pull into the small parking area, closely followed by the pathologist's vehicle.

'I know you're "not contactable",' she said as they headed through the door, 'but I decided it might ease the pressure if I attended the autopsies with you. It might seem like nothing more than a bit of moral support, and that is how I described it to the chief constable, but in reality, there are matters I think we should discuss, and I thought this would be the ideal opportunity, away from prying eyes and ears. There will be plenty of time while the procedures are being carried out.'

Ramirez interrupted at that point, emerging from the small changing room clad in the olive green protective clothing he once described to Nash as his business suit. 'I got my assistants to come in early and remove the victims from the drawers. The remains have been laid out on separate tables, so that should give us a good head start.'

Nash groaned. 'Not more dreadful puns, please.'

'I enjoy seeing you wince,' Ramirez retorted. 'Nothing else seems to upset you.'

Nash was curious as to what Fleming wanted to talk to him about, and even more by the need for secrecy. He refrained from asking questions until they were in the inspection area, shielded from the worst of the macabre activity taking place on the other side of the glass screen, then he asked Jackie what was on her mind.

'I have several concerns I wanted to discuss with you,' she began, for once seeming to be slightly at a loss as to how to put her thoughts into words.

'About this case, you mean?'

'Not only that, although I admit these murders have highlighted the issue in rather dramatic fashion. I appreciate that with you being at Helmsdale you have less direct contact with the chief constable than I do. I talk to her on a daily basis, whereas you might only see her twice or three times every month, barring crises. However, in a sense, that places you at an advantage. Let me ask you directly, Mike, have you noticed any changes in her attitude or behaviour?'

'I'd certainly say this past few days' performance could be classed as a fairly dramatic shift in attitude,' Nash replied. 'And on one or two other occasions, I've sensed that she's rather more impatient and less tolerant than usual. Apart from that, as you said, I don't come in regular enough contact to be able to form an accurate opinion. I assume from your question that you have observed changes that have given you cause to worry.'

'I have, and the ones I've seen represent exactly those traits you outlined. But it was only with the events of the past couple of days that my anxiety about her increased dramatically, culminating in a conversation we had after the report came through regarding the fingerprints at Thornscarr.'

'I know the results seem to indicate that Barton didn't commit the murders,' Nash told her. 'Pearce has a friend in CSI who was involved in the analysis, so we got the results yesterday, probably before you did.'

'I agree that the findings seem to exonerate Barton, but that isn't the way Gloria sees it. She insists that they do not put Barton out of the running, but show instead that he was still deeply involved and that he acted with an accomplice. When I attempted to argue with her, she flew into a rage and accused you of poisoning my mind against her, despite me telling her that I hadn't spoken to you directly since I returned from that conference. When she told me she'd set up the media conference, she said you'd point blank refused to attend because you weren't prepared to admit that your theory was wrong and wouldn't acknowledge that Barton was the culprit.'

'That's definitely not the way it happened. She sprang this media conference idea on me on Sunday, at which point I outlined my concerns about Barton's guilt. She then ordered me to attend the briefing anyway, but by then I'd already committed to coming here.'

'Yes, that's what she told me when I got back, yet only twenty-four hours later, she's spinning the whole story in a totally different direction. Now you can understand why I'm worried.'

'I concede that there is a remote possibility that Barton could be involved along with an accomplice, but given the nature of these murders, I think it's highly unlikely. There have been instances of two totally depraved characters getting together to commit heinous crimes such as these,' — Nash gestured to the work being carried out beyond the glass — 'but far more often, they're the work of one psychopath acting alone.'

'I agree. But when I tried to ask the chief to specify what your concerns were about Barton, she went off on one and told me if I wanted to side with you, I'd better ask you.' Fleming paused before adding, 'So that's the real reason I'm here, not to side with you specifically, but to ask what you believe to be the flaws in the Barton culprit theory.'

Nash outlined his thoughts much as he had presented them to the chief constable, but this time to a much more sympathetic audience.

'I need to think this over,' Jackie told him. 'It's a very tricky situation we're in. Normally, I'd say let's go to the pub and thrash it out, but that scarcely seems appropriate. Give me a while to digest all the implications.'

Nash didn't reply, and when Fleming glanced at him, looking for a response or some sign that he'd heard her comments, she noticed that he had that familiar, faraway expression on his face. Something she'd said, or something he'd repeated, or perhaps even something he'd witnessed in the mortuary had triggered a train of thought, and she knew better than to interrupt. Along with her colleagues, Fleming was aware that often, when he appeared to be daydreaming, Nash later emerged with facts or theories that would lead to a case being solved. She wandered a couple of yards away and attempted to compose her own thoughts.

The pathologist's prediction about the shortened timescale of the procedures proved correct, and they emerged soon after lunchtime into the pale sunlight of a cold April day.

As they walked across the car park to their vehicles, Fleming spoke; the first time either of them had said anything since Nash had outlined his reservations about Barton's guilt. 'Having heard your side of the story, and with the benefit of the fingerprint evidence, I'm convinced that your theory is the correct one. Like you, I don't believe Barton acted with an accomplice, and that means we'll have to start looking for someone totally different. But the question is, where do we go from here? We can't simply act in direct defiance of Chief O'Donnell's orders.'

'Although Barton might not be the murderer, we still need to account for him,' Nash pointed out. 'He disappeared as completely as those poor women, leaving the cottage he'd rented without a trace of him ever occupying it apart from those fingerprints. That being so, the chief's nationwide hunt for him is as equally relevant as a missing person as it would be if he was a murder suspect, and the media coverage could be extremely useful in our efforts to locate him.'

Nash paused to allow Fleming time to digest this before changing tack slightly. 'As for trying to track the guilty party, there's absolutely nothing wrong with pursuing a different line of enquiry. Simply because we have what, in the chief's eyes, is a prime suspect doesn't prevent us from exploring other avenues of investigation, or lead us to ignore other potential culprits. I admit that as things stand we're faced with the difficulty that there are no such candidates, but that's partly due to this being the early stages of our inquiry, and we haven't been given the opportunity to look elsewhere. Doing so wouldn't be running contrary to the chief's orders; it would simply be good police procedure. At present, for example, although we have suspicions as to the identity of the victims, we have no concrete proof that these are four of the five missing prostitutes, and until we follow up on Viv and Lisa's work in tracing their relatives by obtaining DNA, we can't even dignify them with their real names.'

'I agree with everything you've said, Mike. But that leads me back to my original question, how do we proceed from here?'

'I've been dwelling on that while we were in there, and I have a couple of ideas, one of which I have to thank you for. I believe our priority should be to get those DNA samples. In the meantime, I'm off to the pub tonight.'

Fleming stared at him in astonishment. Nash wasn't a great drinker; that she knew, and such behaviour was most unlike him. She began to wonder if the chief constable's intransigence was contagious. Nash saw her surprise and grinned. 'Don't worry, the case hasn't turned me into an alcoholic overnight. Your mention of a pub sparked a memory, so I'm going to seek out an old friend who might have some interesting background material. Whether my research will yield anything pertinent or be simply a wild goose chase is open to doubt, but last time I saw him, he mentioned a couple of facts that have roused my curiosity.'

'Good enough. I'll leave you to get on with it, but keep me in the loop if you do find anything worthwhile. In the meantime I'll ask Andrews and Pearce to get those samples ASAP.'

* * *

The local news bulletin was on TV, and one of the room's two occupants was watching with rapt attention as the details of the events at Track End Cottage unfolded. The media conference footage was followed by an image of Donny Barton's face, ironically culled from the artist's own website, to which, in addition to the caption entitled 'The man police want to interview'. The anchor described Barton as a "well-known artist who is believed to be the prime suspect in the gruesome murders of at least four women. The artist rented the cottage for a six-month period late last year and hasn't been seen since then."

As the bulletin changed to another topic, the viewer switched the set off. 'I know it isn't perfect,' he told his companion, 'but it's the best I could have wished for in the circumstances, don't you think?'

She failed to respond, and to be fair, he no longer expected her to. He'd become used to Samantha ignoring him ever since he'd brutally raped and strangled her. He walked over to where she was lying on the settee, as if asleep, and noticed with satisfaction that the effects of rigor mortis had worn off. 'I think it's time for your operation, my dear,' he told her. 'I know you're going to be a bit cut up about it, but it can't be helped.'

He giggled slightly at his pun before continuing, 'Storage has become such a problem since the police put a stop to me using my last venue. But then,' he added reflectively, 'come to think of it, storage has always been something of a concern round here.'

CHAPTER TWENTY

It was shortly after eight o'clock when Nash reached The Miners Arms, but he was still there before Jonas Turner. The old man Nash wanted to talk to arrived only a few minutes later, by which time the detective had already ordered him a pint and purchased a packet of crisps. Turner's dog, whose sense of smell had not declined with advancing years, detected Nash's presence immediately and deserted his owner, knowing that the friend would have some form of tasty sustenance for him.

By the time Turner joined Nash at his usual seat at the table by the window, the terrier was already munching his way through a handful of crisps thoughtfully provided for his enjoyment.

'By gum, Mr Nash, ah'm reet surprised t' see thee 'ere,' Turner greeted him, 'be what ah 'eard and saw on t' telly, I thought thee'd be up t' thy armpits in corpses, not sittin' 'ere swiggin' a pint. What's going on up t' road, then?' Turner accompanied the question with a gesture in the general direction of Thornscarr.

Nash shrugged. 'There's not a lot I'm allowed to say, Jonas, except what you might have gathered from the news. I will say that it has to be one of the most horrific and gruesome cases I've ever had to deal with. You'll have heard where those corpses were found, no doubt?'

Turner nodded. 'Aye, somewhere in Thornscarr, weren't it? Funny we were only talkin' abaht the place a week or so back. Mind you,' he added, 'there's little 'u'd surprise me abaht yon spot. A rum hole at best o' times.' He leaned forward and lowered his voice to little more than a whisper as he asked, 'Is it true they were all chopped t' bits?'

Nash shook his head. 'I can't comment one way or the other, Jonas. Let me explain why I wanted a word with you. Last time we were talking, you mentioned something horrible that happened up there a while back, a suicide, I think you said, but you left out all the details. Would you care to elaborate on that?'

'Aye, well it were twenty years or so since. It were another rum do; but then the bloke as topped hissen were a weird sort o' character.'

'Tell me more.' Nash encouraged the old man, listening intently as he continued feeding the Jack Russell with crisps.

Turner eyed him with suspicion. 'Is this what they call professional interest or just a load o' gossip?'

Nash smiled. 'Maybe a little of both, Jonas. How did you mean when you said the guy who committed suicide was a strange bloke?'

'Aaron Nelson his name were — 'is missus were a reet eyeful, made me wonder what she saw in 'im, but then she 'ad other things t' think abaht. Anyroad, story were that she upped and buggered off wi' a fancy man. After she'd gone, Aaron couldn't thoile to be on his tod wit' young un t' mind. It got too much for 'im, an' he stuck a .12 bore in his gob and pulled trigger.'

'Oh, very messy.'

'Aye, well, young Elijah, Aaron's kid, found t' body when 'e came home from school. That's tale as went the rounds and t' coroner were obviously happy abaht it, cos 'e ruled it as suicide, but ah reckon there were a bit more to it than that.'

'You don't think it was suicide?'

'Oh aye, 'e topped hissen reet enough. It were t' rest o' t' yarn I 'ad me doubts on.'

'What do mean by that?'

Turner scratched one ear reflectively as he thought about the best way to put it. 'What puzzled me then, and allus 'as, is 'ow come nobody's seen 'ide nor 'air of Elijah's mother since the day Aaron told everyone she'd scarpered wi' 'er fancy man. That were weird too, almost like 'e were trying t' convince folk that were what 'appened.'

'You think something else went on?'

'I dunno.' Turner looked at Nash slyly. 'I'm not a detective same as thee. Ah never gave it much of a thought till ah started talking wi' Elijah's missus. She told me Elijah's never 'eard or seen 'is mum either. Now that's not reet. She were fond enough o' t' lad when 'e were a nipper, so ah'd 'ave thought she'd 'ave come running when she learned what happened to 'is father, wouldn't you?'

'It seems logical. You said it was the son Elijah's wife you were chatting to. I take it he still lives round here.'

'Aye, 'e does that; in t' same 'ouse on t' estate. That must be 'ard after what 'e saw there. Elijah's 'ead gamekeeper fer t' estate.'

'I guess it must be. But if he's happily married with kids to care for, a tied cottage will be worth a lot.'

'I dunno so much abaht happily married, but ah do know there are no kids. Elijah's every bit a difficult character as 'is father were, so mebbe all's not well in t' bedroom department. That'll be summat else you're more of an expert on than me.'

Nash grimaced. 'Not so much these days, Jonas.'

'Aye, well yer still young. Plenty o' time to put that reet.'

'When you said Elijah is as difficult as his father, what did you mean?'

'Ah mean 'e's got a reet short fuse and a mean vindictive streak. Got in trouble over his temper a while back, an' that were another reet rum do.'

'In what way?'

Jonas studied for a moment. 'It were afore old man Harland kicked t' bucket. Lad got into a fight in Helmsdale; reckoned some bloke 'ad made a comment abaht 'is missus. Anyroad, Elijah were up afore t' beak and got hissen a conviction fer assault.'

Nash smiled at the reference. He supposed anyone under forty years of age would be a lad to Jonas. 'What was odd about that? Such things happen quite often; otherwise, we might be out of work.'

Turner chuckled. 'What were rum were t' way estate owner stuck up fer 'im; allus 'ad done. Old man Harland took care of 'im after 'is father's death. Then didn't sack 'im when they should 'ave, an' gave 'im a glowing reference in court. Rumour 'as it they got 'im a fancy solicitor. Ah reckon that probably saved 'im from going inside. Got off wi' a fine, and that there community service. Wi' Harland's reputation wi' t' lasses, it med me wonder if Elijah might a been one of 'is bastards. There cud a bin a few o' em, ah reckon. Might also explain why Aaron Nelson weren't over bothered about leavin' t' lad alone when 'e topped hissen'

'You said you'd met Elijah's wife; what's she like?'

'Kim, 'er name is, and she'd be reet up your alley if she weren't spoken fer. A reet bonny lass, wi' a sweet smile and a cracking figure. As bonny as Elijah's Mum, ah recall — in fact, now ah come t' think on it, if the light weren't too strong yu'd almost tek 'em fer sisters.'

'How come you know her so well?'

'Ah wouldn't say ah know 'er that well, but ah chat t' 'er every week on t' Dales Bus. I allus get t' sit next t' 'er if ah can — or at least ah used to.' Turner's face clouded with disappointment as he continued, 'I reckon either Elijah's bought 'er a car or she's got use o' one from t' estate, cos she stopped using t' bus a while back.'

'When was that, can you remember?'

'Ah'm not reet sure, Mr Nash, mebbe six months or so since. It were afore Christmas, ah can tell thee that.'

'How come you're so certain?'

The old man chuckled. 'Ah picked a sprig o' mistletoe and kept it in me pocket every time ah took bus, in case ah got to sit wi' 'er, but ah never got chance t' use it; more's pity.'

'You're an old rascal, Jonas. Do you fancy another pint?' Nash got to his feet, but only picked up the old man's glass.

'Aye, why not, all this gabbin' meks you thirsty — and not so much o' the old, there's no need t' rub it in. Going are ye?'

'Sorry, Jonas, can't stay. Early start tomorrow.'

Back home, Nash glanced at the clock before picking up his mobile. He decided to make the calls. He spoke to Fleming first and outlined what he'd heard from Turner. 'What concerns me most is that Nelson's wife hasn't been seen since around the time these other victims started to go missing. That may be coincidental, but—'

'I know, I know, you don't believe in coincidences. OK, what do you suggest?'

Nash outlined his idea. Normally, he wouldn't have needed to consult before acting, but given the chief constable's opposition to alternative theories, felt it wise to cover his back.

Fleming gave her approval, adding, 'I'll come into Helmsdale first thing tomorrow and see what you've discovered. Then we might be able to move forward.' She paused, before adding, 'Are you thinking what I am about Barton's disappearance and the fact that Kim Nelson hasn't been seen for several months?'

'I'm afraid I am. The fact that there's no trace of him at Track End cottage and that Nelson's house is around a mile away concerns me deeply. If I remember correctly, no one's been to Nelson's property to make inquiries, probably because they didn't know it existed. By what Turner told me, Kim Nelson is extremely attractive, and if Barton and she became close, her husband might have gone off the rails. And if my theory's right, that might mean we've another two bodies to account for.'

After ending the call to Fleming, Nash rang Pearce's mobile. Lianne answered, explaining that Viv was changing the baby's nappy. After asking her how she and the baby were, he reassured her, 'It isn't urgent. But I know Viv is intending to go to Teesside tomorrow to collect a DNA sample. However, there's been a change in plan. He might still be able to do that, but I want him to come into Helmsdale station first thing — in fact, as early as he can manage.'

'I'll make sure Viv's in early. I'll move Brian's crib so it's on Viv's side of the bed. That will act better than any alarm clock. Hold on, Mike, he's here now.'

'I know this is unorthodox, Viv, but is there any chance you can have a quiet word with your neighbour Alf from the CSI squad? Ask him for a favour, we don't have time to join a queue on this. Try bribery, tell him next time you're on leave or rest days you'll neglect to notice if he pops home during his shift, or something like that.'

* * *

Sergeant Jack Binns wasn't easily shocked, but when he arrived at Helmsdale Police Station that Wednesday morning he was startled to see that three of his colleagues' vehicles were already in the car park; this was becoming too regular. He might have expected Mike Nash's car to be there, as the detective often came in early, especially in recent times, when there were no female distractions to keep him in bed late. On occasion, DC Pearce had arrived before or at about the same time as Binns, but to see Detective Superintendent Fleming's car in Helmsdale at that hour was virtually unheard of.

Binns hurried into the building and almost ran upstairs to the CID suite, concerned that an emergency or something equally momentous had happened of which he was unaware. He opened the door and the trio of detectives in the general office turned from their inspection of the computer screen in front of them, to glance at the intruder.

'Morning, Jack,' Nash greeted him with a smile.

Binns took a deep breath. 'Is something wrong? Have I missed a shout, or have you caught that Barton guy? If not, all I can think is that there's been an outbreak of a new disease called contagious amnesia.'

'There's nothing to panic about, Jack,' Fleming reassured him, 'it's nowhere near as serious as you might think. All we're doing is following up on some information Mike obtained last night. It's imperative that we tackle it as our first priority.'

Binns sighed again, this time with relief. 'Thank goodness for that. I was afraid somebody had discovered yet more bodies.'

Nash shuddered as Binns' suggestion matched his worst fears. 'Don't even think about it.'

'No, I won't. Instead, I'll think about brewing some coffee, if anyone's interested.'

There was complete harmony in the three replies — all of them in the affirmative. As he was heading for the kitchen, Binns heard Pearce say, 'Here it is, I think this is the file we're after.'

During Binns' absence, the detectives read the information on the screen pertaining to the arrest of Elijah Nelson. 'I find it interesting that the Harland Estate made a specific request for Nelson's firearms licence not to be revoked, citing possession of such weapons was necessary given his occupation,' Nash commented. 'That would seem to bear out Jonas Turner's insinuation that Nelson was somehow being looked after.'

'Yes, look who represented him! That would have cost a fair bit. Perhaps Nelson has some sort of influence over the estate owner,' Viv said.

'Something on the lines of blackmail, do you think?' Fleming added.

'If we accept what Turner alleges about the seedy past history of the hotel and the sexual proclivities of more than one generation of the Harland family, it would seem the most likely explanation. However, Jonas also suggested that there might be another, even closer connection. He wondered, given Elijah's mother being part of the brothel set up, if Elijah might be one of Harland senior's illegitimate children. That's of less importance right now than what else this file contains. And that's sufficient to convince me this line of inquiry is worth pursuing,' Nash said.

'Me too,' Fleming agreed. 'Did you alert your CSI pal, Viv?'

Viv looked alarmed.

'Don't worry. I'm turning a blind eye, as the saying goes.'

'Er, yes, I did. I asked Alf to check this guy's prints against that bloodstained one we found in the kitchen of Track End Cottage.'

'Good. Because if he doesn't rule it out in the same way as he did Donny Barton's, we'll have to consider ways and means of taking the inquiry to the next level.'

As they were sitting with their coffee awaiting a response from the forensics officer, Nash asked Fleming if she had any ideas on the subject. 'No, to be honest, I haven't. I'm open to suggestions; in fact, I'd positively welcome them.'

'There is one thought that occurred to me, based on something Mexican Pete said after he inspected the crime scene. He warned me the person who committed these murders is so far off the radar of normality they should only be approached with extreme caution, having taken the utmost in protective measures; a bit like going into a lion's cage. To my way of thinking, when we do have a confirmed suspect, that involves everyone being suited up in body armour and with an armed response team present — the latter part of which can only be achieved with the chief constable's approval.'

Fleming grimaced at Nash's final words. 'I agree, and I was thinking along similar lines, but given her previous attitude, how we hope to persuade her to go along with any plan to tackle a different suspect is quite another matter.'

'Of course, all this theorizing and planning is going to be meaningless if those prints rule Nelson out in the same way they did Barton,' Pearce pointed out.

'Being up early after a broken night attending to the baby has done little for your optimism,' Nash retorted.

Pearce's apprehension was allayed a while later, when his mobile rang. 'It's Alf,' he said before answering the call. Minutes later, he put the phone back in his pocket and smiled at his superiors. 'That's going to cost me a few pints.' He laughed. 'And you'd better prepare yourselves to face the wrath of God. Alf says there is an unusual characteristic common to both sets of prints. It's a break in the pattern that might be genetic, or the result of a severe gash or burn. Alf reckons despite the blood-stained one from the cottage only being a partial, it's highly unlikely that the two prints belong to different people.'

There was silence for a few minutes as they pondered the news and the problem of the chief constable, until Nash exclaimed, 'Got it.'

'Go on, Mike, what have you thought up?'

'If we were to go to God with Elijah Nelson's file and the background Jonas Turner provided, we could explain that we've identified him as a likely candidate for Barton's mystery accomplice, via his fingerprint. We could back it up by pointing out the proximity of Track End Cottage to the place where Nelson lives. We could also point to the fact that the abductions started soon after Barton arrived, and Mrs Nelson hasn't been seen since shortly afterwards. All of which is factually correct; we're simply not putting the same inference on the evidence as she will.'

'That's a great idea, Mike, let's hope it works. I know it's early days, but well done,' Fleming told him. 'But for your deductions and information gathering, we might never have got as far as we have.'

'Alf said he's preparing an email to you, Mike, giving confirmation of what he just told me. I'll leave you to it while I go to Teesside to collect another DNA sample,' Pearce told them. 'We still need to give some form of closure to the victims' families.'

'OK, Viv, and thank you — both for your work this morning and your concern for the victims,' Fleming said. 'I think, on balance, I'd prefer to be in the car with you than travelling to Netherdale to confront the chief.'

* * *

Contrary to their worst fears, the interview with O'Donnell went extremely smoothly. At one point, the chief constable even suggested that their privately held opinion might be correct. 'I agree with everything you've said,' she responded; then added, 'but I think we must surely consider another option — that Nelson is the sole culprit. And that, far from being complicit, Barton could be another of his victims, along with Nelson's wife. As you said, neither of them has been seen since late last year. I for one find it deeply worrying that they haven't come forward. Simply because we found four bodies at one of his dump sites doesn't mean there aren't more elsewhere. We still have at least one potential victim unaccounted for, and now you've brought me evidence that could point to two more.'

'I agree, ma'am, and I believe we should remain open-minded to both theories until we've searched Nelson's place and brought him into custody for questioning,' Fleming replied. 'With your permission, I'll apply for the warrant and set up an ARU team to back up the officers carrying out the search. He does have a rifle and a shotgun,' she added.

'Very well then; off you go.'

As Fleming and Nash walked down the corridor, they both shrugged their shoulders, raised their eyebrows in confusion, and shook their heads.

'Well, that went well,' Nash said, as Fleming bit her lip to suppress a giggle.

CHAPTER TWENTY-ONE

It was still dark next morning when the briefing took place at Helmsdale Police Station, where Nash addressed the officers assembled in the crowded reception area.

'The man we're seeking to detain for questioning is called Elijah Nelson. Nelson is a gamekeeper by profession, and as such, we are aware via his firearms licence application that he possesses one high-powered stalking rifle, plus a .12 bore shotgun. Those are the weapons we know of — there could well be others. It is our belief, based on mostly circumstantial, but reasonably convincing evidence, that this man has murdered four people in a most gruesome manner. He might well have killed at least three more. Given that horrifying tally, and if our suspicions are correct, I have absolutely no doubt that he will not hesitate to kill again. I hope that dispels any complacency you might have felt going up against one person. One further word of warning. As I remarked, our suspect is a gamekeeper, so there is the strong possibility that he will already be up and about by the time we reach his house — I think it's safe to discount the element of surprise. But I want silent approach, is that clear?'

Nash paused and asked for questions. One of the members of the ARU team cleared his throat and asked, 'Do you have a photograph or description of this man?'

'Yes, DC Pearce will be distributing photocopies of Nelson taken from his firearms application, plus the one on his PNC record following a conviction for assault. Those are the best we have. Anything else?'

'Are we to take critical shots?'

Nash looked at the ARU leader. 'Superintendent Fleming will give the order should critical shots be deemed necessary. I want this man alive if possible.'

'Sir. Do we have medical backup?' a second officer asked.

'We do, but they have been instructed to remain at a safe distance on the main road.'

He looked at Fleming, who was standing alongside him, clearly inviting her to add anything he might have missed. Her response, a headshake, enabled him to end by saying, 'OK, let's go. But remember that your own safety and that of your colleagues has to be your first — and most important priority.'

* * *

It was shortly before 6 a.m. As he watched, through the trees, the string of vehicle lights in the far distance heading in his direction, Elijah Nelson sighed. He was in no doubt that the vehicles were those of police cars, and equally certain they were heading for Keeper's Cottage. There had always been a chance that things would end this way, despite every attempt Elijah had made to sidetrack the focus of potential investigations by leaving sufficient evidence, or lack of it, that would implicate Barton. Elijah was consumed by fresh rage at the thought of the artist's name and wondered how his efforts had failed. It was obvious he had done so; otherwise those cars wouldn't be heading this way.

Nelson had watched enough TV documentaries featuring police activity to realize that they were acting at this early hour of the day because they hoped to rely on the surprise factor. The programmes he'd seen often had comical results, as the suspects were hauled from their beds. However, in this instance he believed the police had reckoned without his occupation, which saw him up and about long before the average citizen.

He was pleased that they hadn't arrived earlier, before he'd finished checking the pheasant pens and feeding the early poults. It would have been most unfortunate if that task had been interrupted prior to completion. He hoped the estate's other workers would remember to continue the breeding and rearing programme.

The police vehicles were still almost a couple of miles away, he estimated, far enough for him to complete his preparations and take up his selected position. Although Nelson had hoped this day would never arrive, he'd planned for it as if it was a certainty. He would visit the house before relocating to the old piggery, where he had already removed some of the boarding from the windows. That outbuilding offered ideal cover, and was highly appropriate in so many other ways.

He slung his rifle over one shoulder and picked up the half-empty feed sack. Others might have chosen to ignore this seemingly irrelevant item in such dramatic circumstances, but Nelson wasn't prepared to leave the contents for foxes and other vermin to feast on. Whatever else they said or wrote about him afterwards, no one would be able to accuse him of being negligent.

As he walked towards the house, Elijah refined his plans. He would switch on several lights inside, giving the impression that he was in the building. That would distract their attention long enough for him to gain the upper hand in the early exchanges of the inevitable firefight that would follow. As he was leaving the house he thought of one final touch, literally an open invitation to the unwelcome visitors.

The outcome would be a foregone conclusion; Elijah accepted that fact, but pride demanded that he gave as good a showing as possible. Giving in or surrendering tamely would go against his nature, and he wasn't prepared to bring such disgrace on the family name. Curious, he thought, but he was actually looking forward to it, now that the moment had almost arrived. But then, violence had been his stimulant for quite some time now.

As he took up position he looked at the weapons at his disposal and the boxes of ammunition at his feet. He'd start with the .12 bore, he thought. Then, once they were convinced that was the only threat, he'd switch to the rifle. He'd taken a stag down at over five hundred yards using that weapon — a man at half the range would be no problem.

* * *

The police vehicles pulled to a halt at the end of the track leading to Keeper's Cottage. As the ARU team leader dispersed his men, to form a ring that encompassed the front of the house, Nash, together with Fleming and Pearce, surveyed the scene.

'He's obviously inside the house,' Pearce said, 'there are lights on, and unless it's a trick of what little light there is, the front door appears to be open.'

'I reckon that's exactly what he wants us to think,' Nash said. 'It's all a little too obvious for my liking. I suspect he saw the headlights and guessed we were coming. The only way he could have advertised his presence more openly would be by hanging a sign out of the window saying, "I'm in the lounge, come and get me". No, I think it's a bit too good to be true.'

'What do you suggest we do?'

'I think we should sit here and wait. If I'm wrong and he is inside the house, there's nothing lost, but if I'm right, we won't be in danger of walking into an ambush. My guess is that he's probably rumbled our presence and is after making a fight of it. If that's so, he'll be pumped full of adrenalin, and if the action he's craving doesn't materialize, he'll try and force the issue.'

'OK, that suits me fine; I'll go and speak to the ARU leader,' Fleming said.

After a long wait, stretching beyond a quarter of an hour, nerves on the hillside and in the piggery were becoming stretched like piano wires. It was only a matter of time before someone snapped. In the end, it was both parties. Having tested Nash's theory without finding any evidence to support it, the ARU team leader gave quiet instructions to three of his men.

Inside the piggery, Nelson darted from one to another of the partially covered windows to observe what was happening outside. The answer for long enough was — nothing. Eventually, the waiting game got too much to bear any longer. 'OK,' he muttered, 'if you won't accept my invitation at the first time of asking, let's see if I can persuade you.'

He raised the shotgun and aimed it in the general direction of the nearest police car. The vehicle was almost at the full extent of the weapon's range, but a blast from both barrels might provoke some reaction.

On the hillside, the police marksman adjusted the elevation on the tripod supporting his rifle slightly. His first shot, taken in response to the hail of shotgun pellets issuing from the outbuilding, had been too high. The sniper peered through the viewer of his telescopic sight caught a glimpse of someone he assumed to be the wanted man, and lined up the shot in the cross hairs. He squeezed the trigger, but as he did so, he saw Nelson move, and reacted quickly to realign the shot. Before he could fire again, the target had disappeared.

Cautiously, not wanting to present a further shooting opportunity to the sniper, Nelson peered around the edge of the window frame. Using the distraction of their colleague's shot, three armed officers had crept close to the front wall of the house and were heading towards the piggery. Nelson spotted them. He couldn't allow that. He wasn't ready. Nelson lifted the .12 bore and aimed it at the man nearest the window, hoping to avoid the string spreading as far as his

Land Rover, which was parked close by. He fired, and was sure he'd been successful.

From his concealment behind a clump of bushes at the end of the drive, Nash heard a gunshot. He saw a member of the ARU team half-stagger, then collapse to the ground close to the house. 'Officer down!' he barked into his radio. 'Officer down, take the shooter out. Get him out. Now!'

There was very little cover in front of the house, but Nash could see the injured officer dragging himself towards the Land Rover. If he reached that, he would be safe from further attack, but getting him out of danger and treating his wounds would be far more difficult. Obeying the order on their radios, the rest of the ARU team had withdrawn to a position they believed to be out of shotgun range, and the lull in the shooting made for an eerie, tense silence as they watched their colleague's painfully slow progress.

Two more shots rang out. Obviously, the besieged man couldn't stand the silence either. The officers ducked as a curtain of pellets swept overhead, emphasizing the vulnerability of their position.

Nash bent low and ran back to where Fleming was standing alongside her car. 'Who the blazes ordered those men to make that sortie towards the house?' he asked.

'It wasn't me; it must have been the ARU leader.'

'Well the result is that one of his men is lying wounded near the shooter and we've no means of getting him out or bringing assistance to him.'

Fleming gestured to the bonnet of her car, where she had spread out a large map that was weighted down with stones. 'I've an idea that might work. I've been looking at the Ordnance Survey. There's what appears to be a track leading to the yard at the back of the house. It looks as if it goes all the way to the main road. If we can distract Nelson long enough to get a vehicle round there and in the shelter of the building, a couple of our guys could get to the far side of the Land Rover and carry our injured man to safety. It shouldn't be dangerous either, because unless I'm mistaken, Nelson wouldn't have a clear shot at them from where he is.'

She saw Nash was about to say something and raised a warning hand. 'This is a job for the uniforms. He's their colleague, and they're better protected. Besides which, they can return fire if Nelson does take a shot at them. I'm not having you or Pearce taking any risks. That's an order. Remember, Mike, you don't only have yourself to think about nowadays.'

'OK, Jackie, but all I was going to say was, let me have a look at the lie of the land first, before anyone goes charging in and putting themselves in danger.'

'All right, you do that while I brief the ARU leader and give him a piece of my mind over that reckless action.'

She summoned the officer and explained what she had in mind. Having delivered a severe dressing down, which included a warning that he would have to answer to the Police Complaints Authority over his actions and disobedience of orders, she told him, 'As soon as the rescue vehicle gets close enough to the house, I want your marksmen to commence firing at the outbuilding. I need them to keep Nelson too occupied to have any time for what's happening across to his right.'

Nash, who had returned from his survey, interjected, 'It might be a good idea for them to shoot at the piggery door as well as the windows, aiming at the lock. If we destroy that, as well as taking out the rest of the barricaded windows, we'll have a few possible entry points available should we have to storm the building. Alternatively, do you have any percussion grenades?'

'We can try that. It might disorientate him.'

'Good, then get going.'

When the chastened ARU leader had radioed the brief to the snipers, Nash told Fleming, 'I have only one reservation with all of this.'

'What might that be?'

'We don't know if Nelson is alone, or whether he might have a hostage with him.'

'If he had, he would have made it known before now. I think that's a chance we'll have to take. I'm not prepared to let one of our officers bleed to death while we're making our minds up about something that is nothing more than a possibility.'

The diversion worked. Once the rescue vehicle was in position, the marksman was given his cue and fired a percussion grenade though the window. Then the others commenced shooting at the outbuilding, carefully selecting targets to intimidate rather than inflict injury. The loud accompaniment of shattering window panes added to the dramatic effect. Moments later, their fusillade provoked an angry response from within, delivered via a rapid succession of shots fired haphazardly, which caused no injuries but enabled them to identify the shooter's weapon. 'It's a five-shot semi-automatic pump action shotgun,' the ARU leader reported. 'From what we've been able to tally up, we reckon he's already used well over two full boxes of cartridges; that means in excess of fifty shells. All of which would be useful if we knew how many he had to start with.'

As he was speaking, the rescue party completed their mission, and it was with some relief that they were able to watch the tail lights of the vehicle reach a point that was out of range of possible retaliation. Further good news came from one of the first-aiders inside the car, who reported that the wounded officer's injuries were not as bad as they appeared, and they were nearing the ambulance.

'Tell them we need a replacement ambulance. We must have the reserves on hand the way this is going,' Fleming ordered.

Inside the piggery, Nelson waited, taking time to regain his composure. He stared at the remaining ammunition. It had only seemed like minutes ago that he'd had plenty, boxes of the stuff. Now he had only a handful of cartridges. 'This is proving to be a very expensive morning,' he muttered, 'I think it's time we upped the stakes somewhat.' He placed the shotgun carefully on the bonnet of an old vehicle that was standing to one side of the piggery stalls, its outline draped in dust sheets. 'Look after that for me,' he said, although there was no one else in sight. 'I might need it again soon.'

He reached down and slid the stalking rifle from its gun slip and checked the telescopic sight, making a minute adjustment before he was satisfied. 'Now it's time to really party,' he said as he took aim.

Nelson only managed one shot before a bullet missed him by inches. He ducked, hoping to go beneath the line of fire. The result wasn't exactly what he was hoping for. The second bullet that would have hit him in the abdomen pierced his right eye socket and exited the back of his head, spilling part of his brain tissue as he crashed, lifeless, to the ground.

There was a long silence.

* * *

Nelson might have only managed one shot, but its effects were catastrophic. The bullet aimed at Detective Superintendent Fleming's head missed its target by a fraction. In his overheated excitement, Nelson had forgotten that his rifle always shot lower than the telescopic sight allowed for.

The bullet hit the bonnet of the detective's car, ricocheting off to strike her shoulder. She cried out in distress as she slumped to the ground, losing blood and consciousness fast when her head hit the stony ground.

'Officer down!' Nash shouted. He dived across and covered the wound with the only thing he had available, a handkerchief, applying pressure as he tried to use his free hand to call for assistance. 'Viv, go to my car and get the first aid kit. Then contact Netherdale control. I need that other ambulance here quick. Jackie's been shot and it looks pretty bad.'

The ARU team member with specialist first aid training in gunshot wounds took over from Nash, and by the time the ambulance arrived, Jackie had been stabilized. Although she was still unconscious, they had at least managed to stem the blood flow.

As soon as Nash was free of his medical duties, he reassessed the situation. There had been neither sight nor sound from the piggery during the period they had been attending to Fleming. The focus now was on whether it would be advisable to risk approaching the building.

He rang the chief constable at home and put the problem to O'Donnell as succinctly as the situation allowed. 'It could be that Nelson's playing a waiting game, and as soon as we're exposed, will inflict further casualties. Alternatively, he could have run out of ammo — or we might have wounded or killed him. I need some guidance as to how we should proceed.'

'I'll get there just as soon as I can. In the meantime, you have my backing whether you decide to go in or not. Just don't take any chances, either yourself or with any of our men.'

If that was intended to comfort him, Nash thought, it was cold comfort at best. He called the ARU leader across, and as they sat propped up against the side of Fleming's car facing away from the piggery they discussed the situation.

'We could try a limited exposure tactic to try and provoke a reaction,' the firearms officer suggested. 'If two of my men appeared at either side of his line of sight briefly, fired a couple of shots each and then ducked back under cover, we'll see if he's capable and prepared to respond.'

Nash agreed, albeit reluctantly, and after briefing the men and selecting their positions carefully, they waited, the tension visible on everyone's face. The minutes passed agonizingly slowly before both men reported they were ready. The team leader gave the order. The others watched as the men appeared, crouching as they ran forward, to use the garden wall for cover as they edged towards the outbuilding, their attitude one of obvious menace. Shots rang out, one from each officer, before they ducked down to safety. The silence after the echoes died away was long and heavy with suspense.

'Now what?' Nash asked.

'I think we have to risk a more meaningful approach. What if we get someone up the path at the rear and he works along under the shattered windows with a periscope mirror. That way, we can find out exactly what's going on and the others can cover him from here. Nelson would have to show himself if he tries to shoot the officer under the window.'

The decision made, Nash left it to the ARU team to carry out the risky operation. Ten minutes later, having successfully got within range and used his periscope mirror, the officer got to his feet.

'All clear, the only occupant is dead from a single gunshot wound. If that's Nelson, he's taken after his namesake, the Admiral.'

'Sorry, what do you mean?' his superior asked.

'He's only got one eye. We must have shot the other one out.'

The rest of the ARU team advanced slowly to the barn; the leader kicked the splintered door open. 'We're just checking the rest of the building.' There was a pause before the man exclaimed in horror, 'Oh shit!'

'What's wrong?' Nash was afraid they had encountered unexpected problems.

The man's tone was grim. 'We've found a head. A woman's head. It's been hacked from her body.'

It was Nelson's final flourish, leaving Samantha to greet the incoming officers.

CHAPTER TWENTY-TWO

Having secured the outbuilding, the ARU team went on to check the house. While they were crossing to the cottage, Nash spoke to the chief constable again.

'I'm just leaving,' she told him, 'have there been any developments?'

'Nelson's dead. One of the ARU team's bullets must have struck him soon after he shot Jackie. I don't suppose you've had any news about her condition yet, have you?'

'Only that she's scheduled for emergency surgery, and first indications are that the wound isn't life-threatening, which is a huge relief. Have you found any evidence that proves Nelson is the killer? I assume he must be, otherwise, why resist like he did?'

'I haven't been inside yet, but according to what the armed officers told me, there's a dismembered head in the outbuilding close to where he was holed up. So I think it's safe to assume that we've got our man, but we don't know the full extent of his killing spree yet. I'm very much afraid that we might discover yet more victims.'

'What do you need?'

'Once we've had the all clear to enter the house and the outbuilding we'll need Mexican Pete and a full CSI team here

— a large one at that. Also, in view of the fatality and Jackie's injury, I suppose we'll have to notify the Independent Police Complaints Commission. No doubt they'll want to see that we handled this correctly.'

'OK, I'll contact CSI and the IPCC. I don't suppose there's any requirement for me to drive out there now, so I can be of more assistance acting as liaison from this end. Let me know if you need anything more.'

'I will do that. DC Andrews should be on her way to Netherdale by now. She collected a DNA sample from a potential relative and was scheduled to drop it in first thing this morning. If you see her will you divert her here, or if not, leave a message with Jack Binns? We won't be able to enter the premises until the CSI boys arrive, but after that, I reckon we might need all the help we can get.'

'OK, Mike, leave that with me. I must go now. I've just had a message that somebody wants to see me as a matter of urgency. I don't know what that's about.'

The chief constable must have used the full authority of her office, because the CSI team arrived much earlier than Nash anticipated. Within minutes, he and Pearce had donned their protective suiting and overshoes and accompanied them into the outbuilding. For once, Ramirez refrained from making any remarks about Nash's seemingly infallible ability to attract corpses. Obviously, the fresh horror of this scene, coming so quickly after the appalling discoveries at Track End Cottage, had dampened his tendency towards sarcasm.

With no evidence of rodent or insect predation to mar the appearance of the head, Nash was quickly able to identify the remains from the woman's MISPER file. 'That's Samantha Frost, the most recent of the missing women,' he told Ramirez.

Pearce hastily averted his eyes from the ghastly image of the human head staring sightlessly at them, and from the corpse of the killer gazing with one eye towards the roof. Pearce glanced nervously towards the corner of the building closest to him, apprehensive as to what he would see there. His interest was caught by a pile of objects, and after a moment he identified one of them in particular. Recognition made his heart sink.

He put his hand on Nash's arm. 'Mike, look over there.' He pointed to the corner. 'Unless I'm very much mistaken, isn't that one of those portable easels that artists use when they're travelling?'

Nash's expression was grim as he replied, 'It is. I guess we now know why we didn't find any of Barton's possessions in Track End Cottage. The only problem we now face is finding out what happened to him. I reckon that means searching for his body. For that matter, we also need to discover what happened to Kim Nelson, and I'm afraid that might mean we're also looking for her corpse.'

He turned and spoke to Ramirez and the CSI leader, explaining the significance of the property they'd found and the grim implications. 'I think we're now looking for at least two more sets of remains, plus the rest of Samantha Frost's corpse. The other victims could have been dead for at least six months, so heaven knows what condition they'll be in.'

Before the search began, DC Andrews, dressed in the same protective clothing, appeared in the doorway. 'I was in Helmsdale station when I got the chief's message,' she told Nash, 'and apparently she's been trying to call you but without success.'

'Probably because there's no signal in here,' Nash said, glancing at his mobile. 'What did she want, did she say?'

'No, it was Jack Binns who passed me the message. All he said was that it was extremely urgent.'

'OK, I'd better go outside and phone her. I won't be long. Let's hope it isn't more bad news.'

His call to the chief was diverted to her secretary. 'She's got someone with her,' the secretary told him, 'but she wants you to return to Netherdale station immediately.'

'Do you know why?'

'No, but she made it abundantly clear this was an order, not a request.'

'OK, I'll brief the crime scene people and my officers, then I'll be on my way.'

When he re-entered the building to the flashes from the photographer, two of the forensic officers were in the process of removing the sheeting that covered a vehicle in the far corner of the piggery. Nash just had time to notice that the car was a BMW 3 series. It looked to be in almost showroom condition, despite the fact that the number plate indicated the vehicle was at least twenty years old.

He collared Andrews and Pearce. 'The chief wants me back at Netherdale. In the meantime, if you discover anything relevant I want to know about it immediately, OK? Even if it means ringing me while I'm en route — or in with the chief.'

As he began the journey from Thornscarr, Nash puzzled over the bizarre discovery of a high-quality good condition car in such a strange location. There had to be a logical explanation for it, but at that moment he couldn't think of one.

* * *

Nash had only been on the road for a few minutes when one of the CSI team made a new discovery. Andrews was checking the mound of baggage and artist's materials in the corner. Pearce was checking the BMW with the forensics officer who had removed the cover when a startled cry from the opposite end of the building attracted everyone's attention. The CSI man who had called out was standing next to a black bin liner, but as they watched he backed away hastily; a look of revulsion on his face.

'There's a body in there,' he said, his voice unsteady, 'it's all chopped up.' He gulped and then added, 'But there's no head. It must be hers.' He gestured towards the object near the entrance, now masked by an evidence bag.

Ramirez and his assistants hurried across to take possession of the remains while Pearce, now joined by Andrews, watched the other CSI members continue to check over the

BMW. 'There's a tax disc on the far side of the windscreen,' Andrews pointed to the left of the car. 'Although it's badly faded, the expiry date appears to be July 1997.'

The saloon section of the vehicle yielded nothing until they opened the glove compartment, where they found a large brown envelope containing two slim volumes that turned out to be diaries. These were handed to the forensics men for later examination. As they were sealing the books in yet another evidence bag, Pearce muttered to Andrews, 'It's to be hoped they brought a big enough supply of bags. They've used a few already, and we haven't even started on the house.'

They moved to the rear of the vehicle, where the CSI men were about to open the boot. As they looked inside, all four officers took an involuntary step back, as if choreographed. 'I think you should get Mexican Pete,' Andrews told Pearce, 'while I update Mike. He said to let him know if we found anything relevant, and I reckon this certainly qualifies.'

Pearce was still staring at the twin sets of human remains in the boot. 'I agree,' he said after a moment, 'there can't be an innocent explanation for hiding two sets of remains inside a car stored in a locked, disused outbuilding in the middle of nowhere.'

Andrews left Pearce to liaise with the pathologist and went outside, where she took a deep breath of fresh air before calling Nash.

'Lisa, what have you got?' Nash asked immediately.

She could tell by the tension in his voice that he was expecting bad news. 'We've found the missing body parts we believe belong to the head you identified as Samantha Frost,' she began, 'then, just a couple of minutes ago we opened the boot of that old BMW.' Lisa gulped before continuing, 'Inside we found two more bodies. Like the others, all chopped up, but these were skeletons. We're waiting on Mexican Pete to examine them. I think we might have found Donny Barton and Mrs Nelson.'

'This nightmare just continues to get worse,' Nash said. 'Are you OK? How about Viv?'

'We're fine, Mike. It was a bit startling, that's all, even though we half-expected something like that.'

'OK, stick with it, and let me know if anything else turns up. Which means,' he added, 'that I'm hoping not to hear from you. I'm nearly at Netherdale.'

'And I'm hoping I don't have to call you,' Lisa muttered as she turned and headed back to the barn.

* * *

Nash was relieved to reach the car park at HQ without receiving further grim tidings from Thornscarr. Thinking over what Lisa had told him he was now convinced that the bodies found in the boot of the BMW would turn out to be those of the missing artist, Donny Barton, and Nelson's wife, Kim. He wondered if the two had been lovers, and if so, had their liaison led to their murders and the killing spree that followed. Alternatively, it could have been nothing more than the fevered imagination of Nelson's sick mind that had prompted him to go on the rampage, seeking out vulnerable women as victims. If Barton's relationship with Kim Nelson had been merely a casual acquaintance, they had both paid dearly for it. Being in close proximity in such an isolated spot might have caused Nelson to put a totally erroneous spin on their behaviour.

When Nash entered the headquarters building he headed straight to the top floor, where the chief constable's suite was located. On reaching the outer office, he waited for a second as her secretary was on the phone, but immediately she looked up he was given hand signals pointing towards the inner sanctum. He knocked on the door and was bidden to enter.

In addition to Chief Constable O'Donnell, there were three other people in her office. The chief greeted Nash and introduced him to the first of these, a man of about Nash's age, who rose to his feet and shook hands. 'This is Detective Sergeant Baines from Greater Manchester CID,' she told him. 'He and a colleague have driven over from Manchester this morning bringing with them a man and woman who were arrested when they got off the Paris flight first thing. I believe you might recognize them.'

One of the couple, the male, who had been seated with his back to Nash, stood up and turned to face him. Nash's jaw dropped as he stared at the features that had become familiar to him and to many millions of television viewers and newspaper readers. The chief constable, who was clearly enjoying the drama, continued, 'This is Donny Barton, and the lady is Mrs Kim Nelson.'

Barton's companion, an attractive woman in her late twenties, struggled to rise from the chair and turned to be introduced. Kim Nelson was clearly heavily pregnant.

The astonishment Nash felt was reflected both in his expression and the less-than-diplomatic nature of his response. 'I thought you were dead — both of you.'

He turned to the chief constable and continued, 'That's obviously not the case, so whose are the two sets of human remains Andrews and Pearce have just found in the piggery at Keeper's Cottage?'

It was the turn of the others to stare at Nash in amazement. After several seconds, the chief constable broke the stunned silence. 'I thought you only found part of the other missing prostitute?'

'That was the case when I left Thornscarr, ma'am, but while I was driving here, DC Andrews phoned to say they'd discovered two more sets of remains and the rest of Samantha Frost.'

'There must be two more of Nelson's victims we haven't yet accounted for,' O'Donnell responded.

CHAPTER TWENTY-THREE

Nash looked at Donny Barton. 'I'm still struggling to understand this. We were convinced that Nelson had killed you both and then staged the crime scene at Track End Cottage to implicate you in the murders of those prostitutes. What I'd like to know is how you managed to escape him?'

It was Kim Nelson who provided the answer. She took her seat and, speaking for the first time, she told Nash, 'We were extremely lucky. Elijah claimed he was going away for a week. Obviously, he suspected that Donny and I were attracted to each other and lied to me to try and trap us. I found out the truth by chance from one of the assistant keepers, who said Elijah would only be gone for three days. Knowing what Elijah was like, I panicked and pleaded with Donny to leave, go home, and to take me with him if he wanted to. The morning I believed Elijah was due to return we grabbed what we could carry and caught the Dales Bus into Helmsdale, then took another one to Netherdale, got on a train to London and then flew out from Gatwick to France. I daren't stay in England; I was terrified Elijah would try to find me. We've been in France ever since. That was until we saw an English newspaper with Donny's photo plastered all over the front page along with that ghastly story of those poor women. Donny knew he had to come back to clear his name, and I had to come with him, despite the risk. I got the local doctor's permission to fly, and we took the first available flight. We were arrested when we landed at Manchester.'

'I take it you two are an item?' Nash indicated Kim's condition.

Barton took Kim's hand as he replied. 'We certainly are. Kim said we were lucky, but it's me who's the lucky one. Kim is the best thing that could have happened to me.'

Kim blushed and looked adoringly at her lover.

'Then I think it's in order for me to tell you, Mrs Nelson, that your husband was shot and killed this morning while trying to avoid capture.'

Kim nodded. 'The chief constable has already told me, but thank you, Inspector Nash. I think he got not only what he deserved, but what he wanted.'

Before Nash had chance to ask further questions, his mobile rang. He glanced at the caller display before telling the chief, 'This is DC Andrews. I just hope she hasn't phoned with more bad news.'

O'Donnell nodded approval for Nash to leave the room and answer the call.

'Professor Ramirez has inspected the remains found in the boot of the BMW,' Andrews began, 'and he reckons that they can't be those of Barton and Mrs Nelson, because these victims have been dead for much longer than six months. I'm afraid that means we're still looking for two more bodies.'

Andrews' use of the pathologist's formal title suggested he was standing close by.

'No, we're not,' Nash replied, 'because they're here.'

'Who are?'

'Mr Barton and Mrs Nelson. They're here with the chief constable and I'm delighted to report that they're both alive and well.'

'That's terrific news.' The relief in Andrews' voice was evident. 'But we still don't have the foggiest idea who the victims in the BMW were.'

'We might get a clue if we can discover more about the vehicle. The registration or VIN numbers would be a great help.'

'OK, I'll text it through to Tom Pratt, shall I? One thing I can tell you is that the car is in almost showroom condition and has only done just over six thousand miles. That might have been a long time ago because there's a tax disc on the windscreen with the expiry date of July 1997.'

'That would make sense, because August used to be when the new registration prefixes came in.'

'One other thing, Mike, Professor Ramirez would like a word. I'll pass you to him, because I'm wanted back inside that hellhole of an outbuilding.'

Seconds later, the pathologist spoke. 'I have more information on the remains found in the car. Although I've only had chance to conduct a preliminary investigation, I can confirm that they are the bodies of one male and one female. The remains are skeletal in nature, and the female one isn't quite complete. I believe the missing segments are the two digits that were found in the hotel near here, and which are now lodged in my mortuary. Hang on, Mike, DC Andrews is back and would like another word with you.'

Nash thanked him and waited. 'Sorry, Mike, but we've just made another discovery. There's a chainsaw underneath the car. It's absolutely smothered in what the CSI blokes confirmed to be human blood.'

'I see, is there anything else to report?'

'Only those diaries from the BMW, but you already know about those, don't you?'

'What diaries?'

'Oh, I'm sorry: we must have found them after you left. There were two diaries secreted in the glove compartment of the BMW. CSI have taken possession of them now.'

'We'll need to inspect them ASAP. They could be vital in piecing together exactly what happened and when.' As he spoke, Nash noticed the chief constable's secretary wince at his unintentional pun.

'That's as may be, Mike, but you know how touchy CSI are these days about contamination of evidence — especially after that unfortunate incident a couple of years back.'

Nash recalled the case, which involved a prosecution for theft that collapsed because the defence alleged that the evidence had been contaminated and tampered with prior to analysis. 'OK,' he told Andrews, 'we'll have to be patient until they release them, but ask them to ensure that those diaries are their first priority.'

After he put his phone away, Nash returned to the room and stood for a moment without speaking. Kim Nelson was about to say something but, knowing Nash of old, the chief constable held up a warning hand. She was aware that he could produce a piece of deductive reasoning. Nash remembered his conversation with Jonas Turner and the old man's comments regarding the events that preceded Aaron Nelson's suicide.

"What puzzled me then, and allus 'as, is 'ow come nobody's seen 'ide nor 'air of Elijah's mother since the day Aaron told everyone she'd scarpered wi' 'er fancy man. That were weird too, almost like 'e were trying t' convince folk that were what 'appened. Elijah's never 'eard or seen 'is mum either. Now that's not reet. She were fond enough o' t' lad when 'e were a nipper, so ah'd 'ave thought she'd 'ave come running when she learned what happened to 'is father, wouldn't you?"

After a long silence, Nash turned to Kim Nelson and asked, 'Did your husband often mention his mother? Did he know where she'd gone or who she was with?'

Kim's reply was immediate. 'No, he never spoke about her. There were no photos of her, or his father, for that matter. I knew that his father had killed himself after she left, but that's all. On the one occasion I did ask, Elijah flew into a terrible rage and became extremely violent, so I never dared mention the subject again.'

Nash glanced at the chief constable and saw the look of dawning horror on her face.

'Would you mind stepping into the other room for a moment, ma'am?'

The chief followed Nash through the door. 'Tell me I'm wrong,' she pleaded. 'Tell me it isn't what I think.'

Nash shrugged. 'It's only a theory, ma'am, but it does fit with what little we've found so far. We believed Elijah Nelson had killed his wife and her lover in a fit of jealousy and then went on to kill those prostitutes. However, what if our thinking is a generation out? It might well transpire that those remains in the car belong to Aaron Nelson's wife and *her* lover.'

He repeated the gist of what Jonas Turner had told him before continuing, 'Perhaps the father killed them and dismembered their bodies before committing suicide because he couldn't live with the guilt of what he'd done. And possibly young Elijah discovered the truth after his father's death. Then, if he suspected his wife was also having an affair, he decided to emulate his father. Fortunately for them, Kim and Donny evaded him, so he took his vengeance out elsewhere. We might never know for certain, but I've a shrewd idea that when we inspect some diaries that Andrews and Pearce found in the BMW, we might learn a lot more about what went on all those years ago.'

'They might not contain anything significant,' the chief constable pointed out.

'That's true, but if they don't, why would anyone go to the trouble of secreting them in a place they were extremely unlikely to be found?'

They returned to her office and thanked the Manchester officer, who de-arrested Donny and Kim before departing to collect his colleague from the canteen and head home. The chief constable asked Nash what he thought would be the best way to handle Donny and Kim's delicate situation.

Nash smiled at the couple. 'I think it would be advisable for you to stay close at hand for the time being,' Nash explained. 'If you're content to remain incommunicado in a hotel suite, I think that would be the safest solution.' He turned to the chief. 'That way, they'll be protected from prying eyes, which will avoid potential embarrassment, if not worse. Given the immense amount of publicity this case has attracted, there is a very strong possibility of someone recognizing Donny, jumping to the wrong conclusion, and making trouble for them. Of course, once we're in possession of the full facts, we should hold another media conference as soon as practicable to explain the changed situation.'

O'Donnell and the young couple agreed to the idea and Nash left her to make the arrangements.

'I'm going to see if Tom Pratt's got any news about that BMW, and then I'm off to Helmsdale to meet up with Viv and Lisa. I feel sure they must be nearly finished at Thornscarr; it's getting dark. Given the remoteness and the location of Keepers Cottage, perhaps you could also liaise with uniform branch, ma'am, suggesting that it would be advisable to have at least two officers on duty until CSI declare it free of a crime scene. The last thing we need is the media or ghoulish voyeurs invading the site.'

'Very good, sir,' O'Donnell agreed mockingly, 'and as soon as possible, you should get off home. You've had an extremely long and stressful day — coming on top of a load of long and stressful days.'

Nash took the stairs and headed down to find Tom Pratt, who was seated at his desk when Nash walked in. He picked up a thin sheaf of papers which he handed to the detective. 'That car was at the centre of a huge, hitherto unsolved mystery dating back twenty years,' Tom told Nash. 'The owner worked for a brokerage firm on the London stock exchange and was reckoned to be one of their rising stars. He told colleagues that he needed a break from the stressful daily routine of the job and took a fortnight's leave. Neither he nor the car was ever seen again. The assumption was that he'd suffered some form of mental breakdown and either committed suicide or begun a new life elsewhere. As the man was an orphan, there were no estate problems to sort out, so the matter died a natural death.'

Nash winced at Tom's final remark. 'What a very sad story, especially now we've an idea what really happened to him. Thanks for that, Tom. I'm off to Helmsdale now. With luck Viv and Lisa will have finished soon, and I'll get an update from them.'

It was nearly seven o'clock when the two detective constables walked into CID at Helmsdale, having advised Nash that they were en route. The stress of what they'd witnessed was visible in their expressions. Nash gave them a brief update on events at Netherdale, including the mystery surrounding the BMW and its owner. In return, they told him what had been discovered in Keeper's Cottage following his departure.

Andrews began the account, 'The house was a tip. Nelson either didn't know how to look after himself or he'd totally lost interest. The kitchen and sitting room were filthy, and there was a layer of dust covering every item of furniture. It was so thick you could write your name in it — probably in triplicate. There were pans and crockery in the kitchen sink with green mould growing on them and the fridge had food inside that was covered in fur. I didn't go upstairs, I gave that pleasure to Viv, but apparently that was even worse.'

'It certainly was,' Viv grimaced as he took up the tale. 'Lisa's definitely not guilty of exaggeration. The dust was equally bad, but that was by no means the worst part. The bath was half full of unwashed, sweaty clothing and the whole room smelled of rank body odour. However, the bedroom at the back of the house, the one overlooking the woods, was absolutely sickening. The stench in there was even worse and there was a double bed that obviously hadn't been changed for ages. The sheets were covered in all sorts of stains and blotches. The CSI boys conducted some on-site tests and reported that they comprised semen, urine, vaginal fluid, and faecal discharge. Further tests will have to be made to establish whether, as they so tactfully put it, the samples are "single source or mixed donor." And that wasn't all. There were also lengths of rope that appear to have been used to hold victims captive, because CSI found traces of skin and blood on them. All in all, it was one of the most revolting scenes I've ever witnessed, apart from that charnel house at

Track End Cottage. The press were already assembling in the main road when we left.'

Nash snorted. 'Mexican Pete reckons I've got a nose for blood but theirs is even keener.'

Once Viv had finished his graphic description of the bedroom, Lisa told Nash, 'I passed your message about the diaries to the CSI blokes and they promised to have them available ASAP. Said they'd ring when they've finished with them, but they reckon it will take days to process the whole site at Thornscarr. They wanted to know if you need them sent here or if they're to remain in Netherdale.'

'When they do phone, ask if they'll deliver them to the chief constable's office. Now go home, both of you. It's been a highly stressful day, and I for one am dead beat, so I suggest you must be feeling as bad. In fact, those are the chief's instructions.'

CHAPTER TWENTY-FOUR

The next few days were spent revisiting the crime scene, reading statements taken by officers from the estate workers and builders at the hotel, writing reports, and fielding enquiries from the press. 'Don't these people know we have a press officer,' Nash snapped. 'Tell Netherdale to stop putting calls through unless they ascertain the identity of the caller first.'

Nash had interviewed Donny Barton and Kim Nelson, taking their statements and confirming that the press would be informed of Donny's innocence. The work seemed endless, before a forensic officer rang to say the diaries had been delivered to the Chief Constable's office.

'Good, because I'm going to Netherdale tomorrow.'

When Nash entered the chief constable's office the following morning, he was later than she'd anticipated. O'Donnell had already completed her study of the first of the diaries, and was almost at the end of the second, by the time he arrived.

She looked up in response to his greeting and stared at him for a moment. 'My word, you look tired this morning.'

'It's been a long week and several short nights. Are those the diaries from the piggery? Is there anything relevant in them?'

'I've already skim-read the first of them. It was written by the father, Aaron Nelson, and is dated 1997. The contents more or less confirm what you already suspected. You were right in guessing that his wife intended to leave him. She had fallen in love with the owner of that BMW, who was a regular visitor to the hotel. Their relationship had developed far beyond that of a prostitute and her client, and when Nelson found out, he was consumed by rage and jealousy. Reading between the lines, her decision to leave was less to do with a grand consuming passion and more because she was terrified of Nelson. He reveals all this in the diary, and when she announced that she was going, she told him he was a sick, sadistic pervert. That was too much for him, so he strangled her. Then, to cover his tracks, he also killed her lover and then chopped their bodies up in the hotel kitchen before putting them into the storeroom. Once the coast was clear, he moved the dismembered remains into the man's BMW and hid the car in the disused piggery. Then he started having nightmares in which the bodies re-formed and haunted him. He announced in the diary that the torment was such that he dare not go to sleep until he had consumed a huge amount of alcohol, but eventually that became insufficient to keep the demons at bay. When he realized that it had become too much for him, he decided to do away with himself. That is the final entry.'

'What's in the second diary?'

'That was written by Elijah Nelson, and is even more shocking than that of his father. It covers several years, as though he only made an entry when he felt it worth noting. In it, he tells how he in his childhood he had seen Squire Harland cavorting at the Boar's Head with his mother. Didn't your friend Jonas Turner imply the hotel had been used as some sort of house of ill repute?'

'He did, ma'am.'

'It appears that Elijah Nelson used the fact to blackmail the squire. Nelson knew what his father had done to his mother, and knew he had to remain on the estate to avoid the discovery of the remains in the BMW. I think that explains a lot. The diary goes on and more or less confirms what Kim Nelson told us, but with one additional piece of information. The first part described how, before Elijah went to that agricultural show, he apparently spied on Kim and Donny from a hiding place he'd used as a child to watch hotel guests having it off with their tarts. When he'd seen his wife betraying him, making love in Keeper's Cottage, he decided to kill them, emulating his father. Luckily for Kim and Donny, he didn't have time to act on this knowledge before he had to get to the Game Fair, and by the time he returned, they'd gone.'

'What about the other entries? Does he mention the killings?'

'He does, and in graphic detail.' The chief constable grimaced as she told Nash, 'They make horrific reading. It isn't simply what he did, but the cold-blooded, factual way he describes it — like ordering a takeaway pizza. At a guess, I'd say those prostitutes represented a mixture of his wife and mother, and in his disordered mind, they fully justified the treatment he doled out. To put it bluntly, he abducted them, held them prisoner and repeatedly raped, sodomized, and tortured them until he grew sick of them. After he strangled them, he dismembered their bodies using a chainsaw and left them in the holiday cottage.'

Nash shook his head and sighed loudly. 'One thing that did puzzle me was how Nelson gained entry to Track End Cottage. The CSI people reckon none of the locks were forced, but that was before Donny Barton gave me his statement. He told me in their haste to escape, he left the keys on the kitchen table in the cottage, along with a note addressed to the estate manager, apologizing for not returning them.'

'Nelson mentions that as well. Apparently, he went there looking for his wife and her lover, found the keys and kept them. Later, once he'd formed his campaign of vengeance, he removed Barton's belongings, destroyed the note, and used the house as a body dump in the hope of incriminating Barton.'

'His plan almost worked,' Nash observed, his tone non-judgemental.

'Yes, Mike, I know. It was certainly clever enough to fool me, but luckily, you and Jackie saw through it.'

'How is Jackie, have you heard?'

'The news is that although the operation was a success, it appears the damage to her shoulder is worse than they thought. It will take some time before it is totally repaired, but at least she won't have to take retirement on medical grounds. That leads me onto the other point I wanted to tell you about this morning. I've called a media conference for eleven thirty. The main part of it will be taken up with the Thornscarr case, and Donny Barton will be there. I will exonerate him in front of the cameras.' O'Donnell smiled. 'He said it should increase the demand for his work. But I will also use the conference to update the reporters on the success you've had solving the market muggings. Those are two major achievements, Mike.'

'It was a sort of chain reaction,' Nash replied. 'Sorry, bad pun,' he added with a grin, seeing O'Donnell wince. 'I wasn't referring to the chainsaw. What I meant was that the market muggings led me to speak to Olivia Brook — she advised me to talk to Jonas Turner, who, in turn, supplied background information about the Harland Estate. By the way, I think a vote of thanks should go to Lee, our teenage photographer. Not only did he take the video providing the identity of the mugger, but he and his girlfriend also led us to Track End Cottage on the estate, which then led us to investigate Nelson for the murders. That was part of what I meant by a chain reaction. The other part refers to what Aaron Nelson did — the effect it had on his son, and Elijah finding the template for his own actions.'

'That might be so, Mike but it was still outstanding detective work. I would like you to attend the media conference and sit alongside me. Will you feel able to do that, given our disagreement over this case?'

Nash hesitated for a second, and O'Donnell thought he was about to decline. Instead, Nash told her, 'I will, but only if it doesn't drag on too long. I need to take tomorrow off. Daniel and Clara are due back, and I've to collect them from the airport. I want to try and clear my desk of at least some of the remaining paperwork before I leave tonight.'

'Don't worry, I'll keep it as brief as possible. In fact, why don't you take two days' leave, because DS Mironova *will* be back, and she can cover the weekend as well? You deserve the rest, as long as you're back on Monday.'

She then broached a difficult subject she'd touched on earlier. 'I'm aware that I've made one or two big mistakes recently, for which I apologize; especially if in doing so I've upset you. The plain fact is that I've been distracted and extremely worried by a personal problem,' she paused before continuing. 'Charlie, my dear husband, has been very ill. He's got a heart condition and been waiting for surgery. But that's over with now. He's being discharged from hospital next week.'

'You should have said something, ma'am. We could have rallied round.'

'Why? There was nothing anyone could do.' She paused before adding, 'That means I'll be off work for at least the next one, maybe, two months, so with Jackie also out of action, you'll be the senior officer and will be running the show.' She smiled and commented, 'Much as you always do. I've tried to find cover, but you know how bad staffing levels are nationally. Sorry to drop all this on you, but of course, we didn't anticipate Jackie getting shot.'

Nash tried to hide his disappointment. He'd been hoping to ask for some holiday leave, but in the circumstances that was obviously completely out of the question. Once again, it seemed that he'd have to subjugate his personal life for the good of the team. His reply was all that O'Donnell hoped and expected from him. 'Don't worry, ma'am just concentrate on getting Charlie well again. Please give him my regards.'

As he waited for the media conference to begin Nash wondered how the new situation would affect his own plans. Hopefully, the delay wouldn't make any difference — except possibly to his sleep patterns.

CHAPTER TWENTY-FIVE

It was still daylight when Nash reached home. He turned on the coffee machine, filled a mug, and wandered into the lounge. He stood staring out of the large picture window towards Stark Ghyll, where the lower pastures were populated by sheep. But despite the beauty of this scene, Nash felt depressed. The grisly outcome of the case was only part of the reason for his low spirits. Again he felt lonely, and missed Daniel's company. As if drawn by some invisible magnet, his eyes went to the painting on the wall, and his mood darkened further. He was still gazing at the landscape when the doorbell rang. 'What now?' he muttered. He'd had enough to deal with for one day. He put down the empty coffee mug and trudged wearily down the hallway to open the door.

If a picture paints a thousand words, then Nash's expression would have written a book when he found Daniel standing in the storm porch.

'Hola, Papa,' Daniel greeted him, with a big grin on his face.

'Daniel! What are you doing here?' Nash gasped with surprise.

'We had to get an earlier flight. There wasn't enough room on ours.'

'I don't understand. I thought it had all been booked before you went away. Why didn't you let me know, so I could collect you from the airport?' Nash looked beyond him to see Clara and David taking luggage from a taxi, acknowledging him with a smile and a wave.

'We didn't have time to warn you.' He glanced over his shoulder. 'But I've brought you a present.' He ran back to the taxi, opened the back door and an attractive woman with short dark hair, large brown eyes, and tanned complexion, stepped out. She stood alongside him, looking towards his father.

It wasn't often that Nash was speechless, but it was several seconds before he managed to splutter, 'Alondra?'

Without a word, Clara and David got back into the taxi and continued their journey home, unnoticed by Nash, who stood staring at the woman before him.

'Papa, do you think we can go in the house now?' Daniel asked.

'Yes, yes, of course.' He looked at her again, she hadn't said a word, but her eyes spoke volumes. He signalled with one hand, an invitation to enter, before he grabbed the cases and struggled to carry them indoors, as Daniel watched in amusement and delight.

'Shall I make coffee for you both, Papa?'

'Er. Yes please, Daniel. Er, there's some in the machine.'

Leaving his bemused father in the hall, Daniel smiled as he headed to the kitchen, wondering how long it would be before he got any sense out of him.

Alondra spoke at last. 'Hello, Mike.'

Again, all he could say was, 'Alondra?' He ushered her through to the lounge, where she stood in front of the hearth staring at the painting and smiled. 'I see you kept it.'

'I'd never part with it. It means a lot to me.'

Daniel appeared with a mug of coffee, carried in his one good hand, before returning seconds later with another.

Nash reached out and hugged his son. 'Daniel, I'm so sorry, how are you feeling? How's your shoulder?'

'I'm OK. It's much better. The swimming helped. In fact, I think I can manage to unpack.' He turned towards the stairs and grabbed his bag. 'That's what I'm going to do now. Hope you like your present.'

Neither of them noticed that he had failed to close the door fully, leaving it slightly ajar.

Nash at last found his voice. 'Alondra, why are you here?'

'Someone convinced me it was the right thing to do.' She smiled, knowing she had her instructions, given explicitly by the young man who was stage-managing the production.

Standing outside the door, Daniel crossed his fingers and bit his bottom lip, hoping Clara's and his plan would work. He heard a mug being put on the coffee table and listened as Alondra continued to explain.

'Daniel came to see me along with Clara and David. He'd persuaded them that as they were in Spain, they should pay me a visit.'

She was doing her best to stick to the script, implying it was all Daniel's idea.

'I imagine my expression when I answered the door to them must have been a bit like yours when you saw me. What Daniel told me concerned me. He said you'd been extremely unhappy since I left, and that you mope around the house like a grumpy old man. He said he missed me too, even when he was at school, because he'd nobody special to talk to and confide in. He actually accused me of deserting him when he needed me most. That made me really sad.'

Daniel heard her sigh.

'In that moment, I realized that he takes after his father when it comes to his ability to charm women. Then Clara told me how much you'd changed at work; being short-tempered and never seeing the funny side of things. She said that in the past, whenever a relationship ended, you quickly found consolation elsewhere. But after what happened between us, you've never looked at another woman. She thinks you are overdue a little happiness to make up for all the heartbreak you've suffered. It was then that I knew I had to come and talk things over with you and see where we go.' Her voice faltered as she added, 'If anywhere. So here I am.'

'I have tried to phone you.'

'I know, but I wasn't ready.'

Nash reached out and took her hand. 'How long can you stay?' He asked the question quietly, dreading the answer.

Daniel leaned nearer to the open door; this was the vital moment as far as he was concerned.

In the room, Alondra looked into Nash's eyes; the loving expression in them gave her hope. Her voice was little more than a whisper as she said, 'That depends on you, Mike. I'll stay as long as you want me to.'

'I want you to stay forever,' he said, his tone ardent, the sincerity in his voice evident.

'That's OK, then. Forever suits me fine.'

From his position outside the half-open door, Daniel gave a huge grin of triumph. He punched the air with delight, then winced as pain shot through his damaged shoulder.

THE END

ACKNOWLEDGEMENTS

I would like to express my gratitude to everyone who has contributed with guidance, professional knowledge, and criticism throughout the DI Mike Nash series.

In this particular instance, thanks to knowledge I've acquired along the way, I have been able to construct the plot of *Chain Reaction* with little outside advice.

However, I am, as always, very grateful to my readers, Wendy McPhee and Julian Corps, and above all my in-house editor and critic Val for their invaluable assistance. I should also add Jasper and all the team at Joffe Books for the faith they have shown in my work.

ABOUT THE AUTHOR

Having taken early retirement from the finance industry, prolific writer Bill Kitson enjoys the challenge of writing both crime and general fiction, often with a twist of humour. Both his series, the DI Mike Nash crime thrillers and his Eden House Mysteries, are set in North Yorkshire, the county of his birth.

He also writes his Greek Island Romances under the pseudonym William Gordon.

Living and working throughout most of the North of England he is now settled on the east coast along with his wife.

His writing never stops, and when he isn't seeking inspiration from the surrounding countryside he can be found in a small fishing village on one of the Greek Islands, staring out to sea — laptop at the ready!

For further details go to:
www.billkitson.com
www.billkitsonblog.wordpress.com

ALSO BY BILL KITSON

THE DI MIKE NASH SERIES
Book 1: WHAT LIES BENEATH
Book 2: VANISH WITHOUT TRACE
Book 3: PLAYING WITH FIRE
Book 4: KILLING CHRISTMAS
Book 5: SLASH KILLER
Book 6: ALONE WITH A KILLER
Book 7: BLOOD DIAMOND
Book 8: DEAD & GONE
Book 9: HIDE & SEEK
Book 10: RUNNING SCARED
Book 11: THE BLEEDING HEART KILLER
Book 12: CHAIN REACTION

FREE KINDLE BOOKS

DO YOU LOVE **FREE AND BARGAIN** BOOKS?

Do you love mysteries, historical fiction and romance? Join thousands of readers enjoying great books through our mailing list. You'll get new releases and great deals every week from one of the UK's leading independent publishers.

Join today, and you'll get your first bargain book this month!

www.joffebooks.com/contact

Follow us on Facebook, Twitter and Instagram

@joffebooks

Thank you for reading this book.

If you enjoyed it please leave feedback on Amazon or Goodreads, and if there is anything we missed or you have a question about, then please get in touch. The author and publishing team appreciate your feedback and time reading this book.

We're very grateful to eagle-eyed readers who take the time to contact us. Please send any errors you find to corrections@joffebooks.com. We'll get them fixed ASAP.

Printed in Dunstable, United Kingdom

71499753R10133